FADE TO GOLD

STEFON MEARS

Thousand
Faces
Publishing

Also by Stefon Mears

Cavan Oltblood Series
Half a Wizard
The Ice Dagger
Spells of Undeath

Spells for Hire
Devil's Shoestring
Zombie Powder
Spirit Trap
Dragon's Blood (coming December 2019)

The Rise of Magic
Magician's Choice
Sleight of Mind
Lunar Alchemy
Three Fae Monte
The Sphinx Principle

The Telepath Trilogy
Surviving Telepathy
Immoral Telepathy
Targeting Telepathy

Edge of Humanity
Caught Between Monsters
Hunting Monsters

Power City Tales
Not Quite Bulletproof
No Money in Heroism

Devil's Night
Portal-Land, Oregon
Stealing from Pirates
Fade to Gold
With a Broken Sword
Twice Against the Dragon
The House on Cedar Street
Sudden Death
On the Edge of Faerie
Confronting Legends (Spells & Swords Vol. 1)
Uncle Stone Teeth and Other Macabre Poems
The Patreon Collection, Vol. 1-4 (Vol. 5, coming soon)

Published by Thousand Faces Publishing, Portland, Oregon

http://1kfaces.com

Copyright © 2018 by Stefon Mears

Front cover image © Glock33 | Dreamstime.com

ISBN: 978-1-948490-13-9

FADE TO GOLD

PART I

ARRIVAL

1

A-Day. Nine-Eighteen A.M. Pacific Daylight Time

The trucker blared his tuba of a horn again, and this time Charlie Evans gave the jerk a one-finger salute over his right shoulder.

Charlie knew his compact Garfield Caravel sedan wasn't exactly the fastest car on the road. In fact, it wasn't the latest and greatest anything. Not even when it was new, which was three owners and twelve years ago. Not to mention some two hundred twenty thousand miles.

The Caravel smelled like old French fries with a hint of cough syrup, the latter a side effect of Charlie's record two-month cold last year. The air conditioner would have been fine, if Charlie could afford to get it recharged so that it blew actual cold air instead of recycling the August morning wind, which was warm enough at this early hour to warn of a scorcher by the afternoon. And the car's exterior was an armada of parking lot dents and dings on a sea of hazard-cone orange that Charlie's most recent ex-girlfriend, Lucy, had dubbed a violation of the Geneva Convention.

But the smart cruise control worked just fine, and it would keep Charlie moving up One-Oh-One through the heart of Silicon Valley at a generous eight miles per hour above the speed limit. Or at least as close to that speed as the traffic allowed in lane three.

If that wasn't fast enough for the trucker, the jerk was more than welcome to go around.

And Charlie had set his cruise control and kept one ear open for the instructions from his GPS so he wouldn't have to waste precious firing synapses on his speed or directions or obnoxious truck drivers. Charlie wanted all his faculties focused on the reason he was on the road right now, and not tucked away in his San Jose apartment — his upcoming interview with Frenzy, "the ultimate search utility for all your devices."

After two years of post-college freelancing scramble — ten years freelancing total if you counted high school work — Charlie wanted, *needed*, to find out what it was like to have vacation time. Sick leave. A 401K.

So Charlie had a red folder full of ideas on the faded tan cloth of the front passenger seat, and he imagined the questions interviewers would ask, the answers he could give that would make him sound confident without veering into arrogant.

And most of all, not desperate, which was closer to the truth than he wanted to admit. Which was why it wasn't just the August heat making Charlie sweat into his nicest work-casual red polo shirt and tan cargo pants, and dampening his short, curly brown hair.

Frenzy was a company that everyone used, but many people loved to hate. They had plenty of market share for their main products — the search utility, of course, but also their streaming video and audio, and their social media tool — but a growing segment of their base was either trying to develop alternative tools or actively supporting anyone else's tools out of frustration with the company's public image.

Charlie had good ideas how to go about changing that public image.

No. Check that.

Charlie had *great* ideas. In that folder next to him sat a mock-up for a potential online campaign to improve Fenzy's image with checkpoints at two weeks, two months, six months and a year. Not a complete reinvention, of course, but a one-eighty on their current direction and progress toward making them seem the kind of company people would *want* to see succeed. The kind they'd trust again.

Charlie knew what size team he'd need, what sort of budget it would take to do it right. He had spent more time and effort on preparing for this interview than he had on anything else in the last six weeks.

Which was part of the reason Lucy was an ex-girlfriend. She could handle dating the professional social media wizard known to the world as "Evansessence." She seemed to rather enjoy it at first, even if Charlie only barely eked out a subsistence living here in one of the most expensive regions of the United States. Probably didn't hurt that he overhauled and idiot-proofed her cosmetics website.

But a professional social media wizard who was spending less and less time with her?

Charlie couldn't really blame her for leaving. Though he tried. At least, in the privacy of his own head. Over beers with his friends he admitted the truth. Charlie Evans spent too much time on the computer trying to earn a living, and not enough time actually living.

When the trucker leaned on his horn long enough to pull Charlie out of his thoughts, Charlie realized he was being passed on both sides. That wasn't right.

Worse, his speedometer read forty miles per hour and dropping.

Charlie stepped on the accelerator. Nothing happened, except that cold fear washed down his body, tightened his bladder. And his sweat kicked up a notch.

The trucker went around now, that tuba horn of his still holding its note while the trucker screamed obscenities and returned Charlie's salute.

Thirty miles per hour now.

But the engine was on. The light on the push-button ignition was green. The oil gauge read in the safe range. The digital readouts on the GPS were all...

All at once, every idiot light on Charlie's dashboard started flashing. The GPS went black.

Charlie gritted his teeth and flipped on the turn signal with his left hand and steered right with his right.

Or rather, he tried to.

The power steering was dead. All the idiot lights kept flashing. Lots more horns and drivers screaming at Charlie. Cars in the right hand lane swerving as he yanked the wheel with both hands now, desperate to get off the freeway before...

The Caravel died, there in the slow lane of highway One-Oh-One. Momentum kept it rolling off the freeway, but the dashboard was dead, the accelerator useless.

But there wasn't a lot of room on the shoulder. Ten more feet of asphalt. Two feet of dirt. Then a tan cinder block soundproofing wall that loomed very solid.

Charlie slammed down the brake pedal. Squeezed his eyes closed.

The power brakes were dead too.

Impact.

Slamming into the wall jarred Charlie's gritted teeth. His airbag failed to deploy. He jerked forward against the seatbelt.

Then slumped back against his seat. Very much alive. Uninjured apart from a kink in his neck and a sore jaw, thanks to the fact that the car hadn't had much speed left when it hit the wall.

Charlie sighed once, hard, then once more, slowly. He opened his eyes. His folder was on the car floor, his papers scattered. Some of them would probably be greasy, and the way his luck was running, that would include his résumé.

Cars whizzed past on the freeway behind him, mockingly fast and operational.

Charlie forced another slow, deep breath. He unplugged his phone, which was no longer charging there on the dashboard anyway. In less than a minute with his flicking finger he accomplished three important things.

First, he checked the local social media ride-sharing apps. No one could get a car to him in less than a half hour. No luck there. Second, he checked the prices of the local taxi services — all of them were urgency-sensitive these days, which meant they cost too much for him. So, third, he hit the distress button on the app for his roadside assistance service, which submitted his GPS coordinates and got him in the queue for a tow.

Estimated response time: forty minutes.

Charlie dropped his head forward and thumped it on the wide center of his steering wheel with its stupid, un-deployed airbag.

Which, when he thought about it, was probably a small blessing in disguise. He wasn't going fast enough to need it, and now he didn't have to pay to repack it.

Charlie sighed again and looked at his phone. He had six friends who all worked within range to pick him up and get him to that interview on time. But the operative word there was "worked." His friends were coders and tech writers. They couldn't just take off whenever they wanted to.

Well, maybe Jimbo could. He was the star programmer at a small company that made games for mobile devices. If Jimbo wanted to get away for half an hour, they would probably ask if a full hour would help.

Charlie crossed his fingers and spun through his contacts until Jimbo's round, smiling brown face with its round, smiling brown eyes looked back at him. Charlie fired off a text message: "Need a lift. 911. Will buy beer tonight."

Seconds later his phone rang.

"Jimbo, you're a lifesaver. I'm at—"

"Are you watching the news?"

"No, man, I've got that—"

"Turn on the news. Pronto."

"I can't. I need—"

"Turn. On. The. News."

"Fuck the news! I have to get to this interview."

"Fuck your interview. Aliens have landed in New York!"

2

_____

It was true that Brice DePaul's favorite place to be was at home with his family. He planned to retire this year so he could spend more time with Inga and the kids in their home in the fashionable Upper East Side.

But right now Brice was in his second favorite place. The bullpen. Well, that was what he called it, and his staff picked up on the nickname. To the occasional tour group who wandered through it probably looked like any other conference room in the GagTV offices, which were much more corporate than their channel's content would suggest. Dull gray table twice as long as it needed to be, black leather executive chairs that rolled and spun, each of which had an adjustable height lever and that rocking option that everyone on the staff used when thinking. Three forty-inch television monitors along the short wall behind him for quick media reference when needed.

But Brice called this conference room the bullpen because here the bullshit flowed freely. Most of it work-related. Some of it promoting the sort of camaraderie that Brice loved. And listening to comedians give each other guff was one of the joys of his day.

The morning meetings had a coffee urn, a deli tray, and a basket of muffins. But the dominant scents were the coffee and especially the fresh bagels and lox. Those were the smells of creativity. Brice always imagined that George Carlin's office had smelled like Brice's morning meetings. If Brice could leave even half of that kind of comedic legacy behind when he was gone, he would be proud of his life.

But Brice knew the truth about his legacy. He would be remembered more for the news he covered on his "comedy news" show, *Weeknightly with Brice DePaul*, than for the humor he injected.

He couldn't even be sad about that anymore, though he spent years — and thousands of dollars — crying and raging about it to a therapist. He was a comedian trying to spin the news funny, not a journalist who wedged in some jokes.

But the therapist had been worth the money. She helped Brice see the sad fact that his show was necessary. That he was saying the things that needed to be said. Things the "journalists" had forgotten how to say, or rather forgotten that they needed to say them.

That he did it with humor only meant that people paid more attention when he was talking.

Still, as much as Brice loved being right where he was and doing just what he did, he was tired. Twenty years of this was too much. He was closer to sixty than he was to fifty these days. His once blue-black hair needed weekly infusions of dye to hold back the flat gray tide. And despite daily trips to the gym, he had developed a noticeable paunch.

Yet when Brice looked around the table at his staff, he always smiled. Here were gathered a dozen of the sharpest wits his budget could buy. Some of them better comedians than he would ever be, and he joyed in the fact that he had found them, nourished their careers.

Brice had a staff of twelve, including five women and a two-thirds majority of minorities, and they all worked and played together well in the most relaxed environment he could give them. The guys wore jeans, with striped shirts or flannel or tee shirts when they felt like it. Like Brice himself, who was wearing a Humor Inc. tee shirt and a

Mets cap. Some of the women dressed that way too, but on hot days like this one they opted for light dresses.

They laughed together. They called him "B." And they listened when he was talking. He would miss each and every one of them when the time came to retire.

"All right, folks," he said, standing up and calling the meeting to order over rehashes of last night's episode of that new Star Wars television show. "I know we're gearing up for the primaries and I know the first debates are coming up, but just once this week — just once, I'm begging you — give me something to lead with that doesn't have to do with politics. Go."

Jenna, as usual, was the first to speak up. She was a third-year writer out of Georgia State, who could mix reds and browns in her dresses well enough to bring out the highlights in her dark skin tone. That she was attractive and spoke with a strong sense of self-confidence only meant that Brice put her in front of the camera as often as he could find a reason.

"There's a guy in Chicago beating up muggers in an honest-to-God Robin the Boy Wonder costume. Best part?" Jenna held up her hands in a wait-for-it gesture. "He's—"

The bullpen door swung open and slammed into its doorstop. One of the interns — Suzi, the tiny blonde from Georgetown, who was more interested in real journalism than comedy which made Brice wonder what she was doing *here* — came running in, her face a mask of fear, lips quivering. Before Brice could even ask what was wrong she turned on the center monitor.

The channel was the last one they'd been watching — Conservative Network News, "All the truth you can handle" — and the screen was split. In the upper right corner it showed a silvery gray flying saucer floating down gently out of the sky, spinning as it came. But most of the screen claimed to show the live feed, which had the saucer, already landed in Midtown Manhattan in front of the Radio City Music Hall on three long, telescoping legs of the same silver-gray metal.

Where was the bubble dome though? Weren't flying saucers all supposed to have a bubble dome on top? Or was the lack of one supposed to persuade viewers that this was real, and not some kind of network stunt? Probably for someone's presidential candidacy.

Across the bottom of the screen, as always, scrolled the latest "headlines," mostly tidbits about gun control, gaffes by liberal politicians, and of course, mentioning that aliens had landed and where was the Air Force?

"Actually," said Brice over the old stuffed suit's narration about hoaxes and the liberal agenda, "that's a good question. If that's supposed to be a real spaceship, how did it land in Manhattan without triggering the air defense systems we've all paid so much money for?"

Silence.

When Brice was a child, he used to watch old Warner Brothers cartoons every afternoon after school. And in the silence following that question he found himself remembering one where Daffy Duck did an amazing dance routine onstage, then presented himself to the audience for his applause. All that could be heard was the sound of chirping crickets.

Brice looked around at the faces of his expert staff, and as one they stared back at him, brows furrowed and some looking for answers in the notes they had not yet written. He could almost hear those chirping crickets.

It wasn't the first time Brice had compared himself to Daffy Duck.

"—the Chinese?" continued the Conservative Network News voice over, "And if so, what level of extant threat dose it pose? And when is the President going to respond?"

Brice's heart was pounding like it hadn't since the last time the President had been on his show. Real or hoax, this aliens thing was the biggest piece he'd seen in some time. Maybe the last big news item of his career.

He could almost taste the jokes bubbling in the back of his mind.

Brice muted the monitor. He stood, letting his chair roll back behind him. He pointed at the screen.

"Ladies and gentlemen," he said, "I submit that we have found our lead for tonight. And that means we need not only the best, the absolute juiciest sound bites we can cull from the cable news networks for their sheer comedic value — and I assure you, these guys are already on the air giving us gold that I pray some of the interns have captured so it doesn't slip past us and into the waiting hands of the late night talk show hosts, who will be all over this, mark my words — not only do we need to tear through this story like we've never been through one before, we need something even more important."

Brice shook his head, lips tight together like they didn't want to let his next words out. He punched his own hand to make them part.

"We need to know what the hell is actually going on out there. And why." Brice leaned forward on the smooth, gray table. It felt cold under his flushing skin. "So I'm going to have to ask you guys to do something I hate to ask of you." He gave a heavy sigh. "I'm going to have to ask some of you to act like journalists. Make the important calls. Follow the important leads. Find out whatever you can find out. There may be more humor in the truth here than we'll ever find in the broadcasts of another network."

"Which team are you heading?" said Jenna.

"Assuming that's real, it's happening no more than four blocks from where I'm standing. So I'm taking a camera crew and going down there myself."

Shock and surprise on every face at the table.

"That's right." Brice straightened up and adjusted a tie he wasn't wearing. "Brice DePaul is going on-location."

3

No one would have ever suspected that Laura Jefferson was riding in the back of this old wreck.

The rental Garfield Frigate sedan was the cheapest thing Laura had sat in since her first big hit movie, three blockbusters ago. Gray cloth seats instead of leather. Bench backseat where she could actually feel springs try to poke through the padding, instead of something more shaped and molded for the comfort of the passenger.

A single rear vent that did not do nearly enough to chip away at the humid New York heat, which was dampening her skin with what the magazines would no doubt call a "glow." As though sweat were somehow beneath her pores now.

Worse, the vent brought in a wet, dead possum smell to mix with the lingering odor of chemical cleaners and cigarette smoke. Might have put Laura off her hunger, except that she hadn't had anything to eat since that bland protein shake following her morning workout hours ago. Raspberry. Laura scoffed. That shake tasted less like raspberry than banana candy tasted like actual bananas.

She wanted a lamb curry wrap from Ranjit's with a side of crisp sweet potato fries. And come hell or high water she was going to have it. Ranjit's was a personal treat she only got to enjoy when she was in New York making the talk show rounds, and there weren't enough dead possums in the whole huge city to make her skip it.

And the smell was definitely dead possum. Laura grew up in Oakwood, Ohio, and she knew the difference between dead possum stink and dead rat stink, thank you very much. Possum had more of a tang, and rat, especially here in a big city, smelled scummier. Filthy, rather than dirty.

Laura would have to remember to mention that in her interview later. The interviewers always seemed to find those sorts of details charming. As though they were surprised to find out that there was a real person behind the twenty-two-year-old face, figure and long blond hair that the media kept describing as "magnificent," or "ideal," or worst of all "perfect."

Laura had never felt perfect a day in her life. Inside she still felt very much like the skinny preteen with the face full of pimples and the mouth full of braces, who couldn't get a boy to dance with her, much less go on a date with her.

The boys looked at her differently now. Steve, for instance, the driver provided by the studio who, from the way he fiddled with the air conditioner at this long red light, was probably wishing they were still in his limo instead of this old wreck. Whenever Steve looked at her he had that same hunger in his eyes that so many guys did. Like she was a lamb curry wrap herself.

At first Laura had found those looks exciting. That skinny preteen girl inside her crying out "The boys like me! I'm *sexy*!" Then they creeped her out for a while, made her feel threatened. Now those gazes were just a fact of life. A certain percentage of the men she met couldn't come near her without experiencing intense lust. It wasn't personal. Probably didn't even have to do with sex. Not really. The way Laura looked at it, she was like a lottery prize to those guys. She just represented something that they thought was missing in their lives. Something they thought they wanted, but wouldn't know what to do with if they actually got.

And their odds were about the same.

Steve the driver was a little different. He had that way of trying to make everything he said sound charming, as though he thought he might have a shot. Enough confidence that Laura wondered if some other starlet had given him a tumble at some point.

She could imagine it. Steve had the kind of clean-cut features and soft hazel eyes that looked attractive and masculine without sliding into threatening. Laura could picture some bored and lonely starlet looking at him differently after a couple of days of riding in his limo. Maybe in a thunderstorm, when the starlet was shaking and chill from the rain and Steve lent her a coat that smelled like some rich aftershave...

Well, Steve could hope all he wanted, as long as he kept those hopes to himself. The last thing Laura needed right now was some random hook-up. Bad enough the interviewers would inevitably ask about her recent break up with Jesse.

Jesse Carter, action film star with blockbuster success rivaling Laura's own, and the bastard who...

Laura spliced that direction right out of her thoughts. This was lunchtime. Laura time. The one hour a day when she turned off her phone, and refused to even think about business, social media, or other responsibilities.

For Laura, film stardom amounted to a twenty-three-hour-a-day job. Even sleep was something she caught when she could, on planes and film sets or in interview green rooms. And it was interrupted more often than she liked to think about.

So her lunch hour was the one single hour of the day she took completely to herself. And she made certain her agents, manager, publicist — and more importantly their assistants — all knew this. One single solitary hour when she was sure to be free from commitment or obligation and they all needed to respect that.

Even family and friends only got to interrupt that hour when they were actually having lunch with her. And when Laura could arrange that, she met them with big smiles and bigger hugs.

Not today, alas. Today she would dine alone.

If that eternal red light ever changed.

Lunchtime privacy was why she asked Steve to drive this rent-a-wreck instead of his limo. It was why she wore a long, plain brown skirt with a bulky but lightweight tan top, cheap sunglasses, and all her hair tucked up under a Cleveland Indians baseball hat.

The perfect disguise. No one would look twice at her while she ate lunch in peace at Ranjit's Wraps on 58th.

Well, no one but the owner, who had figured out who she was on her second trip. On that day he waited until she finished her meal, then asked, in the most politely quiet and discreet way possible, if he could trouble her for an autographed photo for his five children. Laura regretted not having one on her, which was why even now she kept a handful in her oversized brown faux-leather disguise purse.

That day Laura mailed him six autographed photos with a big thank-you card. One personally inscribed picture for each of his three daughters and two sons, and one for Ranjit and his wife.

Since then Ranjit seemed to enjoy the espionage of pretending she was just another customer. He gave no sign that he knew who she was except that he gave her a little wink when he brought her her meal.

Laura restrained herself to tipping the cost of the meal, so as to thank him without embarrassing him.

But Laura was never going to get to Ranjit's Wraps at this rate. Worse, she couldn't see much beyond the huge SUV directly ahead of her.

"What's the deal with this light, Steve?" Laura tried to keep the exasperation out of her voice, but she knew that was a lost cause. Her lunch hour was ebbing away.

"It's not the light. Traffic's completely locked down. And it looks like police cordons are going up at the end of the next block." He turned to look at her, trying to infuse the hope in his eyes with humor and affected a conspiratory tone. "Word on the radio is aliens have landed."

He laughed, but Laura sighed.

"Of course," she said, shaking her head. Then thought about the implications. "Man, the guilds are going to kill that guy's budget.

Working through lunch? And not securing the proper permits to keep this kind of traffic snarl from happening?"

"I don't think it's a shoot. I'd've heard something." Steve craned his neck to see what he could see, but got distracted by an incoming text message.

"Well it has to be some kind of publicity stunt then. I mean, aliens? Landing in Manhattan? Aren't they supposed to buzz the rural states?"

Laura was thinking of the occasional "abduction" story she had heard growing up in Ohio. They always seemed to take place around campouts or late night drives, but Laura had been on her share of campouts and late night drives and never seen so much as a moving light in the sky that wasn't a shooting star.

Personally, she suspected the actual culprit in "abductions" was alcohol. Not aliens.

"Jake from over at the Rock says the police are acting serious enough. And he says news cameras are out there." He looked over his shoulder again. The worried look this time. Protective. "I should get you back to the studio."

News cameras? The only news cameras that showed up at a shoot were supposed to be there. And if the crowd over at the Rock thought this was legit...

Actual aliens? Not latex prosthetics over underpaid actors? A real spaceship?

How could Laura pass up the chance to see that?

Of course, there *were* the news crews to consider. Publicity was just what Laura wanted to avoid on her lunch break. Then again, she *did* have her disguise on. And with traffic gridlocked like this, she was never going to have time to sit and eat the way she wanted to anyway...

Steve was firing off text messages when she looked up.

"Steve, can I ask you a big favor?"

No teasing. No flirting. That wouldn't have been playing fair, and Laura never played games with the real important people in show business — the support staffs. So her tone was straightforward and honest. And she didn't assume he'd say yes. She waited until he replied.

"Don't ask me to try to take you into that mess. The studio would—"

"Nothing like that." She waved the thought away like brushing off a fly. "Why, if you were responsible for getting me close to whatever's going on up there you might get fired, even if nothing bad happened to me. What I was going to ask was, would you swing by Ranjit's and ask him for 'Laura's usual' to go?" She handed him a twenty. "This will cover it, and let anything extra be a tip." She handed him two more twenties. "Your lunch is on me, of course. Just take mine back to the studio. I'll warm it up when I get back."

"Back?" Steve's hazel eyes widened in actual fear. How could he not be excited about the chance — even just the chance — to meet people from a whole other world? His voice trembled as he said, "Tell me you aren't—"

"Me? I'm just going for a walk. It's a lovely day, and the sun is actually shining up there between the skyscrapers. I'll toddle along back to the studio before they need me."

"Laura, you can't. Please. What if—"

"Steve, as far as you know, I'm just going for a walk. I could be going any direction at all. In fact, I'm pretty sure I'll be walking back toward the studio." Which she fully intended to be true, even though it wasn't the first destination she had in mind. "So you have nothing to worry about and no reason to be concerned. Do you?"

Laura really wanted to flutter her eyelashes, but she kept her sunglasses on to prevent herself from doing it. Instead, she leaned a little closer.

"It's my lunchtime. You know I'm not going to tell you where I'm going anyway."

Steve gave a relaxed sigh, probably realizing that those words released him from immediate culpability. Which meant he was smart enough to realize he couldn't stop her.

"So," he said, "if you hear anyone talking on your walk — anyone who actually did venture near the so-called aliens — and you hear anything interesting, you'll tell me, right?"

"Of course, Steve!" Laura opened the door and put one brown sandal out onto the hot asphalt. As she got out, she said over her shoulder, "But what are the chances of that happening?"

4

From the smell of the yellow tow truck's passenger seat, Charlie would have sworn he was already at a garage instead of standing in morning heat on the side of a freeway. Even past the exhaust of the truck's combustion engine, he detected gasoline, motor oil, antifreeze ... even beer if Charlie wasn't mistaken. Not the cleanest place to sit in his best cargo pants.

But he climbed aboard the cracked black leather bench seat inside the rumbling tow truck, to wait while Carlos — who was hardly any taller than Charlie's five-foot-ten himself, and whip-lean like his pencil mustache — convinced the whining hydraulic winch to lift the front of Charlie's little car.

Just Charlie's luck. Aliens had landed. Biggest new story of the century — maybe all of human history — and blogger extraordinaire Charlie "Evansessence" Evans was stuck on death watch for his car when he should be streaming video and audio, reading every news report, finding some angle to...

Didn't matter. Not yet. Soon. But not yet.

Charlie was stuck in the netherworld between exits. He had to get to civilization before he could start pulling down information from multiple sources at once. His phone was good, but...

"Be just another minute," called Carlos. "I want to disconnect the drive shaft for you. Make the tow easier on your car."

"That's fine," Charlie called back, scrolling through images of the aliens on his Frenzy!Feed, the social media stream of the company he was *supposed* to interview with today. Not that anyone answered when he tried calling to let them know about his car.

Any one of the three times he called. He hoped his voice messages sufficed. Everyone at Frenzy! were probably all clustered around their computers and televisions, getting up to the microsecond news. Like Jimbo was. Like Charlie should have been, instead of bouncing impatiently on the tow truck seat while his phone now spiraled a loading circle because his signal was weak.

All because his nigh-ancient car finally broke down. And the crowning insult? It was going to be hauled into the shop by an anachronism.

This tow truck had been rigged for a phone mount, but that was the only sign that modern life had reached it. The built-in stereo had a tape player, like something out of the Mesozoic Period. No GPS. A chrome slot on the black steering column for an actual ignition key. Analog dial for the speedometer, and no tachometer that Charlie could see. The heater and air conditioner were melded into a single sliding lever, next to another for the fan, instead of twin adjustable thermostats.

This truck was so old, it might not have a computer at all.

And even it was still running while Charlie's car died.

The driver's door opened and Carlos gave Charlie a big smile as he hoisted himself behind the steering wheel. "You're going to Orkney, right?"

Charlie nodded, trying to return the smile even though impatience twisted all through his guts. Tied up his shoulders like a snarl of cables. His smile probably came out a snarl, but Carlos didn't seem to mind. He just clunked his truck into gear and pulled onto the freeway.

"Thought so. Best place for the older cars. Especially the one I'm taking you to. Ask for Jackie. She—"

"Can we put on the news?"

Carlos' smile faltered, then stretched wide again. "Help yourself. Don't see the point, though. They're all caught up in that alien scam."

"Scam?"

Charlie tried to sound interested while he spun an actual dial moving a marker horizontally across a line of numbers. There was no precision to this! How was he supposed to find an exact frequency?

Buzzing static filled the air, interspersed with ghostly voices as stations tried and failed to reach the archaic truck radio.

"Sure, man. Aliens are like ghosts. Lies we tell ourselves based on urban legends. Everyone's carrying a camera and a camcorder these days. If those things were real, we'd have solid evidence by now."

"No doubt." Charlie kept making small adjustments between 102 and 103 FM, until finally...

"This is Ramona Gutierrez at 102.3 The Scoop, continuing our live coverage of the strange craft that landed in New York City just under an hour ago. Early reports claim that the craft is an alien spaceship, but other stations are now speculating that it's a terrestrial craft after all. So far our calls to the White House and the Pentagon have not been returned, but you listeners know our motto: 'We Don't Just Report the News, We Dig for More.'"

"Ever see that Ramona Gutierrez?" said Carlos, waggling his eyebrows. "Beautiful as she is smart."

Charlie's nerves were bad enough that he had to check himself from telling Carlos to keep his eyes on the road. But traffic had eased up over the last hour. In fact, Charlie couldn't remember seeing One-Oh-One this empty before...

"Wait," said the Ramona Gutierrez, "I'm told there's activity at the vessel. We're going now live to our New York affiliate."

"...crush of people all around me," said a man's tight voice, over the shouts and honking horns and excited babbling of the people around him. "Police are doing their best to hold back the crowd, but they're holding back the media beyond the cordon too, so we're ... we're having trouble holding our position here."

"Probably a brother," said Carlos. "You know if he was a white boy the cops would be helping him out."

"It's gotten worse since the saucer started humming, just a few minutes ago. People all around me jostling and shoving. Trying to get closer or trying to get away."

In the background Charlie could hear police on megaphones admonishing the crowd to stay calm and stay back.

"Wait. Wait. Something's happening. Yes. I see it now. It looks as though another giant tentacle leg is coming down. No, wait. This one is smoother, and it's coming straight down from the center of the craft, expanding like a telescope toward the ground. Could it be an elevator? Could it be that we are about to get our first look at the aliens? Yes! That looks like a door at the bottom, and it's—"

Dead air, with a side of static.

5

A-Day. One-Ten P.M. Eastern Daylight Time

All around Brice's small crew, dozens of real news crews were broadcasting already. Cameras rolling, lights blaring, and attractive men and women in suits speaking very seriously into microphones but saying nothing of consequence. Effectively, every one of them were saying the same thing — holy crap, will you look at this thing behind me? What do you think it is? Here are a few possibilities…

The blessing and the curse of doing these things live. They would get the first word about what was going on here in Midtown Manhattan, right outside the Radio City Music hall of all places, but they would have flubs and dead air and other problems that made Brice glad he was a comedian, not a newscaster.

More or less.

All around him, in the sweltering New York heat that made his own Navy blue wool suit itch and cling, the crowd managed to pack in close while still leaving room for the news crews to do their jobs. At least, if anyone was getting hassled by the crowd, Brice couldn't see or hear it.

Still, the crowd was schizophrenic. Curious onlookers in suits and dresses, waiting for the punchline or movie ad. Hopefuls and doomsayers in sundresses or skirts or shorts and shirts made from denim or hemp cloth or loose cotton, waving hastily scrawled signs with slogans like *The End is Near, Gort Go Home!, We welcome our new alien overlords, U.S. out of outer space*, and others.

Plus, of course, the requisite Bible verses and *Free George!* sign. Couldn't have a crowd without those. Even the hot dog and falafel vendors were finding places for their carts and cutting into the grimy street smell with options that made Brice's mouth water, despite his stomach's fullness from the morning meeting.

Some were cheering and whistling like they were trying to encourage a band onstage for an encore. Others chanted little phrases, but the only one Brice could make out was *I want to believe*. Most of them, though, were just talking among themselves, saying pretty much the same things as the people with suits and microphones.

All these people. Thousands by now, causing a nasty enough level of gridlock that Brice and his team had to get here on foot. Brice just knew he'd have blisters where his loafers rubbed.

And all of these people here for their first glimpse of what might be an actual alien spacecraft.

Up close — or at least as up-close as the police cordon allowed, which was some hundred or so feet back — Brice had to admit that the flying saucer looked legit. Wider across than the length of two city buses. Perfectly round, and gleaming like it had been polished.

Even the three telescoping legs that supported the craft some fifty feet up looked like they'd just had a professional-grade detail job. Brice could see rainbows and reflections in their silvery metal.

That made Brice suspicious. How could anything travel through two atmospheres — and presumably billions of miles of space in between — and look like it just came off the UFO lot? Shouldn't there be space dust on it at least? Heat-dulled spots from entering the atmosphere? Maybe a ding or two?

Brice shook his head and rolled his neck. Time to get to work.

"You getting that thing, Mike?"

Mike the cameraman had a dozen pockets in his long-sleeved tan shirt, and Brice suspected there were even more in the man's matching Utilikilt. Mike was a good enough cameraman that he could have had any job in the city. Used to work Mets and Jets games, and shot more than a few studio films. Even if Brice didn't know Mike's C.V., Mike showed his experience in the way he held even the remote camera steady on his shoulder as he nodded confirmation. Shiny black shoes the perfect distance apart for balance. Back as straight as a kung fu master. Hands positioned for minimum effort and maximum control.

Brice had no doubt that the frame never wavered.

Mike liked to say he worked for *Weeknightly* to work with Brice. Brice thought it was because most jobs would have required Mike to wear pants.

"Get me a sweep of the crowd next, then let's find a place you can get a good shot of me with that thing in the background."

"Best spots are taken," said Mike, sweeping the camera in a slow pan. "But I've got an idea or two."

Two minutes later, Brice was standing unsteadily on the steel lid of an old blue Dumpster, trying not to worry about how much rust he saw on the side, or the way it creaked and wobbled every time he shifted his weight. He told himself that the sweat on his brow and in his pits was just from the heat. And that his heart was pumping because he was feeding on the crowd's nervous energy.

Not because the saucer had started emitting a deep, loud hum.

Certainly not because he was afraid of heights. Not much of one, anyway. And this hardly counted as a height. As long as he didn't look anywhere but at the camera.

Brice was high enough now to catch a little bit of breeze in his hair, which had the benefit of bringing a smell to compete with the old garbage warmed over odor of the Dumpster. The drawback was that the breeze also carried more of the hot dog smell from a nearby cart, and now Brice knew he wouldn't escape the area without devouring two chili dogs with extra cheese.

Going on-location was clearly bad for his diet.

But Mike was in position, shooting up at an angle that put the edge of the Radio City Music Hall sign in part of the frame, and situated Brice dramatically against the body of the so-called spacecraft. Or so Mike had promised it would when he talked Brice into climbing up here.

Brice took a shaky deep breath.

"Okay," he said, "and in three, two, one." Brice snapped his fingers.

"Folks, I don't want to say that this story is trash, but I'm standing on a Dumpster to bring it to you—"

"Brice!" said Mike, swinging the camera to a different angle. "Something's coming down!"

6

A-DAY. ONE-EIGHTEEN *P.M.* EASTERN DAYLIGHT TIME

All of Laura's old concert reflexes still served her well when it came to moving through a crowd. Most people would given up when they saw that steamy city-block-plus of flesh between her and the maybe-spaceship she could only just see in the background. Gone home to get a better view from their televisions.

But Laura didn't get where she was today by giving up.

The trick was body language. Clutch the oversized purse tightly, but only use one arm. Act important, don't make eye contact, sound like she was in a hurry. Mix in the occasional concert-trained "nudge" with an elbow or shoulder and soon she was drifting through a human steam bath of colognes and perfumes, and people who used too much deodorant and people who didn't use any.

Probably helped her progress that the crowd wasn't sure it wanted to get closer. There was an uneasy tension in the air. Like the crowd knew something was going to happen soon.

Between the mid-day heat and the press of bodies, she'd need a shower when she got to the studio.

Maybe two.

But the sheer number of people was only one impediment to her progress. God knew the noise was a kind of barrier on its own.

Honking horns from the traffic in the background. Shouts and whistles closer, and excited babbling all around, plus various groups of people chanting phrases that must have had some kind of purpose. The *Plan 9 from Outer Space* chant made a cockeyed kind of sense, but some of the other ones she could pick out above the general crowd noise were lost on her completely. Probably something to do with a video game or science fiction show.

But she made it past the bulk of the crowd and now she was up by the police cordon, tucked into a pocket of onlookers away from the dozens of news crews.

Yellow "police line do not cross" tape. Scores of police officers in riot gear, looking like they weren't sure whether they should watch the crowd or the saucer. As a result, the ones that weren't actually standing at the yellow tape were just sort of milling about with their hands on their pistols. Or automatic rifles in some cases.

Laura knew a thing or two about guns. Some from training for her spy movies *Dressed to Kill* and *Dressed to Kill 2: The Bitch Is Back*. More from her childhood days of hunting with her father. And she knew that there were four types of people who should never be holding guns — the angry, the drunk, the tired, and the scared.

And those police officers all looked scared. Tight grips on their gun handles. Quick, darting head and eye movements. Visible sweating and swallowing.

Laura had that feeling in her gut, like she got sometimes at parties. A tightness that said *something bad's going to happen*.

She was just about to use her concert-fu to get away from the frightened, armed men when the saucer started to hum. A loud, low tone that found resonance between the buildings on either side of the flying saucer, made the windows vibrate. Not loud enough to drown out the chanters, but enough to set her teeth on edge and tremble through her head and chest.

Police officers on the megaphone now, telling everyone to remain calm and stay back.

Laura supposed they knew that "return to your homes or places of business" had no shot at success.

The crowd got louder. Screams and shouts and more whistles like the house lights at a concert just came down. Laura's heart raced like it had when she got called up to the stage to accept that Academy Award for *A Distant Light*.

She felt just as flushed and breathless. Even her stomach forgot how hungry she was. Ranjit's Wraps barely an echo in the back of her mind.

Then a tube jutted down from the main body of the flying saucer. It came straight down, telescoping. Stretching its way toward the ground.

Screams and shouts got louder. They were everywhere now. People started shoving. Some to get closer. Others to get away.

Laura set her sandals shoulder-width apart and lowered her center of gravity. She wasn't big — "except in the ways that counted" as she had heard an eye-rolling number of times before — but just knowing how to stand counted for more than a little. Crowd pressure was like water pressure. It pushed through the weakest points first, and while Laura would never be the strongest point, she knew how to not be the weakest.

The tube reached the ground. Laura had to crane her neck, but she could see what looked like the seams of a slightly-recessed, round-cornered door, just as silver-gray and shiny as the rest of the flying saucer.

The door opened.

Definite screams now. And shoving. Laura shoved back. Pushed and elbowed. Had to stay on her feet. Had to see.

Police officers formed a wall between the tube and the crowd, riot shields raised and side arms drawn now. Others with assault rifles took up posts. Some on the megaphone, imploring everyone to please stay calm and move back.

Laura kept her belly to that yellow tape, not daring to move beyond it, but determined not to fall back from it.

She could hear a hiss, like air releasing. But she couldn't see past the wall of police officers in riot gear.

She couldn't make out anything the police officers were saying to each other, but one word drifted back for her ears to pluck from the air.

Alien.

There was an alien. Those police officers were seeing an alien.

Some people tried to push through the cordon. Drew the police officers' attention from whatever they were seeing, and bringing night sticks and pepper spray into play.

Then the screams changed. Got piercing. Pained. Citizens clashed with police. News crews got bulldozed as eager youths charged the police line. More of the officers turned from whatever they saw to aggressively keep people back.

Someone grabbed Laura's decoy purse and she let it go. Her cash and I.D. were tucked into her pockets, and she wasn't going to fight over some makeup and a half-dozen head shots.

Just then a voice echoed loud and clear above the racket. It sounded for all the world like a sport broadcaster she'd heard before, but Laura couldn't name which one.

"Please," the voice said. "there's no need for this violence."

Supported by nothing but good wishes — and probably technology never before seen on Earth — the alien floated twenty feet into the air.

He looked ... disturbingly human. Laura was expecting something wild, something amoeba-like, or insectoid maybe. But no, the alien really did look human. Apart from the deep green skin and oversized cranium, anyway.

He — and Laura assumed it was a he because of the voice and the human-male-style build — looked to stand about six feet tall, with a long nose, a bald head, high cheekbones, narrow black eyebrows, and a sharp chin. He looked slender, but toned in his skintight silver spacesuit. Long arms and long fingers, but the same kind of articulated joints and opposable thumbs human beings had.

Laura would still be suspecting a publicity stunt, except for the floating-in-mid-air bit. This was Midtown Manhattan at high noon, and the alien was surrounded by people. There was no way this could be some kind of camera trick or magician's stunt.

Laura was looking at an actual alien.

7
_____

The Orkney Auto Service garage was busy, of course, so Charlie rushed through paperwork to learn that he would have to wait two hours just to find out if his car was worth saving. That meant suffering through stiff plastic chairs in the waiting room, with its garish red and green tile flooring, and noisy, oscillating fan up in one corner that did nothing to break the building heat of the day. Lowering the blinds on the three walls of windows would probably have done more good.

Also, they offered free microwave popcorn from a one-touch machine on a little table beside the door. The smell of that popcorn was a pleasant change from the tow truck.

Despite the number of cars ahead of his, only two other people waited for their vehicles onsite — a Vietnamese woman in a pale blue suit who worked on her laptop and spoke quickly and softly into her hands-free phone, and a fat, scraggly white man in shorts and a tee shirt that were both too small for him.

But Charlie was more than happy to ignore the other occupants. Orkney had free WIFI and a thirty-inch flat screen television angled out from the wall above the service desk in their waiting room.

Civilization, at last.

"See, that's how you know it's a publicity stunt," said the fat man, pointing at the floating green alien on the screen as Charlie sat down. "He looks human. He—"

"Shhh," said Charlie, not looking away from the screen. Trying to burn the image of the floating green man into his head. Looked like something from an old movie. Spacesuit could have been silver lamé. Bulbous cranium and pointed chin and nose could have been prosthetics. But he floated free in the air, in front of a presumably unbiased crowd, and that was no small trick. "Please. I want to hear."

"...for restoring order," said the alien, in a voice like Chris Burghoff, color commentator for The Hoops Network, "all basketball, all the time." The alien continued, "It looks as though I have to start with an apology. When you study a planet through its media, you inevitably will miss some of the finer points, but that's no excuse. We knew there was no way we could get your attention without causing fear in certain quarters, but we really did not expect my appearance here on your street today to incite a riot."

The alien brought his hands together, fingers intertwined in a gesture of pleading.

"Speaking on behalf of my people, we are most devoutly sorry for that. Please don't let this misunderstanding color what I'm about to tell you."

"Bet a few tomahawk missiles—" started the fat man, but both Charlie and the Vietnamese woman cut him off.

"Shhh!"

"Call me Mynack. And my people go by all kinds of names, but we think the one you'll like best is the Greenies. Deep space exploration is a hobby and sport to our people, and we love nothing better than finding a planet on the verge of space travel. Kind of like your NBA scouts combing the ranks of the college leagues for future stars."

"Why does he sound like a sportscaster?" said the fat man. "This guy thinks he's—"

"Please!" hissed Charlie, feeling hope well up in his chest. Was Mynack here to help the human race get its shit together?

"Now the problem with college stars is figuring out if they have what it takes to make the transition to The Show. That comes down to evaluating core skills and potential."

Mynack moved his hands while he talked, just little gestures that didn't mean anything in and of themselves, but they were very human. These "Greenies" must have been studying human media for some time.

"A lot of my colleagues wanted to pass you guys over. Said your whole species wouldn't last longer than a cup of coffee. But I know differently. I can't tell you why right now, though, because that's what I'm here to prove. And I think you guys will prove me right."

Mynack brought his hands together and swept his eyes over the crowd.

"Some of you are wondering why I didn't approach your governments. That's an easy answer. Governments, by their nature, put themselves ahead of other governments. And we're not interested in your politics. We're not interested in your national borders. We're interested in your *people*. Who you are deep down. What you can do."

That brought a cheer from the crowd that put a smile on Mynack's face. The words sounded good, but the smile was all lip, no teeth, and Charlie wondered what that meant.

"So we need to take some of your people to training camp, to test you and evaluate you. But how do we choose?"

Mynack raised his hands in a bent-arm shrug and volunteers cried out their willingness by the dozen.

"No, no." Mynack made palm-down calming gestures to the crowd. "We can't just take volunteers. But we didn't want to take your politicians or captains of industry either. And we don't abduct people in the night, like some of you are no doubt thinking."

"Yeah, right," said the fat man.

"I'm not saying there aren't other spacefaring peoples who do that kind of thing, but it's not how we get down."

Charlie slapped himself in the forehead at that turn of phrase.

Did Mynack understand the sexual side of it? He had to have gotten it from...

Wait. The sportscaster voice. The metaphors. The old B-movie look. If these aliens had been studying human culture, especially Western culture...

"Fortunately," continued Mynack, "you humans have given us a very easy way to determine our choices for your representatives. You have, in a way, chosen your representatives for us, by making them popular though your global networks."

Charlie got a sinking feeling in his stomach that felt as though it pulled down all of his bones with it. Some of his blog posts were *very* popular...

"My team has done an in-depth study of your global networks and the systems your people use to indicate pleasure and agreement versus displeasure and disagreement. And we've come up with a list of the six individuals who have the most appeal among your people, both in and of themselves and for what they represent."

Cold sweat broke out on Charlie's brow. But it couldn't be. There was no way.

"Here is the list of names you've been waiting for." Mynack cleared his throat, fingers alighting the base of his neck in another very human gesture. "Frenzy!Video sensation Dubba J, Jerome Whitehead. International singing sensation Alita Luna. Film star Jesse Carter. Film star Laura Jefferson. Talk show host Brice DePaul. And finally, the blogger most of you know as Evansessence, Charlie Evans."

8

A-DAY. TEN-TWENTY-NINE A.M. PACIFIC DAYLIGHT TIME

Charlie's phone wouldn't stop ringing.

He slumped, staring at it as he sat fully clothed on the toilet in the Orkney Auto Service's small, unisex bathroom. Harsh fluorescent lighting. The odor of bleach cleansers with hints of urine.

Each time the phone rang, Charlie aborted the call. Thirty-five times, at least, in the few minutes since Mynack the Alien had declared that Charlie was one of the Chosen Ones to represent the *entire human race* in their little evaluation.

No pressure.

The moment he could move after hearing his name called — which must have taken a couple of minutes — Charlie marched right into the bathroom and locked the door. His name was on the forms he had to sign so the shop could evaluate his car. His worthless, broken heap of a car, the perfect metaphor for his worthless, broken heap of a life.

A life so low and pathetic that on the day he actually got an interview with the biggest tech company on the planet — an interview he could ace, for a job he could rock — his car died and wrecked and then...

Charlie sighed and tapped his forehead softly against the cold, white tile wall. Every muscle in his body felt like it had been wrung out, stretched in unpleasant ways, then put back wrong. Sweat stains from his pits and back like oil spills on his red polo shirt.

He wanted to throw up. On some level, Charlie was certain that throwing up would make him feel better. Get some of the emotions out. Because there were just too many to deal with.

His eyes squeezed tight as tears began to flow. He started rocking back and forth, muting yet another phone call by reflex. This was too much. This was all just too much.

Charlie should have been on his laptop, writing about the aliens. Writing about what it meant that they came. Speculating about the people who were called, and what their tests would be. What it would mean to humanity if the Chosen Ones passed. What it would mean if they failed.

These were the things Charlie was good at. These were the things that sent his blogs viral. Got so many views and reblogs and quotes that Charlie should have been rich. Didn't know why he wasn't.

Might never get the chance now.

Charlie aborted another call.

What a stupid selection method! Actors and singers and talk show hosts and one nobody: Charlie. The aliens would have done better to grab the first ten patrons through the door in any bar or restaurant on any given night. Random people. Real people. People who didn't ... who weren't....

People who weren't narcissistic enough to put themselves out where the world could see and judge them.

Charlie hadn't thought about it that way before. Not with himself on that list. Actors and singers, sure, they had to have huge egos just to survive in their industries. Talk show hosts and video stars, probably the same category.

But a blogger like Charlie? Was he just as self-involved?

Hadn't Lucy said as much when she dumped him?

Charlie moaned, then went to tap his head on the tile wall again and hit too hard. A dull thump that jarred pain and reminded his jaw and neck that they had been through too much already today.

Perfect.

The phone rang again. Lucy this time. Charlie aborted that one too. He couldn't believe anyone would actually want to talk to him right now. Why were these people calling? Why weren't they just sending text messages like everyone else?

Text messages didn't even take Charlie effort to ignore. Some two hundred of those must have come in already. Plus the e-mails. Private messages through social networks. Notifications chirped nonstop about all the places online he was being cited and noted and linked to and...

Charlie should just turn off his phone. He knew that. But there was no way he could do it. He could never bring himself to willingly cut himself off from his connection to the wide world, even if the one thing he wanted more than anything else right then was to be by himself.

Dizziness now. He was panting for breath. When did Charlie start panting? When did his heart speed up like this? Why was everything going red at the edge of his vision?

Charlie slapped himself, a stinging blow that sharped the pains from his neck and jaw. He had to calm down. He had to ... he had to ...

...breathe.

Just breathe. In and out. In. And out. He skipped an incoming call with a reflexive thumb flick. One breath came in and Charlie held it through four rapid heartbeats. Then shuddered as he let it out.

Charlie sat there, just breathing and skipping phone calls. Ignoring every ping and chirp and vibration of notification as word spread throughout the world that he, Charlie Evans, Evansessence, had been called out by name by the aliens.

When his heart rate slowed to heavy, almost lurching thumps, Charlie stood up. His butt reminded him that sitting on a toilet for too long is never comfortable. He could just imagine the ring shape in the flesh of his butt.

But Charlie could think again, and the moment he could he realized something.

Charlie could say no.

Just that thought made him shiver in relief. He could say no, thank you very much, and get back to his life. The aliens would take someone else in his place. Charlie was sure of that. That Mynack sounded like he wanted humanity to pass the test, so he would surely be willing to find substitutes for those who were unwilling — or maybe unable, that would sound even better — to take up the challenge.

Perfectly understandable. No hard feelings.

Charlie could get back to his normal life. Heavy, relieved breaths now, muscle groups considering relaxing.

Someone pounded on the bathroom door.

"Just a minute," called Charlie, flushing the toilet. "Let me wash up."

Wasn't even a lie. Charlie had no intention of leaving the restroom without washing his face.

Charlie scrubbed his face as best he could under the small sink with its once-chrome hot/cold lever, using lather from the disturbingly gooey white soap. He dried his face with rough brown towels that felt like they had more plastic content than paper, then tossed out the towels and opened the door.

Standing in the doorway was a big, Hispanic member of the Sunnyvale Police Department. Clean cut, muscled and with a look in his eye that told Charlie not to start any trouble. The policeman wore a nameplate that read Hernandez, and had a little video camera clipped to his badge.

Suddenly Charlie was sweating again, and his bowels informed him that a trip back into the bathroom might be advisable.

"Charlie Evans," said Officer Hernandez in a baritone voice with a slight Mexican accent, "you are not under arrest nor are you being charged with any crimes at this time. However, my department was asked by the Department of Homeland Security to detain you for questioning in connection with a possible invasion from outer space.

And while I do not personally believe that this lies within the scope of that department's mandate, my superior officer disagrees, and has given me the direct order to comply."

Officer Hernandez leaned forward just a little, tapped the badge below his camera, and winked before continuing.

"If you refuse to comply, I have been told to arrest you for violation of the Patriot Act, and *turn you over* to the Department of Homeland Security."

"So if I willingly comply as a good citizen..."

"Then I am a witness to your compliance and your eagerness to assist those agents of the United States government who no doubt have only the best of intentions. And you will remain in my official custody."

"Then, of course, Officer Hernandez." Charlie forced a smile that must have looked like a wilted noodle. "I like nothing better than serving my country."

9

"No, I don't want to do it," said Brice, pacing back and forth behind his oak desk. He was back in his office now, but his Navy blue wool suit still itched everywhere, and he definitely had blisters forming from double-timing it through the streets of Manhattan. To his right was a beautiful, eleventh-floor view of the city. But on his left were his producer, Yolanda, and two nondescript white men with black hair and black suits who wore sunglasses indoors.

Yolanda was leading the charge to get him to go with the Greenies. With her dark skin and red dress she didn't look like a Cossack, but her tone brooked no refusal and her hands waved as she talked like she was conducting the New York Philharmonic.

"You owe this to your viewers. To your nation. Hell, you owe this to the whole human race!"

"What about my family?" Brice threw up his hands. "What about what I owe them? You think Laetitia will agree to this?"

"We think she will, Mr. DePaul," said the high tenor of one of the men in ... black.

"Just who are you guys, anyway?" Brice stopped and put his fists on his hips. "Don't think I don't know that rumors about you guys go back long before those movies, and your reputation isn't nearly as funny."

"Those movies did more harm than you can possibly imagine. Even more than that old television show." The man shook his head. "We're not here to cover anything up and we're not here to make you disappear—"

"So without two dozen or more news networks broadcasting that alien's words live to an international audience, those would have been possibilities? Is that what you're saying?"

The man waved one hand to try to calm Brice, while his partner put his hands behind his back.

No way Brice could be calm now. Fear ran rampant through his system. He felt twitchy. Shaky. Sweaty. And he could smell that his deodorant had given up for the day.

"We're just here," said the man in black who did the talking, "to make sure the government's concerns are considered."

"Let me handle this," said Yolanda, stepping between the two plush red visitors' chairs and leaning forward on the desk. "Brice, think about what you're saying. Think about what you're giving up if you don't go. This is the chance of a lifetime! Travel aboard an alien spacecraft. Meeting aliens. Talking to *aliens*. You have any idea how many other television personalities would give their eye-teeth for this chance? The book rights *alone* will be worth millions."

"True," said Brice, tapping his jaw with the index finger of his right hand and grabbing his elbow with his left, jaw slightly up as he mocked deep thought. "Now let's consider what I give up if I *do* go. Growing old with my wife. Watching my kids grow up. Maybe having grandchildren someday—"

"They don't want to kill you!"

"You don't know that!"

"Actually," said the speaking man in black, whom Brice now designated 'Talky,' which made his partner 'Walky.'

Once Talky had Brice's eyebrow-raised attention, he continued.

"We're of the opinion that they have not come to kill anyone. Not every department in the government agrees with us, but they don't have ... shall we say ... the history with this sort of situation that we do."

"This has happened before?"

This was too much. Brice dropped down into his big, comfy executive chair, not feeling very comfortable or much like an executive.

"Not this exact thing, no. Of course not. But let's just say" — Talky wiggled his hand — "Mynack and the Greenies are not the first aliens to contact the human race. You heard the part, I presume, where he confirmed that another alien race has, in fact, been in the habit of abducting humans for experimentation?"

"Grays are real?"

"That's not their preferred term, but yes. And we think the timing of Mynack's visit is not coincidental. I can't go into details, but let's just say—"

"No." Brice slapped the table. "Let's not 'just say.' No pussyfooting around. No bullshit. Tell me what the hell's going on here."

"So you're agreeing to go?"

"If you don't tell me everything right now, I'll walk out that door and go home to my wife and kids. If the Greenies ask, I'll tell them to go abduct somebody else."

Talky tried to stare down Brice, and Brice's guts started quivering even harder and the little voice in the back of his head reminded him that Talky had already all but confessed to 'disappearing' people, which made pissing him off a class one Bad Idea.

But Brice held firm.

"All right," said Talky quietly. "Ms. Cromartie, I'm afraid you'll have to leave."

"Excuse me?" Yolanda straightened up, arms crossed. "This whole floor is mine, and—"

"Ms. Cromartie, you'll have to leave or you will be guilty of interfering with a Federal agent in the performance of his duty."

Yolanda's mouth kept moving for a few seconds, but words stopped coming out. She drew her lips into a hard line, as though those unspoken words tasted bitter. Her eyes darted back and forth between Brice and the men in black.

Finally she snorted and left, shaking her head and slamming the door behind her.

"She will find a way to make you guys pay for that, you know," said Brice.

"I'll make sure we get hazard pay then."

Talky sat in one of the visitors' chairs, but Walky hung back behind him, hands still behind his back.

"All right. What I am about to tell you is even more classified than we are. We cannot risk your revealing this information to anyone, but I was told that if you pressed the issue, I had permission to impart it. But before I do, you need to understand the consequences. Your just knowing what I'm about to tell you means that someone will be keeping an eye on all your personal communications for a length of time I cannot divulge. Best to assume the rest of your life."

Talky drummed his fingers on the soft, padded fabric of his chair.

"Do you still want to know?"

"Are you guys going to push me to do this test for the Greenies?"

"Your producer seems to think you respond best to the stick, and I admit that she knows you better than I do. But it seems to me that you have your mind made up about your responsibilities. And I don't blame you. If I had a wife and kids, I couldn't do what I do. And neither could my partner."

Walky shook his head.

"But you need to understand something," said Talky. "If you guys pass the Greenies' tests, we stand to gain a substantial amount of technology. Not just space travel. Heck, we can already get to Mars on our own, and we're close to a whole lot more whether the Greenies help us or not. But *with* the Greenies, I'm talking about food production. Water reclamation and purification. Recycling on a level we've never dreamed before. Energy technologies so cheap and efficient they make solar and wind look like coal and oil. We're talking about the chance to not only stop abusing this little planet of ours, but also to repair some of the damage we've done while improving the lives of every human being."

"How do you know this?"

"If I can convince you that it's true, will you go on the tests?"

Brice sat back and thought about it. The wonders sounded too good to be true, which was usually an indication that they were. Hope warred with cynicism in his chest. The young idealist who started *Weeknightly with Brice DePaul* would have jumped at this chance. But the cynicism of twenty years working on the show couldn't believe it.

"You know," said Talky. "Lots of people look up to you. You call out both the left and the right when they're wrong. You represent the liberal ideal in what it's supposed to be, not what the politicians try to make it."

Brice saw where Talky was leading with this, and the realization began to chill him from the face and neck on down in a slow sweep.

"But all you do," Talky continued, "is talk. Night after night on your show you talk about what we Americans *are* doing and contrast it with what we *should* be doing." Talky raised his right fist, not as a threat but as a call to action. "Well here is your chance to *do* something. To show that you're more than just talk. Here's your chance to make a difference."

Talky didn't repeat the question, but it hung in the air between them.

Brice sighed and sagged in his chair.

"Fine. *But,*" — Brice raised his index finger — "you still have to tell me how you know all this first. Otherwise I walk."

"Fair enough," said Talky with a nod. "It all started in Roswell, New Mexico..."

10

A-DAY. TWO-THIRTY P.M. EASTERN DAYLIGHT TIME

"Laura! Honey, you've got to be kidding me."

Laura lowered the bill of her Cleveland Indians cap and folded her arms as she sank lower into the limousine's molded leather bench seat. With a dark gray interior, tinted windows, cherry potpourri air freshener, this was the sort of car Laura was used to riding in these days. If a little smaller than most. After all, it only had room for four rear passengers — six if they were friendly — on two bench seats facing each other, and only a tiny little excuse for a fridge. Barely enough to hold four water bottles.

But the air conditioning felt delightful after that humid outdoor heat. It gelled her sweat — her so-called "glow" — as she rode slowly through the streets to her interview.

"What are you even doing in New York, Harvey? And don't tell me you're here to support me in the interviews. You haven't done that since—"

"Don't try to change the subject on me. You're being very selfish here."

That got Laura to raise her head just enough to see her agent, sitting across from her. The great Harvey Roth, who hated facing backwards in limousines but would do it for his top clients. And he only worked with top clients. He had forty years at the helm of the Roth agency, handling Hollywood's elite.

And even at sixty-eight he spent hours in the gym every day to fit into his slick light gray Italian suits, bound at the neck with his trademark blue and yellow striped tie.

"Selfish," Laura said softly. "This coming from the man on his fifth marriage, each wife younger than the last."

"Yes, selfish," said Harvey, who had a way of sounding respectful and indignant at the same time. "A lot of people are counting on you."

"Really? That's your argument?"

Laura tilted her head back against the cushion and raised the bill of her cap so she could look at Harvey properly. Not an edge-of-silver hair out of place. He looked cool and collected like this was a Los Angeles spring and not a New York summer. As though he hadn't spent enough time outside of air conditioned cars and buildings to even consider breaking a sweat. Part of the image, she supposed, of the consummate bullshit artist.

"Yes," said Harvey, talking with his hands now as though he simulcast everything he said in a sign language of his own invention. "And I don't just mean your fans here. Or the money-men who make these things happen. I'm talking about the other people you care about. The support staffs. The grips and lighting crews and makeup artists and—"

"I have a chance to help the whole human race, and you want me to say no because it might — *might* — interfere with my shooting schedule this *October*?"

"You signed a contract, Laura. You have an obligation to be in Vancouver on October—"

"Tenth, ten a.m. I know. And that's just for the final medical pass, before the table reads start. I do actually read my own calendar, you know."

"Then you understand why you can't do this. You don't want to break a contract with these people, Laura. You'll never work again."

"If — and I do mean if — I don't make it back in time for the start of shooting, I wouldn't be the first actress to break a contract. Bet I wouldn't be the last either. But I can tell you this." Laura sat up straighter. "I'd be the one who had the best reason for doing it."

"Oh, so you think going off and getting yourself killed is a good reason to break a contract?"

"What makes you think I'll get killed?"

"What makes you think you won't?" Harvey grabbed the knot of his tie and tugged it as though he had to let out steam. His face *was* turning kind of red. "Laura, this isn't some movie. Margie won't be there to do your stunts."

"I do about half of my stunts these days—"

"*These aren't stunts!*" Harvey punched the seat beside him. "We don't know anything about these 'Greenies' or what kind of tests they have in mind for you. And what if they don't *kill* you? What if they just hurt you? What if you come back with a whole second case of PTSD? Or they mar your—"

"If you say 'your beautiful face,' I swear to God—"

"*This is no time for your impostor syndrome bullshit!*" Harvey's breaths came heavy through his nostrils, and he ran both his hands through his hair, trying to calm himself. "Look. I know it's cute how you always say you don't feel gorgeous or whatever. But if you think talent and hard work were enough to get you where you are—"

"There are a thousand girls in Hollywood who are better looking than I am. There are—"

"*Fine!*" Harvey had to loosen his tie now. He'd finally broken a sweat. "Fine. Don't believe me. Don't believe the casting directors or your fans. Don't believe the photographers who drop supermodel shoots just to snap one magazine pic with your face. Don't believe any of us. Or better yet, go pay a second shrink to help you deal with this bullshit, because the difference between a movie star and a film legend is owning exactly who and what you are."

That stunned Laura enough that for a moment she forgot what they were arguing about. But Harvey wasn't finished.

"But you know as well as I do that if you come back scarred you get character roles instead of lead roles. Is that what you want?"

"What I want." Laura's voice sounded distant in her own ears. She stared down at her unpainted toenails, only just visible past the brown leather of her sandals. "Do you really care, Harvey? Do you really care what I want? Or are you just worried about your ten percent?"

"You know the answer to that. Both. You hired me because I can get you the best deals for the best projects. You hired me because you know I will make sure of two things: you always get paid, and I always get paid. I worry about the bottom line, so you don't have to."

Harvey sighed, and for a moment looked every one of his sixty-eight years, plus maybe a few extra.

"But, Laura, of course I care about you and what you want. And I'm telling you the same thing I'd be telling any one of my own daughters, if they found themselves in your position. Don't just say 'no.' Say 'Hell no.' Let the Greenies pull from any of our fine special forces—"

"They don't want soldiers. They—"

"They're aliens." Harvey shook his head, sighed and tightened his tie. "Honey, you can't expect that they know us any better than we know them. This is probably just another way of saying, 'take us to your leader.'"

"I'm doing this."

Harvey looked her over, and Laura knew he could see the steel in her straightened posture. He sighed.

"Fine. Let me talk to Sylvia before you tell her. Or were you going to keep your publicist out of the loop and surprise us all by announcing it on Late Night?"

"I'd never do that to her. Or you."

"You're doing enough."

Harvey made the call and Laura pulled her hat back down over her eyes. This was scary and amazing and wonderful all at once. Part of her wanted to thrill to the moment, while the rest of her studied every iota of her reactions so she could summon them again the next time cameras rolled.

Harvey had just finished his call when the limo stopped outside the Late Night studio. Laura's stomach growled, and she hoped Steve had that lamb curry wrap waiting for her.

The door opened and Laura's smile froze at the sight of the woman holding the door.

Laura knew a government agent when she saw one.

11

Charlie had to keep reminding himself he wasn't under arrest. It helped that so far no one had cuffed him.

Still, sitting in a police interview room wasn't good for his already troubled nerves. Hard metal chair, probably steel. Metal table too, painted pistachio green. Cool to the touch, but dented slightly on Charlie's side. Almost as though someone had slammed a forehead into the table. Repeatedly.

And there was a small metal loop for handcuffs close to his side too.

But he wasn't cuffed yet.

White cinder block walls with a four-foot-by-six-foot "mirror" and a single door so heavy that every time it closed it sounded like sealing a tomb. Thin gray carpeting, stained in spots by coffee.

At least, Charlie devoutly hoped those were coffee stains.

The room was cool, at least. Probably all the cinder blocks. But that just meant that Charlie's sweat had gelled and now he felt chilly enough to shiver a bit, and the salt from his sweat itched under his red polo shirt.

The room still smelled like the burger and fries that Officer

Hernandez had picked him up at Meat for Your Beast. Charlie had finished the food, but the taste of fast food regret clung to his tongue. That mixture of salt with burger and fry grease that no amount of Diet Eruption Cola could banish. And Charlie was putting a serious dent in his forty-four-ounce drink trying.

Officer Hernandez checked on Charlie every ten minutes, which was nice. But even forty minutes of waiting had not gotten his heart rate quite back to normal. In fact, he was starting to wonder if he should worry about the way it thumped—

The interview room door opened, and this time it wasn't Officer Hernandez.

Two people came in, an African American man and a white woman. Both tall, both thin, both with short hair and dark suits. The man's tie was a rich yellow and purple. The woman's was a light blue paisley. As though the only allowance for personal expression in their dress was the tie, and damn it, both intended to take advantage of that.

The man's face was rounder, the woman's more pointed. But they both looked so serious Charlie had a hard time finding anything likable in their demeanor.

And he was trying.

"You are Charlie Evans," said the man in a deep voice, "alias Evansessence?"

"It's more of a handle than an alias," said Charlie, holding up his hands and doing his best to look nonthreatening. "Just something people call me online, not something my girlfriend ever called me. You know?"

"That would be Lucy Pendleton?" asked the woman, consulting a tablet computer small enough to fit in the palm of her hand.

"Not anymore." Charlie could feel his confusion spread across his face. Why did they know Lucy's name? "I mean, yeah, she's still Lucy Pendleton, but she's not my girlfriend anymore. We broke up."

"Mr. Evans," said the man, "your blog primarily deals with entertainment, is this correct?"

"Before we go any further, can I see some identification? I'm here voluntarily, but to cooperate with my government. I need to be sure you two are—"

"I am Agent Crawford," said the man, "and this is Agent Kolchak."

Both agents pulled badges out of their jacket lining pockets, identifying them as working for the Department of Homeland Security. They held those badges up long enough for Charlie to look closely at them, then put them back.

"Now," said Agent Crawford. "Do you need me to repeat the question?"

"No. I'm mostly an entertainment blogger, though I do talk about the news sometimes. Protests and riots, stuff like that, because I think they deserve all of our attention and notice."

"Do you believe," said Agent Kolchak, "that the protests represent failures on the part of our government?"

Charlie jostled his chair back a little and bumped into the cinder block wall behind him.

"Our government is about representation," Charlie said. "Protests and riots, those are mostly about bringing attention to areas where American citizens don't feel represented."

"Individual failure," said Kolchak, "or institutional failure?"

"Why does this matter?"

The last thing Charlie wanted to do was debate governmental policy with federal agents. Mostly because part of him was afraid doing so would *be* the last thing he ever did.

"You're the odd man out, Mr. Evans," said Agent Crawford. "Jesse Carter and Laura Jefferson are movie stars. Alita Luna is a singer. Brice DePaul is a talk show host. Dubba J is a dancer and comedian. But you? You aren't part of the entertainment industry. You write about the entertainment industry."

"And if what I wrote weren't entertaining, people wouldn't read it." Charlie rubbed at his neck. He felt exposed here. If these two were in the room with him, who knew who was watching through the "mirror?" "I'm an entertainer too."

He hoped at least Officer Hernandez was watching. Just in case.

"The others are famous personalities. Their images recognizable all over the world. The same can't be said of you."

"But my words are. My voice is. No one else writes blogs the way I do."

"Exactly," said Agent Kolchak. "People turn to Jefferson, Carter, Luna, DePaul and Dubba J for escape. Illusion. Distraction. But they turn to you for opinion. And that makes our superiors wonder what the Greenies see in your opinions that we're missing."

"So the question, again," said Agent Crawford, "is why? Why have they chosen *you*, Mr. Evans?"

Charlie stared at them both, mouth slack with incredulity.

"How can I possibly know that?"

"You can't," said Agent Kolchak. "Unless they've been in touch with you before."

The sentence hung in the air. Her words seemed to grow bigger in the silence. To echo within Charlie's mind. They couldn't believe that, could they? Could they really mistake him for some sort of ringer? Some sort of—

"I thought not," said Agent Crawford, with a sigh. "Forgive me if I hoped they had. I didn't want to think ill of you, but it would have made our jobs easier if we had someone to interview who could give us a look into what these aliens have in mind."

"But if they have been in touch with you before," said Agent Kolchak, "you clearly don't know about it."

Charlie sighed so hard he got a head rush. He had to catch himself from falling forward and banging his forehead on the dent in the table.

"I swear. I never—"

"Mr. Evans," said Agent Crawford, "spotting liars is our profession. Agent Kolchak and I are so good we get flown around the country to do it. You're lucky we were already in Los Angeles when the call came. You might have been held here until we could fly in from the East Coast."

"So I'm free to go?" said Charlie, standing up, then catching himself again with one hand on the metal table because that head rush wasn't quite gone.

"Not quite," said Agent Kolchak. "If you can't help us figure out why they want you, then we need to help you figure out how to respond."

"Simple," said Charlie, not ready to sit back down yet. "I'm going to tell them to piss off and go hide in my room and blog. I'm not some kind of action hero. I didn't even have the guts to follow through and go on that one-way trip to Mars. They can take the next runner up."

"Suppose it doesn't work that way," said Agent Crawford. "Suppose your refusal automatically means a one-sixth failure."

"You don't want humanity's future resting on my shoulders."

"No," said Agent Kolchak, "we don't. But this is the hand we've been dealt. Refusal may not be an option, so let's just assume you'll have to go. The question becomes, how can we help you while you're gone, and how can you help us when you return?"

Charlie looked from one agent to the other. They looked more relaxed now. Not quite friendly, but not quite so cold either. They even looked like people who might tell a decent story over a beer. As long as they were off the clock at the time.

"What do you have in mind?"

12

Thirty years together, and the sight of Laetitia still made Brice's pulse quicken. Heavier now than the day they met, sure, but where she saw herself as dumpy, he saw her as enjoying her food. Where she saw lines deepening in her face, he saw the smiles that put them there. When she pointed out gray roots under her chestnut locks, he said, "the couple that dyes together ... lives a long life together because they're already doing one kind of dying."

That always got a laugh out of her.

In her yellow sundress, Brice felt she fit perfectly in the breakfast nook, the lightest, airiest part of their penthouse apartment. She kept it full of ferns and rubber trees and orchids in exotic colors that really set off the Mediterranean tiles and cherry wood table and chairs, and worked with the bay windows to give the impression of sitting out on the deck instead of inside the glass door, where the air conditioner kept them cool.

But Laetitia wasn't laughing now as she slapped a cup of decaf on the table in front of him and dropped heavily into the seat opposite.

"I don't want you to go," she said.

"I know." Brice shook his head. "I don't want to either. But the benefits to the whole human race—"

"I don't care. If whatever we'd learn from these "Greenies" is that important, we'll figure it out on our own, like we have everything else. Surviving is what humans do best."

"Maybe. These Greenies—"

"I don't want to lose you." She reached out one hand to him across the table.

Brice grabbed her hand and hung on for dear life.

"You won't. There's no reason to think this will be fatal. In fact—"

"No matter what happens, I'll lose you." Tears started flowing down her face now, and her voice caught when she tried to speak.

"Never," said Brice.

"Y-yes," she said, gripping his hand every bit as hard as she did during the birth of their first child, Jean Paul. Hard enough that Brice winced, but he didn't interrupt and her voice got stronger as she spoke. "We ... we've shared everything you and I. For thirty years. All our ups and downs. But this. How can you share this with me? How can I begin to comprehend what they put you through?"

"Teesh," Brice said, but she wasn't done.

"They could bring you back in thirty minutes, and the gulf between us would be a lifetime."

Laetitia broke down in tears, her face in her hands now. Brice was around the table and taking her in his arms before the scrape of his moving chair faded from hearing.

He hushed and soothed with small sounds at first, but then Brice sobbed and joined her, mourning a loss that might be.

They hung there together, crying and clinging to each other as though they could merge into one being, until all sense of time was lost. It might have been five minutes. It might have been five hours.

But the sun was not yet down when Brice opened his eyes again, blinking them clear. Laetitia joined him a moment later, and he kissed her tears away as he had that time when she twisted her ankle on their very first hike together in Corsica.

The memory of it brought a wistful smile to his lips, and a moment later to hers. But that did not surprise him. Laetitia always seemed to understand when he smiled, to share a memory before he gave voice to it.

And then they were kissing. And then Brice hoped the kids were out for the night because he and Laetitia did not stop at kissing. They did not stop until they were physically spent as well as emotionally spent, lying naked together on the Mediterranean tiles. He on his back, and she on her side, leg and arm draped across him and head pillowed on his shoulder.

"I'll find a way," Brice said. "I swear to you. I'll find a way to tell you everything. To share every moment of whatever they put me through, good and bad. I'll never utter the words 'you wouldn't understand.' No matter how weird it is, how far outside anything we know. I swear to you I will find a way."

Laetitia tilted her face up to look him in the eye.

"And if you can't?"

"Then I'll keep trying. I love you. More than anything or anyone. More than life itself."

Brice kissed her again.

Someone knocked on the front door.

Jarred out of the moment, Brice and Laetitia laughed like embarrassed schoolkids and rushed to get dressed. And though she insisted that her hair was beyond repair, she was decent first, so she hurried through the living room to the front door while Brice finished dressing.

He had just finished pulling back on his Humor Inc. tee shirt when he heard her call from the front door.

"Brice!" Her voice came tight and shaky. "It's the alien!"

Brice ran to join her at the front door, and there stood Mynack, every green inch as calm and collected as he had been on the streets of New York earlier that day. The alien's eyes were amber. Why hadn't Brice noticed that before?

"It's time to go, Mr. DePaul," Mynack said.

"I'm going to have to say no," Brice said, suddenly realizing he meant it. "As much as I want to help the human race, I can't put my wife through this. Or my kids."

"No," said Laetitia, voice heavy as though she had to drag out her words. "Honey, no. I hate to say this, I really do, but you have to go."

"Teesh?" said Brice, turning to her.

"This is who you are," she said with a shake of her head that was both loving and exasperated. "And this is what you do. You take stands others don't take. You say things others won't say. You make yourself a target for everyone to shoot at, because it has to be done. It frightens me. It always frightens me. But it's who you are, and I love you."

Brice wiped away a small trail of tears with his thumb as he stroked her cheek.

"Maybe I've been that man long enough. Maybe it's time for me to retire."

"I'm going to hold you to that when you come home." Laetitia turned to Mynack, jabbing her finger into the alien's chest with a fierceness that surprised even Brice. "And he better come home. Alive and healthy. Because if he doesn't the stars won't hide you from me. Believe it."

Mynack said nothing.

Brice didn't have to do this. Mynack's silence made that clear. Brice had to choose. With no promise of safety. With no promise of returning at all.

But that didn't mean Mynack couldn't promise something else.

"Let's just say I survive this and return," said Brice, looking into those amber eyes. "Will I get to remember what I've been through? Will my memories make sense? Coherent enough for me to explain to my wife?"

"I would imagine," said Mynack, "that you will create books and movies about your experience. About the experiences of all six of you, succeed or fail. If any of it were beyond your ability to conceive and comprehend, then the tests themselves would have no value."

Brice sighed, and the relief made his body lighten, his back straighten. Laetitia was crying again, softly.

Brice turned and took her in his arms.

"Then this will be an adventure I can share with you, my love, not a gulf that drives us apart."

He kissed her again, and the kiss went on until Mynack finally cleared his throat and said, "It really is time to go, Mr. DePaul."

13

Charlie's Caravel was a lost cause. But it must have had scrap value, because the junkyard gave Charlie a couple of hundred bucks to haul it away.

Sad, but arguably the best thing to happen to Charlie today.

Anyway, he was now driving a rental provided by the Department of Homeland Security. A big Garfield Man-of-war SUV, with all the bells and whistles. Practically drove itself. Seemed like overkill for a guy about to leave the planet, but Charlie did manage to enjoy the riding in it all the way back to his apartment in San Jose, down near Bascom and Hamilton in a neighborhood on the cheap side of safe. His block was full of old construction apartment complexes, old wiring and old pipes, but it had live oaks and wandering cherry trees, and not too much crime.

Once Charlie had said he was willing to play ball, the agents had been downright friendly. Still, Charlie would have been much happier hiding out in his apartment than handing himself over to aliens. Flight was a much stronger impulse in him than fight, and he liked it that way.

But Agents Crawford and Kolchak had a raised a good point —

refusal might have been either a) impossible, or b) damaging to future of the human race.

Hiding in his apartment to preserve his own life was one thing. Living out the rest of his days as the man who doomed the planet through inaction was another.

The SUV barely fit in his parking spot against the redwood fence, and Charlie tried not to think how fast it would suck up the kilowatt hours if he plugged it in. But the charge was still half full when he got home, so he hoped the solar panels built into the windows and moon roof would do the trick.

Charlie lived in a six-plex. The front unit looked like a one-story house, with a branch office coming out the back. In that branch were the laundry room and two units downstairs, then three more units upstairs. The whole thing was stucco painted poop-brown, with lighter brown trim.

Charlie's apartment was the top, back unit. On a day like today, he left the window air conditioner running on low when he left in the morning so he wouldn't broil when he got upstairs. If he hadn't, his apartment would have caught and focused all the heat of the day.

All the bushes and shrubs that grew along the outside of the building had been hacked way back. In theory this was for security. To keep thieves from having a place to hide. At least, that was the excuse the landlord gave when she sent in the "gardeners."

In practice, it cut out the possibility of anything growing lush or flowery within ten feet of the stucco. Like the bushes were half-starved prison inmates.

The lawn out front was yellow, in a shade that, in Charlie's mind, continued the lavatory color scheme perfectly.

At least it didn't smell that bad. Mostly hot asphalt and that dry, summer smell.

Charlie stopped by the row of metal boxes outside the laundry room to check his mail. Nothing but advertising circulars. Printed spam. He tucked them under his arm alongside his red folder with the notes and handouts for his aborted interview.

He trudged up the concrete slat stairs, each step ringing out from their wrought iron frame. He wanted nothing more than to flop on his lumpy, root-beer-brown couch, drink a beer, put on some Three Coyotes music, and forget the world for an hour or two. Then, and only then, he might be ready to face at least part of the sea of messages waiting for him on his phone and in his e-mail. And on his blog. And more places besides, he was sure.

Charlie got one step inside his front door and stopped short.

There was a Greenie sitting on his couch. And it wasn't the one from television.

14

"Hi," said the alien in a friendly, bouncy voice that sounded vaguely familiar. "You must be Charlie. You can call me Kyna."

Kyna was tall. Supermodel tall. Probably taller than Charlie if she stood up. She was slender like Mynack, except that she had curves under her tight silver spacesuit that suggested a very appealing human build.

What was *actually* under that spacesuit, Charlie had no way of knowing. And he found the thought the kind of creepy that itched between his shoulder blades.

She shared Mynack's smooth green skin, high cheekbones, and pointed nose and chin. And she had the same bald, slightly enlarged cranium, though her thin eyebrows were jet black. She had normal human pupils, but vivid orange irises. The overall effect of her appearance was both pretty and disturbing.

Kyna was sitting directly under Charlie's poster of *Barbarella*, and while she looked nothing like Jane Fonda, Charlie had to wonder if her placement was a coincidence. After all, her spacesuit left her arms completely bare. Legs too, except for her knee-high silver boots.

Then again, the couch was the only place to sit in the little living room. The couch, between two unmatched thrift store end tables and behind an oak steamer trunk that served as a coffee table. Generic, puke brown carpeting underneath it all, and the only light source a hanging lamp with a beige shade that Charlie had found abandoned in a hotel parking lot. Across from the couch sat Charlie's old thirty-inch flat screen television.

If Kyna didn't want to stand, she only really had a choice of parking herself under *Barbarella* or *The Empire Strikes Back*. The latter might have sent an even worse message.

But then, the momentary detachment faded, and Charlie realized *an alien was in his living room*. The shock of her presence felt like he'd run straight into a wall. And it wasn't even the first time today he could say that. Though at least this time it was figurative, and by now his body felt too numb to properly panic.

"I ... uh..." said Charlie, trying to think of some way to stall until he could get his brain working again.

"Wasn't expecting visitors? I understand. I'm sorry. I know that in your society it would be more polite to wait until you were home, then knock."

Her smile looked apologetic, but the tone of her words helped Charlie place the voice, which got his mind back in gear.

"Shireen!" he said, snapping his fingers. "The secretary from that sitcom. *Two Friends No Waiting*."

"Yes," Kyna said, without a trace of embarrassment. "I learned your language watching your situation comedies, especially that show. Her voice is my tribute." She sat forward. "As I started to say, I would have waited until you were home, but, well, I would have been somewhat noticeable, hanging around outside your apartment."

"Yeah," Charlie said with a slow nod. "I guess you would."

"Speaking of," Kyna said, pointing to the door. "You might want to close that. Maybe even come sit down so we can talk."

"Right." Charlie shut the door harder than he intended. Locked it by reflex, then cringed at the thought of how Kyna might take that. He shook his head and turned back around. "I need a beer. Want one?"

"Oh! Excellent." She gave Charlie a broad smile that somehow avoided showing any teeth. "Beer is a celebratory thing, yes? And this is an occasion to celebrate."

"It is?"

The walk from Charlie's front door to his refrigerator took only a dozen steps, and brought him from puke brown carpet to scuffed white linoleum. Two rows of pale wood cabinets, above and below a short stretch of matching counter, where Charlie's microwave and coffee maker lived. The only other appliances were the dull brushed steel dishwasher and fridge, both of which were older and noisier than Charlie's departed Caravel.

But the fridge held cheese, and cube steak, and milk, and most important of all, a six-pack of Death Watch IPA, with its skull-and-crossbones clock face label.

Charlie pulled out two, popped their lids on the edge of the counter, and sipped at one as he walked back into the living room. Crisp and clear beer taste, with just a hint of bite.

"Of course," said Kyna, taking the beer Charlie offered as he sat down at the far end of the couch. "This is a great day for both our worlds." She raised her beer in a toast and said, "May this be the start of a long and beautiful friendship between our peoples."

Charlie clinked his beer bottle with hers, but couldn't keep the confusion off his face, even as he drank a swig.

"You make this sound like a done deal. I thought there were tests we have to pass."

"There are. And that's what I'm here to talk to you about. Our studies indicate that of all six of our selections, you are the one most likely to say no."

"Is saying no an option?" Charlie couldn't keep the hope out of his voice. If he could say no, someone else could—

"Not a good one, to be honest." She sipped again, and Charlie joined her by reflex. "If you guys fail, your people will be ... isolated for a long time. Long enough that your race might not survive. You haven't been the kindest to yourselves in how you've handled your planet."

"Hey, we didn't—"

"Forgive me," she said free hand raised in a halting gesture. "I don't mean to sound accusatory. Most intelligent species suffer from myopia in their early phases. That's why we showed up when we did. We wait to see proof that a species has figured out what it's done wrong and starts serious attempts to address its problems."

Charlie took a long swig as he thought about that. What she said sounded familiar...

"Wait," he said. "Are you saying that the human race is somewhere on the verge of growing up? That we've just reached the point that we're thinking about the consequences of our actions?"

"I'd rather not answer that, if you don't mind. No matter what I say, it would sound judgmental."

"But you *are* judging us."

"Not judging. Evaluating." She sipped as though she'd been drinking beer for years. "We're trying to determine where you are in your progress, not whether or not we believe you're making the right choices. Do you see the difference?"

"No." Charlie shook his head. "If we pass your tests, we get your help. If we don't, you quarantine us until we kill ourselves off. That's judgment."

"It's not that at all." She shook her head, her mouth set and brow furrowed in a very human expression of frustration. "Your language is so imprecise. It's like this. Have you seen television advertisements that say you can help a child in another country with a modest financial investment?"

"Yes," Charlie said slowly, eyes narrowed in suspicion.

"Well, the organizations that do that. That take your money and use it to help these children. Can they help everyone? Every child in every village and town across the surface of your world?"

Charlie shook his head and drained his beer while she spoke.

"Of course not. They do the best they can with the time and resources they have available. They have to assess these places. Not only who would benefit from their help, but who would accept it. Figure out where their help would do the most good. That's all we're doing. We need to test your people to determine if you are ready, willing and able to benefit from our assistance. Not every species is. The first couple of planets we helped? They tried to hoard our gifts and use them against their own people. What a nightmare that was."

Charlie screwed up his face tight, but couldn't keep his next words from slipping out.

"We do have people who would do that."

"Of course you do," Kyna said with a shrug. "Every species does, when they're around your stage. That's why we have the tests, to figure out who's ready and who isn't. If you are, great! If not, we have to move on and help someone else. And by the time we get back to you..."

Kyna sipped her beer rather than repeat herself.

Charlie went for another swig, but his bottle was empty. "What do you guys get out of this? Why help anyone at all?"

Kyna raised an eyebrow. "I think you know the answer to that."

Charlie rolled his moist, empty bottle around in his hands while he thought. The answer that came to mind was that they were doing the same thing the human race had started doing. Trying to make their environment better. Longer lasting.

Charlie almost said that. His lips parted and he got as far as the "b" in "Because." But then he realized that making him answer was a con man's trick.

"No," he said. "I know what I *think* the answer is. You tell me what the truth is."

Kyna chuckled.

"Why do humans give to charity? Devote time and energy to helping the less fortunate? Because it feels good. It feels like the right thing to do. Because we've been where you are. And because we can look back later and say, honestly, I helped make that possible."

"That isn't what I thought you were going to say at all."

Kyna winked and finished her beer.

"Your people always look for complicated answers," she said finally, "when the truth is often the simplest option."

"Ockham's Razor," said Charlie, blinking.

Kyna set her empty bottle down onto the table and looked at Charlie sideways. "So, will you agree?"

"I already promised my government I would."

"I figured as much." She leaned back against the couch, which creaked underneath her. She spread her arms along the back and crossed her knees, emphasizing what her tight, silver spacesuit concealed. "That's the other reason I'm here."

"Governments," Charlie said, trying not to let her pose distract him. On a human woman it would have looked fetching. But Charlie couldn't believe she had the same anatomy, for all she mimicked human movements and gestures. "They're the ones you were talking about. The ones who would try to hoard and find advantage."

Kyna said nothing.

"So if I'm going to say yes, I have to do so knowing that I'll be pissing off my government by reneging on my agreement with Agents Crawford and Kolchak."

Kyna only looked at Charlie. Her orange eyes gave away nothing.

"That's my real choice here, isn't it? Saying yes, but planning to work with my government behind your back, that's the same as saying no. The same as failing, isn't it?"

Kyna didn't even blink. She just stared back. Waiting.

This was what it all came down to then, for Charlie. He could say no to everybody and piss off the whole world, and quite possibly doom the human race to extinction. He could say yes, then lie to Kyna and try to work with his government behind her back.

Or he could say yes and mean it. Forget everything Agents Crawford and Kolchak offered and promised. Forget the little ways he was supposed to pass them information if he could.

He would be risking the wrath of his government, but if Kyna wasn't lying, this was the only real way to try to help the whole human race.

When he thought about it that way, it was no choice at all.

"I'm saying yes," he said, setting down his bottle. He dug into the pocket of his cargo pants for a small black disc the size of a quarter. He set it on the table next to his beer bottle. "And I'm promising you, and Mynack, and everyone else involved that I am coming on my own as a member of the human race. I'm not going to work with my government the way I told them I would."

"Excellent." Kyna stood up and held out her hand. "Then it's time to go."

Shifting golden light began to surround her.

Suddenly Charlie couldn't bring himself to move. His breaths came in gasps. "Maybe we should have another beer first. And I've got like a thousand messages waiting for me."

"Come along, Charlie. Everyone else is waiting."

"But ... but I don't want to be broken down into millions of tiny particles and reassembled. What if—"

"Shhhh," said Kyna, one finger over her pursed green lips. "That's not how this works."

Moving slowly, she took Charlie's hand, and he let her do it. Her glow swept around to engulf them both, tingling over every inch of Charlie's skin.

And then, together, they vanished.

PART II

GATHERING

15

A-Day. Seven-Thirty P.M. Eastern Daylight Time

In terms of accommodations, Laura had seen worse.

Her first shoot had been a horror movie, on the edge of Arizona desert. Everyone had been forced to double-up in rooms in this tiny motel that had started life as an office building. Thin gray carpet everywhere, even in the bathroom. Some half-assed installation job on the bathroom sink and shower that would have made Laura's father cringe. Bedsprings so rusty they creaked if you gave them a harsh look. Walls thin enough to hear the name stars going at it three rooms away.

Whenever those two were fighting or fucking, everyone knew it. Hell, even the coyotes in the desert probably heard them. And much to the director's chagrin, his two stars seemed to fight and fuck nonstop when they weren't in front of the camera.

That was Laura's first lesson in reasons not to date a co-star. No one on the set respected those two, and they made the crew's lives hell.

If only Laura hadn't broken her rule for that charming bastard Jesse Carter.

No. None of that.

She spliced that line of thinking right out of her head.

Then there was that scary little Winnebago that had been her first "trailer." The memory of the roaches alone was enough to make her shiver, and there were worse things than roaches in that Winnebago.

But this place where Mynack had dropped her off — teleported, of course, which suggested to Laura that *every* aspect of that big silver ship landing had been selected to draw attention — this place might not have been the Hotel Bel-Air, but it came pretty close.

Two rooms to herself, a little sitting area with Louis XVI décor, down to the couch, chairs, tables, even the writing desk. No art though, or plants. Just a big mirror on one wall, also Louis XVI design. More than six feet tall and easily four feet wide, with gold leaf trim all around the rectangle as well as forming an oval in the center, and flourishes everywhere the oval met the rectangle, especially top and center.

The bedroom was much more modern. California king sized bed, with very soft, pale green cotton sheets and a darker green bedspread. A vanity in one corner, filled with high-end makeup. A deep, broad walk-in closet filled with hundreds of outfits and combinations, that all looked to be her size. Shoes from practical work boots to tiny, frilly little black pumps that would be *perfect* for next year's Academy Awards.

Even the underwear was in her size. There was a time when that might have creeped Laura out, but these days it just told her that these aliens had excellent support staffs.

Mynack had collected Laura... Picked up? Retrieved? She couldn't think of a word or phrase that made it sound any better in her head. Every term she tried made this sound like a date or an abduction, and she didn't want to think of it as either.

Whatever it was, Mynack came for Laura before she could go onstage for her *Late Night* interview. So there, at least, was a small blessing out of all this. And she did get to eat her lamb curry wrap, so as far as Laura was concerned, the day was looking up.

Mynack's timing also meant that she was dressed in her practical disguise outfit when she arrived in her suite.

But that was no longer true. Now she wore a pale green, chiffon sheath dress that would complement the complexion of her host. The dress started at the collarbone, but left her shoulders bare and hugged her curves through the hips before flaring out enough for free leg movement.

Laura almost felt beautiful in this dress, especially after a touch of makeup at the vanity and a hint of rosewater at her wrists and throat.

If she wore this dress on a red carpet, networks would rave. Though on the red carpet she would have worn pumps, instead of matching flats.

And Laura needed that red-carpet-ready feeling right now. Needed an outfit that made her feel powerful, like the woman these aliens must have seen in movies they picked up from our satellites, not the woman who lounged around in floppy gray sweats and didn't always shower if she wasn't leaving the house.

In an outfit like this, Laura felt ready to face almost anything.

Ready as she was going to get, Laura crossed her living room to the only door with a lock. The only door that led somewhere that wasn't part of her suite. The door Mynack had told her to come through when she felt ready.

Seemed like it should have been special somehow. Glowing maybe, or made from some kind of metal that muted sound and felt warm to the touch.

Instead, it was a plain white door with a simple brass knob and a push-button lock. The door even had hinges, on her side.

Laura shrugged, and opened the door.

16

Laura wasn't sure what she expected when she opened that door, but it wasn't a lounge.

It was a big lounge, at least. Twenty foot ceilings, painted sky blue like the walls. Plush carpeting the color of Kentucky bluegrass, and a half-dozen white doors spaced evenly along the outside walls.

One side of the room was set up for games, with pinball tables, air hockey, pool, ping-pong, even a dart board. The near side had a kitchen in the corner, with white oak cabinets and hardwood flooring, and all kinds of brushed steel appliances that looked showroom new. Black marble counters with a deep-looking sink. She could smell that someone had been making coffee and popcorn.

And the rest of the near area was devoted to conversation. Two sectional couches with chaise longues, both of distressed dark leather, and both facing each other, with a flat, white oak coffee table between them.

The couches were in use, and now Laura felt overdressed.

Sitting on the couches she saw talk show host Brice DePaul, in a tee shirt and jeans, with a Mets cap. He sat forward, on the edge of the couch, a slight hunch of discomfort. Sitting next to him was that Frenzy!Video sensation with the short dreadlocks, delightful muscles, cocoa brown skin and wide smile, Dubba J. Dubba J wore red jeans shorts without shoes, and a black tee shirt with the sleeves torn off. He leaned back deep against the cushions, and had his legs crossed with an ankle on one knee.

Across from the two of them sat Alita Luna, the Colombian singer who packed so much beauty and body into her five foot frame that Laura felt momentarily like a prepubescent stick figure. Alita wore painted on blue jeans and a tee shirt cut short enough to show off her honey-brown midriff, and sat deep on the couch with her legs tucked under her. She shunted her mass of copper-brown hair behind her with a rainbow of clips.

Apparently Laura would have fit in better with the crowd if she'd tied back her hair and gone for the other style of outfit that made her feel powerful: tomboy. Didn't matter. Her choice was made. And Laura had years of practice at faking comfort until she felt comfortable.

A big blue crystal bowl of popcorn sat on the table, half eaten. And each of them had a steaming mug on the table in front of them, and now Laura was sure she could detect notes of Arabica beans and perhaps a hint of mocha.

"Laura," said Brice, the only one in the room she'd met before. "Our hosts have great coffee. You should grab a cup and join us."

"Wow," said Dubba J, drawing the syllable out. "*The* Laura Jefferson. Figured a megastar like you had insurance clauses in your contracts that kept you from saying yes to a thing like this. You know," — he wiggled his eyebrows — "no skydiving, no climbing Mount Everest, and no running off with aliens."

"They always forget the aliens clause," said Alita, giving Laura a smile over her shoulder. "And don't think I didn't rub that in their faces. Did your manager fight you as hard as mine fought me?"

"Oh, yeah," said Laura, and just the camaraderie of the question settled her nerves a bit. Made her feel a little kinship with Alita. Laura continued talking as she stepped into the kitchen to get herself some coffee with lots of cream and just a little fake sugar, hoping it would settle the nervous flutter in her stomach.

"In my case it was my agent. Tried to call me selfish for wanting to do this. Said I wasn't thinking about—"

"—about all the people who have money on the line if you miss a day of work," Alita finished for her. "Do these guys all train at the same school or what?"

"Kind of," said Brice, raising his cup to Laura as she smoothed her dress and sat beside Alita. "Most of the top managers and agents go to the same handful of schools. Lots of them meet in Harvard Business School, for example. And those that didn't" — Brice shrugged — "take their cues from the ones that did."

"Make it sound like a conspiracy," said Dubba J.

"More like nepotism..."

Brice continued talking, but that fluttering in Laura's stomach was not going away. No matter how much she wanted to settle into the comfort of business talk, or even getting to know Alita and Dubba J, there was a question she needed to ask and she spoke across Brice to do it.

"Am I the only one who's worried about what the aliens want us to do?"

"Of course not," said a voice she knew all too well. "I'm sure we're all concerned about how exactly we're going to become the saviors of the human race."

Laura didn't want to look up. Didn't want to see him again. Didn't want to hear his stupid voice. But that was a girl's response, and Laura was a woman now. Laura could handle anything this jackass could throw at her.

She set her lips in a line and raised her chin to see Jesse Carter, dramatically framing himself in the doorway to his suite.

Laura had to admit, Jesse looked good. But the bastard always did. That was part of the problem.

Right now he had on a white shirt with subtle, light blue stripes that would bring out his eyes. He had the sleeves rolled up to the elbow, and not just the top button undone, but the second one too, to show that his tan didn't stop at his face and provide the viewer just a hint of chest hair. Jesse wore black jeans that Laura just knew had the special crotch design that would let him show off just how high he could kick.

People always went bananas when he kicked high. Or when he did the splits. Laura could do both those things, but she was a woman. It was expected.

His short black hair was mussed just a little, of course. The whole look was orchestrated to convey that he'd just been working on his house or something. Even had on sneakers for the occasion. Probably the first time he'd worn sneakers since his last film had that pick-up basketball sequence.

And after Jesse's little pronouncement, everyone was looking at him. Just the way he liked it. Probably spent five minutes fiddling with the lights in his suite so when he framed himself in the doorway he would be lit *just so*.

Laura shook her head. At least the flutter in her stomach was gone now. Her insides felt like lead.

Brice glanced at her, then back at Jesse. "Jesse, grab some coffee and come join us. It's been an age."

Dubba J and Alita were watching Laura now, waiting for a reaction. Which just meant that everyone knew about the breakup. She figured as much, but this was the first time she'd actually been in the same place as Jesse since their final fight.

"Glad you could all make it," said Jesse as he passed through the lounge gaming area on his way to the kitchen. "Though I see we're still one short. Anyone heard from that blogger? What's his name? Evanescence?"

Laura felt a tendril of anger thread through the lead and work its way up her spine. Jesse. Talking like he's the host. Pretending he didn't read every word of that blogger's reviews of every one of his movies.

"You don't know Evansessence?" said Dubba J, and Laura liked the tone of his question. Like Jesse had admitted not knowing who was the President. "Man, he did a series of posts last year tying Roe v.

Wade to the casting of female leads in blockbuster movies that was *incredible*."

"I read that," said Alita. "Didn't note who the author was though."

"I admit I missed that one," said Brice. "Though a few of my staff writers have mention the guy before."

"The point is," said Jesse, who poured a cup of black coffee and came over to sit with his knees so wide apart he took up one whole chaise longue. "He's not here."

"You just got here," said Laura.

"I've been here for a couple of hours. Needed a little rest after parasailing down in Malibu."

"So maybe he's waiting in his room too," said Laura. "Not yet ready to come join us."

"So," said Brice, adding enough punch to the word to draw everyone's focus to him. "Assuming he's coming, that'll make six of us representing the entire human race. Do any of you have any idea why they chose you? I mean, there are lots of singers, actors, talk show hosts and home video stars."

"Hey," said Dubba J, "I'm not just posting vids of cats chasing laser pointers. My parkour dance video had more than a hundred million views in just the last week. There's no bigger star on Frenzy!Video than me."

"Laura and I are the top box office draws worldwide," said Jesse, and Laura felt her jaw tighten. Phrasing it so he was speaking for her. Couldn't he even relate a fact without doing it in a way that pissed her off?

"And which of us makes more money?" said Laura.

"Hey, that's not my fault," said Jesse.

"Really? Because I seem to recall you throwing it in my face when—"

"My singles have topped charts in more than forty countries," said Alita. "Honestly, I'm afraid to try another world tour, because so many cities are pestering my manager that it would take me three years to hit everyplace my fans want me to go."

"No," said Brice. "That's not what I mean. You guys are basically giving the same reason the Greenies gave when they picked us. I mean, what don't we know about each other that might make the difference? Assume for a second this isn't a numbers game. What is there about you that they might be looking for?"

"We're all artists," said Laura. "Two actors, a dancer, a singer, and a comedian."

"Bless you," said Brice, and Laura puzzled over the weight he gave those words.

"And the blogger's a writer," said Jesse.

"But that makes him a fine artist," said Alita. "The rest of us are performance artists."

"Good point," said Brice, leaning forward with his elbows on his knees now, like he wanted to call them into a huddle. "Follow that thread."

"You know they've got to be listening," said Dubba J. "Hell, this might be the first test."

"I hope not," said Jesse. "That blogger isn't here yet."

"Yes he is," said a voice over by the kitchen.

As one, Laura and the others turned to see a golden glow resolve into a Greenie woman who looked like Mynack, as interpreted by a pinup calendar or a men's magazine. She was holding hands with a very worried looking man about Laura's age. He had short, curly brown hair, a decent enough frame under office drone clothing, and looked to stand a couple of inches under six feet. Which at least made him a couple of inches taller than Jesse.

The new arrival had a look of wide-eyed shock, like he was trying to take in everything at once.

But the Greenie woman had a beaming, close-lipped smile.

"Now that everyone's here," she said, "we can begin."

17

A moment ago Charlie was sitting on his living room couch, one hand extended to Kyna. And now he was standing in a kitchen that was only small in comparison to the huge lounge around him, complete with a plethora of game tables.

But pinball, air hockey and pool weren't what drew Charlie's attention.

Five big-name stars were sitting on two fancy leather sectionals.

When Charlie had heard his own name spoken by Mynack during that television broadcast, the other names mentioned had flown right out of his head. But here the owners of those names were.

In person. Right in front of him. Five people that everyone he knew could pick out of a crowd. Five people that everyone he knew talked about. Thought about. Had an opinion about.

Laura Jefferson. Jesse Carter. Alita Luna. Dubba J. Brice DePaul.

Five people he had mentioned by name in at least one blog post or comment in the last month.

And dear God how could it be possible that Alita Luna and Laura Jefferson looked even better in person than they did on the big and small screens? Those two women had everything Kyna pretended to have, and then some.

But Kyna was talking.

Before Charlie could catch up enough to parse her words, Kyna vanished in another golden glow.

And five famous people were staring at him.

Charlie could hear his own heart pounding. Feel the sweat forming on the palms of his hands.

Today had to have sucked out years of Charlie's life. This much stress had to be taking a toll.

"Uh, hi," said Charlie, immediately flushing deep red over his lame words.

"So you must be Evansessence," said Brice DePaul. "We were just talking about that series of posts you wrote about female leads and abortion politics. Impressive stuff. Please, grab a cup of coffee and join us. And don't let the big name stars intimidate you. You and me, we're part of this team too."

"Please, call me Charlie."

Charlie thought about coffee, but the Death Watch IPA burbling in his stomach said it was a bad idea. His taste buds tended to agree.

"If you insist," said Dubba J, as Charlie took tentative steps to the couch and perched on one corner of an unoccupied distressed brown leather chaise longue. "Gotta say, though. Evansessence has more style to it. Like me. Dubba J has rhythm, rises at the end like you know something exciting is coming. But Jerome? I hate that name. Jerome. Jer*ome*. Any way you say it, it either sounds like an insult or an excuse."

"Jerome Bouchard really *owns* that name," said Alita, talking about an NBA player.

"He can have it then," said Dubba J.

"Fascinating as all this is," said Jesse, "Now that we're all a little more at ease with each other" — he frowned a little at Charlie, then flicked a glance at Laura — "or at least as at ease as we're likely to get, I'd like to return to the question we've all just glossed over. *Just who the hell was that who brought you in?*"

"What," said Laura, "did you think Mynack was the only member of his entire race?"

"The only one I've met. How about the rest of you? Hands up if Mynack brought you here."

Everyone raised their hands but Charlie. He felt heat rising under his chin.

"Exactly. So how come you rate the hot Greenie escort?"

Jesse turned the full movie star presence on Charlie, complete with a piercing look in those famous blue eyes. As though Charlie were a terrorist hiding information and Jesse the Action Star was going to get it.

Charlie found himself leaning back, wide-eyed and swallowing past a lump in his throat. Half the muscles in his torso locked up. His heart lurched into overdrive.

"I, uh..."

"Leave him alone," said Laura. "He's not some *extra* for you to push around."

"Shhh, baby," said Alita Luna, leaning closer and stroking Charlie's shoulder. "Don't let him scare you. We're all on the same side."

She smiled. Friendly. But for Charlie's exhausted psyche this was just one shock too many. Alita Luna's hand was on his shoulder. The woman his friends described as "walking sex." The woman whose hits and videos had been everywhere for the last five years.

Charlie froze as he looked into her brown eyes, flecked with gold. Embarrassingly aware of her nearness and exactly how well she filled out her midriff top and tight jeans. And her warm scent, a heady mixture of neroli, jasmine iris, toffee caramel, and vanilla that blended well with the couch leather...

Dubba J started laughing, a low, percolating sound, and Charlie shook himself and wondered just what the look on his face had been.

"All right," said Brice DePaul, walking around the coffee table to sit next to Charlie on the chaise longue. In his tee shirt and Mets cap, Brice DePaul looked more like a regular guy than anyone else around Charlie. He held out his hand to shake. "It's good to meet you, Charlie. I'm Brice."

Charlie shook hands by reflex, and looked Brice in his pale gray eyes.

"Good," said Brice. "Now you've had a hell of a day, haven't you, Charlie?"

Charlie nodded, heart still pounding.

"I'll bet you're not used to being the center of attention. And you're not used to meeting celebrities. Not even two-bit comedians like me."

Brice smiled, and Charlie felt a little connection with him. As though Brice really was on his side. Understood what Charlie was going through. Empathized, and wanted to help.

"And now," continued Brice, "aliens, am I right?" Brice smiled and shook his head, and Charlie found himself smiling too. "It's crazy, what's going on. And it's crazy that we're the ones called together. And what's more, I get the feeling that you and me, we're the only ones who didn't jump at the chance to be part of this."

"I ... had a panic attack and hid in a service station bathroom until the cops picked me up for the Department of Homeland Security."

"Panic attack is about right," said Brice, his voice still jovial friendly, but with a calm undercurrent that eased some of the tension out of Charlie's shoulders. Slowed his heart rate just a little. "Most natural reaction in the world. Aliens calling your name on television. Last thing any of us were expecting when we woke up this morning, am I right?"

"Hell yes," said Dubba J with a laugh. Everyone else just nodded and murmured agreement.

"And I bet you were wondering how your name ended up on the list. I'm sure we were all wondering that. That female Greenie who brought you here..."

"Kyna," Charlie said without thinking.

"Yes, Kyna. Did she mention why they chose you?"

"No. She just said that I was the one most likely to say no—"

"And they sent her to" — Jesse cleared his throat — "change your mind?"

"Jesse!" said Laura, while Alita wrinkled her face in distaste and Dubba J laughed some more.

"To talk me into it," said Charlie, voice a little stronger now. Heat in his words, instead of just his face. "Just talk. This isn't some T.V. show, man." Charlie pointed back to the kitchen. "That wasn't some actress in green body paint. That was a fucking *alien*. Yeah, maybe in that suit she looked like she had human anatomy, but *who knows* what's really under there? Would *you* risk that?"

"He would," said Laura without a moment's hesitation.

Jesse nodded and said, "Sure. When would I get a chance again?"

"Definitely," said Dubba J. "I mean, if nothing else you know she has a mouth and a tongue."

"Gross," said Alita. "Could we please stop talking about alien sex?"

"So," said Brice, and though he didn't say the word loudly, he managed to bring all the attention back to himself when he said it. "Even if she wasn't human, Kyna did look like a pretty girl, and I bet she helped you calm down a bit."

"We talked about it over a beer."

"Good. How did she convince you?"

"She ... kind of didn't." Too much had happened today for everything to be clear in Charlie's mind. The conversation was only a few minutes ago, but he felt like so much had happened since that—

"She told you what was at stake?"

"Yes, and that one of us saying no was the same as one of us failing. The same as one of us trying to work with the government while we're here."

Every single one of the others looked away at that moment.

"Huh," said Charlie with a little chuckle. "So I got the Department of Homeland Security. Who'd you guys get?"

"Me too," said Alita Luna. "Homeland Security."

"F.B.I.," said Laura Jefferson and Jesse Carter at the same time, which made them look at each other.

"I got the Bureau of Alcohol, Tobacco, and Firearms," said Dubba J.

"The A.T.F.?" said Brice. "Seriously?"

"Nah. Actually it was No Such Agency. I just thought the A.T.F. was funnier."

"What about you?" said Charlie to Brice.

"I..." Brice pulled off his Mets cap. He spun it in his hands and put it back on. "You guys will think I'm joking, but I'm actually serious about this." He blew out a long breath through his nose, but he looked at Charlie when he spoke again. "I got the men in black."

"That's the phrase I was waiting to hear," said Mynack, appearing behind Jesse in a flash of gold.

18

It was one thing to know that the aliens were listening to them. It was something else entirely for them to be waiting in the wings so they could — what — teleport in whenever they felt like it?

"Hold on," said Brice, standing up. "Was this part of the test too? To see if we'd admit to each other that we'd been contacted by our governments? Or do you have some kind of beef with the men in black that we should know about?"

Mynack only stared back at Brice, patient.

Five other human lab rats around Brice, and not one of them stood up with him. Talked back. They just watched him, content for Brice to take the lead. No surprise from Charlie. That kid was more than half-fried already. But the others?

"Look," said Brice, in the tone he used to tell certain guests how obnoxious they were, "we understand that you want to test us. But you need to remember. Before today, not one of us even knew that alien intelligent life was real. And to have it show up on the news? Tell us you guys are testing us on behalf of our whole planet? Kind of a lot to take in, you know?"

Still no response from Mynack, except the irritating patience in those amber eyes.

"Some kind of format would be nice. Some kind of agenda. Some sense of what you guys are trying to find out."

Nothing.

"You were waiting for the phrase 'men in black,'" said Charlie, standing up beside Brice. "So, you've heard it. What happens now?"

"Have you decided then?" asked Mynack, his tone as neutral as his eyes. "Is that the question you want to ask?"

"No," said Jesse. "I want to know—"

"Wait," said Brice, certain he saw a smile hiding somewhere in those amber eyes.

"No. I want to know—"

"I said 'wait.'"

Jesse cocked his head and raised an eyebrow at Brice.

"And I don't remember anyone putting you in charge."

"Better him than you," said Laura, standing up now. "So far Brice seems to have a brain in his head."

"Oh, and I don't?" Jesse's tone got sharper now, turning face on toward Laura, who had her chin jutted forward, ready for a fight. "You didn't seem to mind—"

"*¡Callate!*" shouted Alita, jumping up to stand on her couch cushion so she was actually taller than everyone else right now.

In the momentary silence that followed her shout, Brice could hear the coffee maker beep in the background, shutting off.

Dubba J just lounged on the leather cushions, watching the others every bit as curiously as Mynack.

Alita gestured for Brice to continue.

"Look," said Brice. His eyes were on Jesse, but he hoped the others were listening to him too. "Mynack said 'Is that the question you want to ask?' To me that implies that we only get one question right now. That's why he's standing there like a statue, staring at us."

"Well that's stupid," said Jesse. "What good is one question? And does that mean the tests are starting?"

"The tests started the moment their flying saucer appeared," said

Charlie, rubbing at the five o'clock shadow on his chin. "Maybe even before. Either way, everything that's happened since their saucer appeared has been part of the test. They've probably been watching the six of us the entire time."

Brice thought back to his interlude with Laetitia, and hoped the aliens weren't voyeurs.

"And if we only get one question," said Laura, eyes widening like she saw where Charlie was going, "the question we choose is part of the test too."

"So's all this back-and-forth then," said Dubba J, cradling one knee as though he were stretching on the couch. "All of it."

"So if we only get one question," said Brice. "We should all decide on it."

"We don't know that we only get one question," said Jesse, throwing his hands up in exasperation as he stood. "You guys are leaping to conclusions. And I still don't see how you" — Jesse pointed at Brice — "figure you're in charge."

"He's not," said Charlie, before Brice could speak. "But neither are you. Neither am I. Far as I can tell, none of us are."

"But someone has to be."

"Why?" said Alita. "Why do we—"

"Probably because we can't decide on a simple question," said Dubba J. "But what do I know?"

"We're not running a goddamn election," said Jesse.

And before anyone could stop him, he asked Mynack, "What do you guys have to do with the men in black?"

"No!" said Brice before Mynack could answer. "That's not our question."

"That's it," said Jesse, fists clenched and turning to Brice with violence in his eyes. Laura started forward to intercept, shoulders set.

"Whoa now," said Brice, stepping back onto the couch, which was not as easy to balance on as Alita made it look. "Let's not get crazy here."

Dubba J extended one long, muscular leg so his bare foot tapped Jesse on the chest.

"Chill, man," said Dubba J, voice still casual. "No need for us all to start hurting each other."

Jesse turned his head slowly to look at Dubba J, who still had a smile on his face. Brice couldn't see the look in Jesse's eyes, but he imagined it was formidable.

"You don't want to start anything with me," said Jesse.

"Not starting anything," said Dubba J, not moving his foot. He just held it there against Jesse's chest, without the slightest tremor of effort. "Just pointing out that if you start something, I'm not afraid to finish it."

"And he's not the only one," said Alita, fingers weaving in a pattern that made her long, glittery nails look like talons.

Laura just stood in front of Jesse now, arms folded and chin down so she could glare. Brice couldn't see her expression, but he imagined she had a pretty intimidating glare.

"Everybody simmer down, please," said Brice, patting Laura on the shoulder to get her attention. "We're all tired, and we're all on edge. Let's just sit down. You too, Mynack. How about I tell you all a little something about the men in black, and then maybe you'll understand why I don't want our question wasted on something that maybe I could have told you."

Brice sat first, and everyone else followed. Everyone except Mynack, who continued to stand and stare. Brice expected Laura to continue shooting lasers at Jesse with her eyes, but even she seemed to put her anger on hold.

Everyone was watching Brice. For the moment, anyway.

"We're closer to space flight, and I mean deep space flight, like interstellar, than any of us knew. The reason is that there's another alien race that's been in contact with humanity for years. They've been in touch with the United States government for decades, but I have no reason to think that these aliens haven't contacted other governments too."

"The Grays?" said Charlie, who sounded too worn out for any more surprises.

"That's right. And Roswell really was the first contact point."

Brice picked up his coffee mug and slugged down half of the rich brew. Charlie wasn't the only one stretched thin and exhausted by the events of the day, but Brice apparently had more experience pulling through such times.

At least no one interrupted him.

"The Grays cut a deal. An exchange. Tech for subjects. The Grays got to abduct individuals, but they had to return them in more-or-less good shape when they were done with their experiments. The government got ... well, not tutoring exactly, but more like guided independent study. Most of what they've learned hasn't been released yet. But some of it has been filtered through channels to the private sector. You can probably guess some of the results."

"Smartphones?" said Jesse.

"Doesn't matter," said Brice before anyone else could guess and sidetrack the group. "What matters is that the government kept this information to itself, and decided how to use it."

"Hoarding," said Charlie. "That's what Kyna said about why the Greenies didn't go to the governments."

"Is that what Kyna said?" asked Mynack, and that the alien spoke at all so surprised Brice that he lost what his next point was.

"Not exactly," said Charlie, rubbing the bridge of his nose as though the simple act would help him keep his thoughts straight. "But hoarding was a concern for the Greenies. Something they've seen before. And it doesn't end well."

"So these guys and the Grays are enemies?" said Jesse.

"They have different goals and methods," said Charlie. "That doesn't make them enemies."

"Doesn't make them friends, either," said Alita.

"Rivals maybe," said Dubba J.

"Maybe that's what we need to ask about," said Jesse.

"The Grays don't matter," said Charlie. "Not for what we're doing here."

"But they do," said Brice, drumming two fingers on the handle of his cup. "That's what I'm getting at. The feds took an extra step to keep all of this secret. They created an organization without a name and hid it deep under different parts of the budget. They cover up for the Grays, and they get the fancy tech toys, so the government can test them without producing so many that they lose track of who's in the know."

"This is sick," said Laura, eyes wide with horror. "The United States government is renting its citizens to some interplanetary Joseph Mengeles? And covering up for them?"

"Our government's done a lot worse than that," said Dubba J. "You want to start a list?"

"Wait," said Charlie. "Are you telling us the men in black tried to talk you out of coming?"

"No," said Brice. "They wanted me to come."

Brice reached into the back pocket of his jeans and pulled out a paperclip. He felt like an idiot doing it. It looked as much like an ordinary steel paperclip as it had back in his office when Agent Talky handed it to him.

But aliens were real. And men in black were real. So maybe this paperclip was exactly what the men in black said it was.

Brice set the paperclip on the table in front of him.

"That," he said pointing at it, "is a recorder and a transmitter, given to me by the men in black. They want that tech from the Greenies, whether we pass the tests or not."

Brice looked up at Mynack.

"And I think the Grays are going to help them."

19

Charlie wrinkled his brow as he looked at the paperclip Brice just set down on the table. There was just something not right about all of this. Everything looked too ordinary. All around him, this lounge could have been a weird nightclub in a converted warehouse.

Leather couches. Game tables. A freaking kitchen in the corner. Nothing alien about any of it. Not even the smells of popcorn and coffee and leather.

The only alien-looking thing was Mynack, and even he looked more like an alien out of a B-movie than the sort of life scientists expected to find on another planet.

But Charlie was in this lounge, with five celebrities no less, because he'd been teleported. No other word for it. One moment in his kitchen, the next here.

So maybe that little steel paperclip they were all staring at really was exactly what Brice said it was — some kind of alien-tech recorder and transmitter.

Still...

"Mynack doesn't look very concerned about the Grays coming," said Charlie, more to Brice than anyone else.

"Hold it," said Jesse Carter, standing up again. "I didn't sign up to be on the front line of a war."

"Details were vague," said Dubba J, rocking his head back and forth as though he were considering Jesse's point. "But yeah, I think that's exactly what Brice just said."

"Is he right?" said Alita Luna to Mynack.

"Wait!" said Charlie. An idea was finally burning its way through his exhausted brain, making him jittery. Though that might just have been the exhaustion. "That's not our question."

Everyone was looking at Charlie now. His tongue seemed to freeze solid in his mouth. His lips moved, but no sound came out.

"It's all right, Charlie," said Brice in a low tone. Fatherly. "Just tell us. Or tell me."

"Homeland Security." Charlie started rubbing the bridge of his nose. Eyes closed so he didn't have to watch everyone watching him. "Tiny recorder. Didn't bring it."

"They gave me one too," said Alita Luna.

How she got her hand into those tight, tight blue jeans, Charlie couldn't tell, but when her hand came back out she held up a tiny black disc the size of a quarter. Just like the one given to Charlie by Agents Crawford and Kolchak. She set it on the table next to the paperclip.

Laura Jefferson rolled in her lips, then let them out with a soft pop. She fished into her cleavage and Charlie looked away over at the pinball tables. Three of them. Not machines Charlie recognized.

When he looked back, Laura Jefferson was holding up a small piece of transparent tape with a black bar in the center that couldn't have been longer than the width of Charlie's pinky. She set it down on the other side of the paperclip, then looked at Jesse Carter with an expectant expression.

"What?" he said.

"You said the F.B.I. visited you too. Where your mic?"

"How do we know we can trust these Greenies?" he said. "If we give these things up, we're giving up our only connection with home. Our only chance at rescue. Survival."

"You trust the F.B.I.?" asked Alita Luna, her narrow eyebrows high.

"They're human at least." Jesse Carter pointed at Mynack. "These Greenies... We don't know what we're in for here, do we?"

"Typical," said Laura Jefferson. "You'd fuck one if her tits were big enough, but you don't—"

"What guarantee do we have we're going to get home at all?"

"No one gives you a guarantee when you leave the house in the morning," said Brice. "But you heard what Charlie said earlier. Working with the government is the same as failure."

"That kid's too shaky to remember his own name. And you trust him?"

"Yeah," said Brice. "I do."

"More than I trust you," said Laura Jefferson, and Alita Luna nodded.

Charlie started to blush, much to his humiliation. His body was just too tired to help it.

"Laura," said Jesse Carter in a penitent voice, "I know we've had our problems—"

"So not the time," said Laura Jefferson. "Give up the mic or go home."

Alita Luna nodded, and so did Brice and Charlie.

Jesse Carter turned to Dubba J.

"You've been quiet through this whole thing. You're on my side here, aren't you?"

"Nope," said Dubba J. "Fuck the Man. Which is what I told Mr. No Such Agency when he offered me his little recorder."

"Seriously?" said Charlie.

"Yep." Dubba J gave Charlie a broad grin. "Mr. and Mrs. No Such Agency looked none too pleased, let me tell you. Why, I think they might have forgotten themselves and intended me bodily harm, if Mynack hadn't shown up when he did."

Charlie glanced over at Mynack, who still stood immobile. Watching.

"So, Jesse," said Brice. "What do you want to do?"

"Fine." Jesse Carter gave a big sigh and started digging around in the change pocket of his jeans. "You guys win."

"No," said Charlie, and everyone looked at him. Charlie felt as though he should have been sweating, but his body just couldn't manage the effort. "This isn't a vote. We all agree what we think you should do. But you have to make your own choice. Give up the recorder if you want to stay here and try to get through these tests with us. Or don't, and go home."

"What if I want to stay and keep the recorder?"

"That's the same as failure," said Charlie. "And I don't think any of us want you distracting us and increasing our chances of failing too."

"You don't know that!" said Jesse Carter, throwing up his hands. "Even Mynack confirmed that's not what your Greenie girlfriend told you."

"He's right, though," said Brice. "If you'd think about it, it makes sense. It's like cheating. Trying to get around the rules they set up."

"What rules?" Jesse Carter stood up now and pointed at Mynack. "He hasn't given us any rules. He hasn't done anything but stand there like a fucking statue."

"And why do you think that is?" said Laura Jefferson. "He's testing us. And I think it's pretty clear that the first test is, 'are we willing to do this on our own?' No outside help. No safety net. Just us."

"Just people, man," said Dubba J, and Alita Luna nodded. "Not organizations. No deals. No debts. No bullshit. Just us, showing our guests what the human race is capable of. Pretty sweet opportunity, you ask me."

Jesse Carter blinked at Dubba J, then looked at Laura Jefferson. Whatever he saw in her eyes, he didn't like it because he set his mouth in a firm line.

He reached under his armpit, pulled out the miniature recording stick given to him by the F.B.I., and slammed it down on the table. He dropped back onto the couch so hard that air hissed out of it.

Everyone stared at one another, shooting glances at Mynack, expecting some kind of reaction. But Mynack only stood and watched. Even Brice seemed at a loss for what to say next.

"If we pass these tests," said Charlie, "how do we make sure our whole planet benefits from your gifts, without our governments hoarding them or the Grays interfering?"

"Is that your question?" said Mynack.

The others murmured assents.

"We will handle distribution, until matters are far enough along that hoarding concerns have been alleviated. And as for the people you call the Grays," — Mynack pointed at the recorders and all of them, even the paperclip, vanished in a golden haze — "they will not interfere with any planet that has passed our tests."

"So what's next?" said Brice.

"Tonight? Nothing. You all need rest. And food. You have tonight to yourselves, and we will continue in the morning."

Mynack glowed gold and vanished before anyone could get another question out. His disappearance was followed by a tumble of words from six different mouths.

Charlie started laughing the way only the truly tired can laugh. It started as a tremor deep in his belly, then shook its way out of him, crinkling his eyes and reddening his face.

Dubba J followed right into the laugh, and his mirth infected everyone else. Soon they were all breathless and flushed from laughing past the point of control.

Finally they all sat in companionable silence, panting for breath on the leather couches and looking at one another with traces of humor threatening another outpouring of hilarity.

But the humor leaked out of them as they regained their breaths. And they stared at one another, sharing a single thought that only Dubba J gave voice to.

"If this was just the first test, we're fucked."

20

A-Day-Plus-One. Eight A.M. Lounge Local Time

When Laura's alarm awoke her at seven, she didn't feel as rested as she should have. Given her usual chaotic schedule, some nine hours of more of uninterrupted sleep should have left her feeling ready to face anything. Instead, she felt awake, but not vibrant. Like she had a jet lag hangover.

But routines were routines, and Laura kept to hers even if she didn't have access to her normal equipment. Instead of time on the treadmill and weight sets, she settled for pushups, sit-ups, jumping jacks, yoga, any kind of workout she could cobble together with Louis XVI furniture in her sitting area.

Not great, but enough, and now she was showered and ravenous. Clad in a red plaid felt shirt — sleeves rolled up to the elbows — and practical jeans that had started life a deep blue color but had faded by now to whites and grays in an uneven pattern she found appealing. Her long hair she bound in a simple knot at the back of her head. On her feet, white running shoes.

Laura opened the door of her suite and stepped out into...

...a small cafeteria.

White marble flooring with veins of bronze, a pattern that continued onto the walls.

Walls that, unlike last night, could not have been more than twenty feet apart, and the matching ceiling they held up was no more than five feet above her head. Still the same six plain white doors around the perimeter, though they had to have been closer together now.

A buffet had been set up on a teak runner table, as by a fine caterer. Large silvered bowls overflowing with fruits and melons from all over the world, both cut up and whole. Six different breads with a six-slice toaster. Bacon and eggs (fried, scrambled, and hard boiled), and vegan options for both. Orange juice, apple juice, and water in large, transparent jugs with spouts at the bottom, and large carafes of coffee, decaf, and tea.

In the center of the room was a teak bench table, with padded seats. Brice sat in the center of one bench. He had on loose jeans, pale blue and cinched with a brown belt, and a Mets shirt faded enough he might have brought it with him. From the crumbs on the plate in front of him, he'd already finished eating and savored his cup of coffee with eyes-closed bliss.

The smell of the light Costa Rican blend put a smile on her face.

"Good morning," he said, still not opening his eyes.

"Do you need a moment alone with your coffee?" Laura asked, only half-joking.

"No, I think we're ready for company." He sipped.

"You know," he said, as another door opened and a sweaty Jesse strolled in wearing a black crew-neck tee shirt and biker shorts, "I should be freaked out by this. The room change, I mean. I should be bouncing off the walls."

Laura added pineapple and kiwi to the chunks of casaba and honeydew already on her plate as she spoke.

"This isn't the same room we were in last night," Brice continued. "It's not even the same size. But I haven't felt anything move. Not a single hint of a seam or change around my door frame either, on either side. Just doesn't seem possible. Why am I not freaked out, do you think?"

"Because we're getting numb to the shocks," said Jesse before Laura could answer. As usual. "We'll be bleating like sheep by the time they drop the hammer."

"You're an idiot," said Laura, irritation filling her as much at the sound of his voice as the content of his words. Too soon after a workout to get so tense through the shoulders.

"These Greenies teleport as easily as we breathe," she continued. "If they wanted to drop the hammer, it would already be dropped."

Alita and Dubba J filed in from their respective rooms, looking as though they expected a picnic. Her in a pink cotton blouse and red corduroy pants. Him in shorts and another sleeveless black tee shirt. He was barefoot again. She had on simple black flats. Both wore their hair loose today. Dubba J's dreadlocks like a mane around his face that bounced with every step. Alita's copper-brown hair flowed down just past her shoulders.

Alita jumped at the sight of the new lounge, but Dubba J just looked around and shrugged.

"Yeah, it's surprising," said Brice, "but admit it. You aren't really shocked, are you? Not like you should be."

Dubba J shrugged again and went straight for the coffee. Alita chewed at her bottom lip as she looked around, but finally joined the food line just about the time that Dubba J and his coffee found a spot next to Brice.

"Think you could have showered first?" Alita wrinkled her nose at Jesse who was toasting six slices of whole wheat. "As a public service, if not for yourself?"

Jesse ignored Alita's question, but Laura gave her a smile.

"All right then," said Jesse, "since you're all so smart and I'm so stupid, you guys tell me. Why doesn't this new room freak us the hell out?"

"I think you're right that we're getting numb to the shocks," said Laura, peeling and salting a pair of hard-boiled eggs to go with her fruit. "It's your conclusion that makes you—"

"Why am I still tired after ten hours of sleep?" said Alita, yawning as she sliced bananas and mixed them in a bowl with cantaloupe and some yogurt that Laura had missed. "This place isn't exactly normal."

"What time is it anyway?" said Dubba J. "My watch says it's just after eight, but that doesn't feel right."

"Ah ha," said Jesse as his toast popped up. He raised one finger in dramatic exclamation. "That just proves they're messing with us. Did something while we were asleep."

"The time thing's probably just jet lag," said Laura, grabbing the seat on Brice's other side and forcing Alita to accept a seat next to Jesse. "We're probably not in New York anymore."

"I was in Malibu," said Jesse.

"Chicago," said Dubba J.

"Mazatlán," said Alita.

"Where's Charlie?" asked Brice. "He's the only one not here yet."

"Again," said Jesse.

"Let it drop," said Laura.

"No." Jesse knocked on the teak of the serving table. "Think about it. He was the last to arrive. He was brought by a Greenie who isn't Mynack. He talked us into giving up our recorders. Maybe he's a plant."

"Ridiculous," said Laura, drawing the word out to emphasize the syllables.

"I don't know," said Alita, slowly. "Maybe he has a point. We all know each other's stories. Or at least what's in our press kits. But what do we know about Charlie?"

"We know he's as human as we are," said Brice, "and twice as scared."

"Do we know that?" said Jesse. He waited until all five of them looked up from their food before he continued. "We know these Greenies can teleport. They completely switched the main room here on us, and we can't even guess how they did that. Maybe Charlie was a Greenie spy for years while he was writing his blog. Deep cover agent so he would look normal when the time came."

"Or maybe he just sleeps later than the rest of us," said Dubba J.

"You've made too many action movies, Jesse," said Laura, unable to hide her smirk. "Bad enough to believe your own press, but your own scripts?"

"If I don't have a show," said Alita, "I don't get up before noon. But I woke up at seven o'clock sharp this morning."

She smacked her hand on the table for emphasis.

"And I'm *tired*," Alita continued. "So I should still be sleeping. Yet we five are all awake. So where's—"

The sixth door opened, and Charlie stopped dead in his doorway. He blinked a few times, then shook his head and tiptoed into the room as though afraid any step could trigger a landmine. He wore the most boring blue jeans Laura could imagine — not tight enough to have shape but not loose enough for the current fashion — and a baggy tee-shirt that depicted an old pixel golf video game. His curly brown hair was a mess.

Laura shook her head. The sad part was that Charlie would have been cute if he had any self-confidence.

"You have a knack," said Brice, "for making an entrance when we're talking about you."

Charlie mumbled something, then cleared his throat.

"Come on, *chico*," said Alita, "what did you say?"

"It's stupid," he said, and as he reached the buffet he started shoveling scrambled eggs and bacon onto a plate as though heart disease hadn't been invented yet. "Just an old Oscar Wilde quote."

"The only thing worse than being talked about," said Laura, and everyone else at the table helped her finish, "is not being talked about."

Charlie gave a sort of sideways nod.

Laura puffed out a hard breath.

"All right," she said. "Enough's enough. There are only six of us here. So let's get everything out in the open. Hands up everyone who was born on the planet earth to human parents."

Laura raised her hand while everyone blinked at her in confusion. Then, with expressions that clearly hoped she was going somewhere with this, all five of the others, one by one, raised their hands.

"Right then. We're all human beings. Every one of us. So, Jesse, no more conspiracy theory bullshit. And Charlie, get over this star-struck crap. Every one of us burps and farts, same as you, and I'm willing to bet that after the right meal, any one of us can stink up a bathroom bad enough to bring tears to your eyes."

Dubba J started laughing, and Brice was right on his heels. Alita blushed a bit, but nodded and soon she and Jesse were caught up in Dubba J's laugh. Laura felt the humor of it crack a smile on her face, but she kept her eyes on Charlie, unwilling to lose control until she saw him relax.

Charlie blushed hard, but then finally started snickering, and soon all six of them were laughing together again.

Charlie looked less guarded when he finally took a seat on the other side of Jesse, across from Dubba J.

"Man," said Dubba J. "Any bathroom I hit after eating Thai food should be declared a hazardous waste zone."

"We don't need details," said Alita, holding up one hand and looking away.

"My point is," said Laura, pleased that some of her own tension eased in her shoulders, "we're all on the same side here. So first names only — or preferred names anyway, Dubba J — and if anybody wants to know something, just ask. No accusations. No third degree. We need to pool our resources, not divide ourselves."

"And what about the elephant in the room then?" said Brice, and when Laura wrinkled her eyebrows in confusion, Brice pointed from Laura to Jesse and back again. "I'm not saying you guys have to tell us a story or anything, but I think the sniping's got to stop."

"He's right," said Alita, digging her spoon around in her yogurt so the spoon clinked against the white ceramic bowl. "The tension between you two is nuts."

Jesse turned on his professional smile. The one he used for poster shots and promotional photos. That smile alone was enough to wedge steel up Laura's spine. Her hand itched to slap him.

"Well, Laura? We *could* kiss and make up."

"I'd sooner kiss Mynack."

"You don't have to make up," said Brice, his voice soothing as only an experienced talk show host can be. Or maybe a father to feuding children. "Just, try to tone down the hatred enough to work together. Think you can do that?"

"I can forgive and forget," said Jesse. "Why can't you?"

Laura couldn't keep the disbelief off of her face. "Do you really want to go into this?"

"Well—" Jesse started.

Laura slapped her palms on the table and started to rise, but Brice gently touched her arm. She glared at him and grimaced, but lowered herself again. She stuffed a hard-boiled egg into her mouth to keep herself from launching into an exhaustive list of exactly what all Jesse had done to wrong her.

More specifically, a list of *whom* Jesse had done.

"You may need to," said Charlie, his voice so soft Laura could barely hear him over the sound of Dubba J sipping his coffee and Alita's nonstop yogurt stirring. Charlie cleared his throat, swigged some orange juice, and said, louder, "I get the feeling that might be part of the test."

"I have to forgive a philandering bastard for cheating on me with every B-star, extra, or groupie willing to spread her legs or her lips?"

"I told you," Jesse said, trying to sound exasperated. "That's not what happened."

"I saw the pictures," Laura said, not keeping any of the bite out of her tone. "And if I'm expected to just forget that, then I'm going to fail."

21

A-Day-Plus-One. Eight-Fifteen A.M. Lounge Local Time

Charlie crunched on a crispy slice of maple bacon and tried to stay unobtrusive. Jesse and Laura — and Charlie had just been told to address *Jesse Carter* and *Laura Jefferson* as Jesse and Laura, which was almost as weird as everything else happening to him — glared at each other across the teak bench table, all thoughts of their breakfast plates apparently forgotten.

And Jesse still had at least three slices of toast to go. Charlie couldn't help wondering how big a breakfast the man ate.

Brice's loafers clicked on the marble floor and Dubba J's bare feet padded as Brice and Dubba J went back to the buffet. Ostensibly they were after more of that light, enticing coffee, but Charlie suspected that they were getting out of the way too.

On the other side of Jesse from Charlie, Alita busied herself and her clinking spoon with her bowl of fruit-filled yogurt. Charlie noticed she never took more than half a teaspoon at a time into her mouth, and right now she gave the process her full and complete attention.

Just a few minutes ago, everyone had been laughing together.

Now everything was tense again, and all because Charlie suggested that Laura and Jesse's animosity might be part of the Greenie's test.

After all, Jesse and Laura may have been at the top of the A-list, but people called it the A-*list* because it didn't stop at only two names. The Greenies could have chosen any two major movie stars they wanted, and they chose two that had just gone through a rough break-up.

"You're being unreasonable," said Jesse, eyebrows raised and head tilted just a little.

"You're being unsafe," countered Laura, jaw forward and eyes narrowed. "You're damned lucky you didn't give me anything. And believe me, I got every test in the book to make sure."

"I—"

"Wait," said Charlie. An idea was burbling around in the back of his mind, but he couldn't quite make it out. He just knew that their fighting wasn't going to help it come clear. "I don't think the Greenies expect you guys to get back together or anything. I mean, this would be a hell of a lot of effort to go to for some kind of make-up scenario."

"But you said—" started Jesse at the same time Laura said, "Then why did—"

"Give me a second, okay?" Charlie swallowed hard around a lingering bit of bacon, holding his hands up to call for a time out. "This is reminding me of something Kyna said yesterday."

"Ah, yes," muttered Jesse, "his Greenie girlfriend."

Laura hushed him, but Charlie furrowed his brow. "It *was* yesterday, wasn't it?"

Laura nodded, encouraging, but her eyes were still narrowed.

"You didn't sleep *that* late," said Dubba J, reclaiming his seat while Brice reclaimed his.

"I hardly slept at all," said Charlie, thinking out loud now, "but that's not the point. When Kyna mentioned hoarders, I pointed out that we have people who would hoard advanced technology like she was worried about. And she said that of course we did. Every planet at our stage of development would."

"So?" said Alita, looking at Charlie sideways, draping her long hair down her pink blouse. "I mean, good that they're willing to work with us anyway, but how does that apply here?"

"Maybe it doesn't." Charlie shrugged. "I don't know. But it seems to me that the Greenies are willing to give the human race a chance, even though we aren't perfect. You guys were talking about making up or forgiving and forgetting. But maybe expecting you to do that is like expecting the human race to be perfect. Maybe that's not what the Greenies need to see. Maybe they just need to see us work with people whether or not we like them."

"That sounds awfully convenient," said Brice.

"Ever have to work with someone you hate?" said Dubba J.

"I work in television. So, yes."

"Is it easy? Or convenient?"

"Point taken," said Brice, who then lost himself in a sip of coffee.

Alita nodded, and though Jesse and Laura didn't nod, they didn't contradict Dubba J either.

"'s my point," said Dubba J. "We've all done it. It's part of being human. This probably isn't any different. So do like Brice said. Grin and bear it."

"That's not quite what I said," said Brice.

"Enh." Dubba J grinned. "Close enough."

Laura and Jesse still didn't say anything. Charlie couldn't read their expressions. But he had to admit that the way Laura set her jaw reminded him of Lucy, when she was really mad at him. If Laura was that made at Jesse, nothing Charlie could say would be likely to help.

But he felt the need to try.

"So."

Charlie looked back and forth from Jesse to Laura, then around at Brice, Alita and Dubba J. But no one looked back at him. Charlie flared out a half-sigh through his nostrils.

"So," he tried again, "do you think you guys might be able to at least be civil to each other?"

"Depends," said Laura, voice still tense. "Jess, can you stop pissing me off with every word out of your mouth?"

"What about my breathing? Can I keep doing that?"

Laura rolled in her lips as though she was thinking about it.

Charlie felt his heart start beating faster. This was about to get worse. Maybe much worse. Laura took a deep breath to say something, but before she could Charlie did the only thing he could think of.

He started laughing.

He was faking it. He knew that. Even he could hear the desperate undertone. But Brice picked it up immediately, sounding so natural he had to have thought of something hilarious from one of his shows.

Alita just stared at them both like they were crazy. At least, until Dubba J started laughing that laugh of his. That low, percolating sound so contagious it could be weaponized.

Then Alita fought a smile, tilting her chin back and forth as though to let off humor steam. But it was a losing battle. She started giggling and she was done for.

Charlie's laugh started feeling more natural. Not because his situation was so humorous, but because it was just too ridiculous. He was laughing to keep movie stars from fighting so aliens would help the human race.

What wasn't funny about that?

Jesse finally started laughing too, and something cracked in the tension between him and Laura. She didn't get sucked into uproarious peals or anything, but she snorted and started chuckling.

And she looked at Charlie when she laughed. That was enough to make Charlie's heart lurch again, and pound harder.

"Well, breakfast is about finished, I see," said Mynack, appearing at the end of the table next to Laura and Alita. "Then I think it's time for the next test."

A golden glow enveloped Charlie.

22

A-Day-Plus-One. Eight-Twenty-Three A.M. Lounge Local Time

The golden glow around Brice faded, and he realized he was no longer in the lounge. Cafeteria. Whatever it was.

He wasn't sitting down anymore, either.

Instead, Brice was standing in the African savannah. Or what looked like it anyway. Golden grasslands all around him, blotched with spots of green and fits of nearly round dark green shrubs. Occasional acacia trees that stretched up bare trunks and limbs until they spread at the top, sprouting leaves like a flattop haircut.

Brice was alone.

No Mynack giving him instructions. None of the others from Mynack's list to face this "test" with him.

Were the others taken away by teleporting glows too? Or were they being tested one at a time? What did they want him to do?

Well, if the Greenies expected him to hike, at least Brice's sneakers were a good choice for the dry grass and dirt, and the warm breeze suited his tee shirt. The air even smelled warm, and dusty like that summer camp in Utah when he was a kid.

To Brice that was the smell of Utah. In California that smell meant fire season. In New York ... it just never smelled like that. Not anywhere Brice had been.

Brice chuckled, despite himself. He was in the middle of nowhere, all alone, with no food or water or bathroom facilities. This was like location scouting without a car or a hotel. At least he still had the light taste of the blonde coffee blend on his tongue, and his belly full of scrambled eggs and bacon.

What he didn't feel was scared, which surprised him. It nagged at the back of his head that he was alone, but he didn't think the Greenies had sent him here to die.

Brice just had to figure out why they *had* sent him here.

"So," he called out. "You guys want me to just stand here and wait then?"

Nothing.

"Hardly seems like a fair test when we don't know the rules." Brice grimaced and shook his head. Finally he sighed. "Fine then. I'll just head ... west...."

Where was the sun?

Overhead the pale blue sky was smeared in places with white clouds, but Brice couldn't pick out any particularly bright spot. The daylight — if this was daylight and not some kind of alien trick — seemed sourceless.

Brice didn't even cast a shadow.

That thought twisted Brice's stomach sideways, and made his gorge rise in his throat. Brice put his hands on his knees. Leaned forward and started panting shallow breaths of the dry air.

He could see the horizon in every direction. Mountains in the distance ahead of him and to his left. So distant they had to have been days' travel away.

So much distance. But no sun.

Not right. Not natural.

Teleporting was one thing. Even the lounge-cafeteria switch could have been explained. But this?

Brice fell to his knees. Kept his slow, shallow breaths to try to ease his querulous stomach while he sought answers. He dug around in the ground. Dry, crumbly dirt pressed against his fingers, but Brice dug into a crack. Pried some loose.

More dirt beneath it.

He brought a handful to his nose. It smelled as dry and dusty as he expected. Real dirt. Not some kind of hallucination. This was real grasslands. But there was no sun in the sky.

Brice started rocking back and forth. He could feel heat spreading through his neck, along his chin, down his chest. Hear his pulse pounding over his shallow panting.

Too shallow for too long. He was getting lightheaded. But he couldn't stop himself.

Why was there no sun in the sky?

"What the hell, guys?" he said, assuming the Greenies could hear him even if he whispered. "Where am I? What are you doing to me? What do you want me to do?"

Finally, over the soft whistle of the wind, Brice heard something. Like a car horn rising and falling.

Just the fact of something happening made him hold his breath.

The world stood still. Nothing but the wind and the thump of his heartbeat.

The sound came again.

No, not a car horn. A trumpet. No. That wasn't right either. It sounded ... familiar somehow. Like something he had encountered in his youth, but couldn't quite place.

He started breathing again, slow and quiet, through his nose.

Finally, Brice heard it again. A long, almost wailing note.

The memory came. Six-year-old Brice, the big birthday boy, taken to the San Diego Zoo by his father during a rare visit.

Still in the parking lot, Brice heard that sound. Laughed an excited laugh.

"That was funny, Daddy. Can I have a trumpet like that?"

"That's not a trumpet." Brice's father shook his head, solemn. Gray and wrinkly already, in his forties, a man who wore a suit to take his son to the zoo. "That is the sound of an elephant in distress."

On his knees in the savannah, Brice forgot about the Greenies.

About the tests. That sound made him feel six years old again, and worried about the fate of a giant creature he had only seen in books. Brice saw elephants that day at the zoo. Even rode one. But still, every so often that long-ago morning he heard the call of the distant elephant in distress.

That elephant he didn't get to see.

That elephant, six-year-old Brice didn't get to help.

And by God, adult Brice was going to find a way to help this one.

The sound came from his left, the direction he arbitrarily decided was west. Maybe the poor creature was somewhere near that copse of acacias in the distance.

Brice took off toward the sound at his morning jogging clip.

23

When the golden glow around Laura faded, she was standing at the edge of a campsite. Clear nighttime sky full of stars overhead. Frogs and crickets a symphony loud enough to overpower the rustle of the cool wind through the oaks and hickories around her. Cool enough to prickle her skin, and make her tuck in her elbows and pull her red flannel shirt closer. Dirt forest floor beneath her running shoes covered in dry leaves and twigs, but not much underbrush.

At least she had jeans on. This was not a place to be wearing shorts.

Over the forest scent, Laura could smell the remains of a fire coming from the center of the clearing, inside a circle of rocks big enough to sit on. Not long extinguished, and carrying hints of burnt marshmallows. The smell tingled at the doors of memory somewhere in the back of her mind.

Two small dome tents in the clearing. Target specials. One blueish and one tan but pretending to be gold in the pale light of the full moon. At least, it felt like moonlight, and was bright enough for the full moon. But the moon she saw two nights ago had been only a sliver on its way toward full. And above her Laura could see stars, but not the moon itself.

The tents were pitched on opposite sides of the fire, for maximum privacy.

Those tents. That burned marshmallow smell.

Laura shook the memory away. The memory didn't matter right now. Wherever the Greenies had sent her, it couldn't have been into the past. If the Greenies could travel through time, then this whole testing process was a farce.

Laura couldn't bring herself to believe that. Wherever she was, it was part of the test.

So yes, it was night, and yes, it was a weirdly familiar place, but Laura had to think of this as stepping onto a movie set. It looked like night, but she knew she'd just had breakfast. Could still taste her coffee, salted eggs, and most of all her chunks of pineapple. The cool air and green trees felt like spring to her, not August. The glow looked like moonlight, but she couldn't see a moon.

So whatever the Greenies had done to put her on a campsite at night, it was all just set design. Sure, the teleporting glow was a special effect she couldn't explain away, but that didn't matter.

Once Laura got to a set, no one cared how she got there. Just what she did while she was there.

And since the Greenies were hands-off directors, it was up to her to figure out what they wanted from her performance, so she could give it to them.

Wherever they were, they were watching. And she only got one take.

That thought was enough to get her blood pumping, but breathing exercises helped her rein that in before it got out of hand. A star couldn't let nerves get the best of her.

Why here? Why now? Why all alone? What beat did they want from her? No other actors to play off of made for a more demanding scene. Especially since she was sure they didn't want her to monologue.

Odd that they sent her here alone.

Or was she alone?

Laura craned her neck looking about the woods behind her in moonlight dimmed by the lush trees, but couldn't see Brice or Charlie, Dubba J or Alita, not even Jesse.

Well, being anywhere without Jesse right now was worth a little... Wait.

This tree next to her. A black oak, with three knotholes coming up the trunk from left to right like a diagonal tic-tac-toe win for the circles. And the frogs and crickets, so loud here.

Those tents.

This wasn't just any campsite.

Laura's stomach started to pucker. Her knees started shaking. Her elbows pulled in tighter against her ribs.

This was Wayne National Forest.

Teenage Laura used to camp here with her friends.

Mom and Dad liked luxury camping, where they could have cabins, or toilets and showers less than a hundred feet away from someplace they could set up an air mattress. And propane this and propane that.

But Laura and her friends liked deeper woods camping. Going away from the easy trails. Taking a whole day to find a spot near enough to a river so they had some running water. Someplace to themselves. Someplace they could pitch their blue and tan tents in peace.

Worked great, until that one time. That full moon night. When Petey got drunk and spilled half a bag of marshmallows into the fire.

The memory hit Laura like a shovel to the face.

The creeper. Big burly woodsman type who got fourteen-year-old Laura alone when she went out into the trees to pee. The creeper with intentions Laura didn't like to think about.

She'd let the details of the encounter blur over the years, to keep herself sane, but she remembered the emotions like it happened yesterday. Called on them for that moment of perfect terror whenever Laura needed to scream for the camera. Like she did in that horror movie she made with Tiffany Shepis and...

Laura heard a scream so sharp and desperate it raised every hair on her body. Stiffened her spine. Widened her eyes. Drained the blood from her face. Even Laura's knees and stomach froze in a moment outside of time.

Laura remembered that scream. Made one like it herself when she was confronted by that creeper.

Oh, God. He found someone else. Some other young girl.

Someone who needed help.

All thoughts of aliens and tests rolled from her mind like sweat from her brow. All Laura could think of was that creeper. Her personal bogeyman in dark places for the past eight years.

And that bastard was trying to get his hands on another little girl.

Not this time.

Some kind of fire flared in Laura's belly. Unfroze time and her limbs.

Laura was running flat out before the scream stopped.

24

"What do you mean 'next?'" Charlie tried to ask Mynack, but too late. The glow took him.

As soon as the golden haze cleared from Charlie's eyes, he whipped his head around, frantic to figure out where he was this time. He immediately stumbled over his own loafers and caught himself with his hands on thin, gray carpet that smelled like rubber and some kind of chemical.

Well, technically not *his* loafers. The shoes, like the loose jeans and Golf Academy video game tee shirt, came out of that clothing store pretending to be a closet in Charlie's suite. But the shoes fit so well that Charlie couldn't even really blame them for leaving him face-down on the floor.

Grumbling about unannounced teleportation, Charlie stood back up and looked around again.

He stood in the center of a row of computers. Each had a flat-screen monitor, maybe thirty inches, and a little beige box running the show. Black gaming keyboards with dozens of extra keys for macros, and gaming mice with so many buttons Charlie wondered if they needed two hands to operate.

Six computers to each brown, rectangular table, three facing each long side, with power cords running down to surge protectors on the carpeting Charlie had just seen up close. Black roller chairs, the kind with armrests and multiple levers for every kind of setting Charlie could want, and a few more besides.

This place was set up for a hell of a LAN party.

The computers were all switched off. And the long, narrow fluorescent lights on the ceiling were off too. The room wasn't pitch black, though. More like dim twilight. Like light was coming in from somewhere, but not anywhere Charlie could see. Just enough to see the tables around him, get a sense that the row was at least three tables long. Maybe more.

Charlie could hear the hum of vending machines at one end. He could see a hint of their red and blue glow, maybe off in a corner. A soft rumble and a coolness to the air suggested air conditioning.

He smelled pizza. Not fresh, but Charlie's experience with LAN parties told him it was more like two dozen pepperoni pies had been eaten about a half-hour ago. Just before everyone left and shut the place down.

Wherever he was.

Charlie sighed. If the Greenies were going to keep teleporting him around like this, he wanted frequent 'porter miles or something.

"You never answered my question," Charlie said, directing his words to the ceiling. "What do you mean 'next' test? Is this the second or the third? What were the others?"

His words didn't echo right. Like the room was smaller than he first thought. He'd figured this place was the size of the lounge — the lounge, not the little cafeteria — maybe sixty or seventy feet across. Maybe more.

But now he thought it had to be smaller. Maybe thirty feet end to end and across. Meant the rows ended near walls he couldn't yet see.

Wait. If Charlie could see the glow of the vending machines, why couldn't he see the machines themselves? They couldn't have been that far away. From fifteen or twenty feet, Charlie should have been able to tell what varieties of soda they sold, and for how much. But instead he could only hear the hum and see their glow.

And they sounded more than thirty feet away.

"Mynack? Kyna? Anybody? I think your room is broken." He looked back and forth. "Seriously, you may need to send down tech support. Sound response isn't right. And I suspect there's a problem in the power systems..."

No response, which made Charlie sigh again. He had hoped that Kyna would show up, like she did at his apartment. Give him hints or clues about what was going on. What the Greenies expected from him. Things Mynack apparently couldn't tell them officially, but maybe she could via some loophole.

He kept thinking of Kyna as a 'she,' but was that the right pronoun?

Charlie shook off the question. Not an issue Charlie felt any need to explore. Clearly Kyna wanted to be perceived as female. She even emulated the voice of a female television star. So the female pronoun would do for Kyna, and the matter could end there.

If Dubba J or Jesse wanted to find out the truth behind those curves in her silver spacesuit, they were more than welcome to explore it for themselves.

For some reason the thought made Charlie remember that moment of meeting Laura's eyes while they were laughing. Now *there* was a pleasant thing to think about. Something he could pretend had meaning, even though he was pretty sure it didn't. If Laura had been saying anything by looking Charlie in the eye just then, it probably wasn't any deeper or more personal than, "thanks for breaking the tension."

Hell. He had friends who would have been burning with jealousy just because Charlie was now on a first-name basis with the other five members of his humanity-saving cohort. Looking for more than that might endanger the whole mission.

But a guy could dream.

Charlie started wandering down the row, toward the end with the vending machines. That was the only real source of light or sound that he could pick out. Maybe it held a clue.

At this point, he'd even settle for being told his answer was in another castle.

Within a dozen steps Charlie knew something was wrong again, but needed another dozen to figure out what. The sound again. His brown loafers should have made more of a scuffing, the way he was walking on the carpet. But his feet sounded distant, like he was hearing himself walking from a row over or something.

Didn't make sense. His feet sounded far away. The vending machine and air conditioner sounded far away. But Charlie's words reflected like the room was smaller than it looked...

And shouldn't Charlie have reached the end of the row by now?

He stopped and looked around. More tables. More computers. All too much the same to give him any sense of whether or not he'd covered much distance. The glow of the vending machines didn't look any closer.

Suspicion started creeping up Charlie's spine, bringing a slight shiver with it.

He tried jogging. Well, more of a brisk trot. Enough to make him puff for air after about twenty seconds or so.

But even Charlie's slow running pace should have more than reached the end of the row by the time his breathing picked up. To say nothing of the sheen of sweat he could feel starting up on his forehead and under his pits.

Charlie was running, and not getting anywhere.

"Okay," said Charlie to the ceiling, "if this is metaphor, you guys are laying it on a little thick."

No one answered.

25

When Brice arrived at the copse of acacias in what might have been the golden grasslands of the African savannah, he felt loose and ready for action. The wind was at his back, and the jog had done him good. Got the blood pumping, the good kind of sweat sticking his tee shirt to him in the heat, and enough of an endorphin rush that he felt as though he could take on the world.

A sensation that was tested by what he saw, just past the trees.

Brice finally got his first glimpse of the elephant that had been trumpeting out its distress.

Its skin wasn't gray, like the elephants Brice had seen at the zoo as a child. More of a reddish-brown. And it wasn't as large as he expected either. It wasn't much bigger than his own sedan. And short, like something had cut it off at the knee. But the elephant had tusks. Great, long ivory tusks, each a yard long easily.

Those tusks were stained dark red with blood.

Two more elephants lay in the trampled, once-golden grass in front of it. Big ones, larger than full-sized SUVs. Gray-skinned and bloody and dead. Blood on their own tusks too. No way to guess who had been fighting whom or why.

The smaller, reddish-brown elephant trumpeted again, and at not much more than twenty feet away the sound was painfully loud. Left a buzz in Brice's ears when it ended.

The elephant strained and struggled like it was trying to move and ... couldn't. Like it was caught from the knee down. Quicksand, maybe, or something like it. Brice couldn't tell from where he stood, under the closest acacia.

Then the warm wind shifted. The foul odor of gore and blood and elephant spoor slapped Brice. Made him gag. He pinched his nose closed and pulled a sweaty spot in his Mets tee shirt over his face. Shallow breaths through his mouth helped, the salty sweat smell preferable to the rank scene ahead of him.

But the moment was gone. The righteous need to right a wrong from childhood fled before the reality of what he saw. He wasn't at the San Diego Zoo, and he wasn't six years old anymore. This wasn't some sick elephant in need of a bowl of chicken soup and a friend to stroke its long trunk and floppy ears until it felt better.

This elephant was a killer. Maybe in self-defense. Maybe murder. No way for Brice to know for certain.

Still, it *was* in trouble. But Brice couldn't tell if this was an opportunity to help an animal in distress, or to take advantage of its immobility and end the life of a hazard to other wildlife.

Brice thought of jungle cats, like lions, and people who tried to keep them as pets. Sooner or later, the stories always seemed to lead to the great cats getting a taste of human blood, which always lead to them having to be put down. Once they'd tasted it, people were sure they'd want more.

Was it like that with elephants? If an elephant started killing its own kind, would it keep going? Elephants were herbivores, so it wasn't as though it would start killing other creatures to eat. Still, Brice felt certain that elephants wouldn't just murder other elephants. That was aberrant behavior. Maybe the equivalent of an elephant as broken as a human serial killer.

Confusion worried at Brice's brow, made him gnaw at his lip. He was no zoologist. He was just a comedian. A talk show host. Heck, some people would have called him a pundit. He had no way of knowing for certain if his memories about animals and animal behavior had any scientific merit at all.

Maybe this was some kind of Greenie metaphor? Was he supposed to learn something from what he saw? Or do something about it?

And what would they want him to do?

The buzz cleared from Brice's ears, and he heard a sound that set his teeth on edge. Spiked fear up his spine.

It was a growl followed by a rising whoop.

That was the sound of a hyena. Not the full giggling laugh. An inquisitive sound. A solo sound.

Brice grabbed the rough bark of the acacia and started climbing. The tree was thin and young. He could almost get one hand around its trunk. But fear was a great motivator, and his slight fear of heights paled before the risk of being torn apart by a hyena.

Brice shimmied up like it was a pole on a playground.

The tree shuddered, dropping leaves as he reached the lower branches, some eight feet up, and started looking around.

There. Blonde with dark brown spots and a long, thick neck. A hyena. Sniffing and studying from a safe distance.

It whooped again, big ears perked. The trapped elephant trumpeted a challenge at it, and the hyena dropped back a half-dozen steps, giggling.

But the hyena didn't seem to hear what it wanted. It whooped one more time, ears still perked and listening. The elephant renewed its struggles to free its trapped legs.

The hyena turned and loped off, looking back over its shoulder and giving its growling whoop every few steps.

Realization shivered through Brice, cold despite the heat of his efforts and the wind. That hyena was fetching its pack. And that pack probably wouldn't be the only one. No vultures in the sky — no birds at all, which disturbed Brice more than he wanted to think about — but Brice knew that the hyenas would have competition for all that dead elephant meat. Lions maybe. Or jackals. Or just other hyenas.

Animals that would kill the trapped elephant and eat it too. And without any freedom of movement, the elephant would be unable to fight back. It would die like the ones in front of it.

No.

26

Twigs snapped under Laura's sneakers with every running step. No silence. No stealth. No time.

Her heart pounded faster than her feet. Fear pushed her for more speed. Fear for the screamer. Fear for herself. Stomach clenching around her breakfast. Nauseous saliva building up under her tongue.

Trees flew past Laura all around. Hickories and black oaks in full moonlight. Just like that night. Just like when the creeper found her.

No. Never again. Not another girl victimized by him.

He got away last time. Police manhunt found nothing. No sign. Took too long to reach the rangers. The police. He had too much time to clear out. Everyone knew. Everyone knew he'd get away.

And no one seemed to care. Oh, her parents cared, and her friends cared, but not the police. Not the people who could help. Not the people whose *jobs* were to help.

Laura had pushed to run the search statewide. Begged for it, crying there, her head down on the file-strewn oak desk of the detective in charge of the investigation. Fat Detective Simmons, with his comb-over, hit burnt coffee, his tacky ties, and his wrinkly, ice-cream colored shirts. Detective Simmons who leered when he thought she wasn't looking.

Detective Simmons, who said no.

Said her description fit hundreds of possibles, even locally, but no known perps. That phrase stuck in fourteen-year-old-Laura's head. No known perps. The creeper hadn't been caught before so he couldn't be caught for what he did to Laura.

Her description could have matched too many people, so it wasn't worth checking. Too many man hours. Too much cost. Wasn't worth trying to find him. Wasn't worth trying to stop him before he did it again.

All Laura heard was that *she* wasn't worth it. Wasn't worth the effort. Done was done, and Detective Simmons plainly thought she needed to move on.

As though it was just that easy. As though she didn't need years of therapy. As though she didn't plunge deep into every character she played to distance herself further and further from the incident.

As though she didn't sometimes still wake up shaking in a cold sweat, certain he had found her again. Certain he was in her house.

Well not this time.

This time the young girl screaming for help was heard. This time Laura's friends weren't sleeping dead to the world or passed out drunk. Laura wasn't the victim now. She was older. Stronger. She had . years of workouts and martial arts training. Laura could handle herself now.

And Laura was going to save that poor, screaming girl.

Only the one scream, but it was enough. This campsite, this patch of woods. Laura knew that girl had to have wandered off to pee just like Laura did. Probably to the same place. That spot of privacy by the boulder.

The creeper probably staked it out, knowing by now it was the kind of place a girl would go to pee.

Laura forced herself to slow down as she neared the boulder. She could just see it through the trees now. A great slab of gray and white rock, jutting out of the dirt to a height of some eight feet. Ridged, which was why Petey had climbed it that day. Made everyone laugh by singing "I Am the Very Model of a Modern Major-General" from the top. The reason she had thought of it that night when she needed to pee.

She spliced that line of thinking out of her head. No time to remember Petey or the others. It was a cool night, so like that night. The frogs and crickets just as loud as they had been then.

Laura focused on her breathing, kept it slow and smooth and through her nostrils. Only the hint of a light sweat on her forehead and neck. That short sprint was little more than a warmup for her now. But her pulse hammered in her neck all the same.

She watched her footsteps, kept her rubber soles easing down onto dirt and avoiding twigs and leaves when she could.

One tree to the next. Each tree a little closer. She needed surprise. She knew that. For all her training, Laura's weight never got higher than one-thirty-five. The creeper might have weighed twice that. And he had reach. She couldn't count on force. Needed precision.

Needed any advantage she could get.

She pressed tight against the deep-ridged bark of a hickory tree, breathed in the minty-turpentine smell. Pretended to be part of that bark. Just tree. Nothing here but tree.

And she listened.

Laura could hear rustling now, in the shadows over by the boulder. Grunting, but effort grunting. Not...

Laura found a sharp rock on the ground. It was red and brown, and fit into her shaky hand for an easy grip. And it had a sharp ridge along one side, like a long knife with a shallow curve.

Decent for stabbing. Better for cutting or slashing. Much better than her knuckles.

Laura lowered her center of gravity, hunching forward. She started trotting toward the rock. Slow. Too slow. But she wanted to see him before she sprinted. Wanted her target in sight. Find the perfect gauge, so she was ready.

Laura came around the curve and saw them. The skinny teenage girl, her spaghetti-string top torn to reveal her white bra. The creeper with his big belly and stained white long john shirt. Ankle high black leather work boots. Black suspenders struggling to hold up blue jeans, ripped at the knees. Lots of black hair on his head, his face, his arms, peeking out of his long johns.

The girl's back was to the sheer side of the boulder. The creeper had her cornered. Had his arms wide to snatch her.

He was going to grab her. He was going to have her. If he got his hands on her...

Laura's plans flew out of her head. Anger and hatred pulsed through her. Turned the world red. Her knuckles whitened, one hand a fist and the other clenching the rock. Her stomach clenched too, along with her jaw.

"Hey, asshole!" she yelled. "Try your luck against a *woman* instead of a girl."

The creeper turned.

The girl shoved a stun gun in his back and pulled the trigger.

27

Charlie wiped sweat from his forehead with the back of his hand. He looked around this room, so full of computers. The way his life was full of computers. Or maybe his life *was* computers. Maybe that was the metaphor the Greenies were going for.

That Charlie's life could be reduced to a dim room and row after row of bleeding edge computers. With hints of pizza and soda in the background.

Not a pleasant thought. But he didn't care for the alternatives either.

"You guys can't seriously want me to turn on one of these computers." Charlie stared at the dark ceiling, with its useless row of extinguished fluorescent lamps. "I could have done a test like that at home, you know."

Still no answer, but Charlie no longer expected one. He just didn't want to talk to himself, and he figured they were watching anyway. If they wanted to insist on testing him, he might as well talk to his proctors.

So what did he know?

Dim room full of computers. Strip-style surge protectors under every table. Faded pizza smell, like this was after a LAN party. Thin gray carpet though. And office-style fluorescent lights. And black office roller chairs, executive style.

Something like an office building then. If he could see a wall, maybe he could tell more. Figure out if this were one of those places people rented out, or the testing room in a game company, or something else. Air conditioning he could hear and just barely feel. And the red-and-blue glow of soda machines that weren't nearly as close as they seemed to be.

Or were they?

Charlie unplugged one of the mice, coiled its cord up tight, and tied it with no regard to the possibility of anyone ever again trying to use it as an input device.

Charlie threw the mouse as hard as he could, aiming for the vending machines. His shoulder, elbow and ribs all complained that he was no baseball player, but that didn't matter. What mattered was that the mouse fell short. Charlie could hear the muted clattering on carpet.

Those vending machines were definitely more than fifteen or twenty feet away.

All right. So if walking down the row got Charlie nowhere, maybe crossing rows would do better.

Charlie got down on all fours and started crawling across the gray carpet, crossing under one table and soon another. Felt like concrete underneath the carpet, cool and solid and not very gentle on his knees. The carpet's rubber and chemical odor stronger at this range.

After two or three minutes of this, Charlie stood up. The glow of the soda machines was in the same place it had been last time. In fact, Charlie couldn't tell that he'd moved at all.

Charlie puffed out an irritated sigh.

He pulled out the four nearest roller chairs and lined them up in the center of the row. He got down and crawled again, counting two or three rows crossed before he looked up to his left.

The same roller chairs, in the same position.

Charlie sat back on his knees, breathing a little harder than he wanted to admit.

"Really?" he said, looking up. "Why not just put me in a small room with a computer then?"

Charlie shook his head and stood up. There had to be another answer. Maybe the test was to figure out a way to escape his life full of computers. Charlie chewed his lip as he considered that. Could that really be the test?

The floor was solid. No way out there. And no way out down the rows, or across them. That left up. More thick metaphor, but a possibility.

Charlie climbed up on one of the brown, rectangular tables. It felt stable enough underneath him. No good though. He couldn't reach the ceiling. Not even with one of the keyboards. He sighed and climbed back down.

Maybe he could stack one table on top of another...

Oh, who was he kidding?

"Fine. I don't see what this is going to tell you, but whatever." Charlie sat in one of the comfy roller office chairs and adjusted it to the height and tilt he liked. He moved the mouse to its proper place so he could have his arm and wrist bent just so, then tapped the power buttons on the monitor and the little box computer.

"It's your dime. Let's see how you're spending it."

A beep. The low whir of a computer fan. The monitor flashed blue, then brought up a web page, using a browser Charlie didn't recognize. It had a green border and a star field symbol in the upper right corner.

The web page displayed an old school bulletin board. Nobody used that kind of outdated design anymore, not in Charlie's time. Had to be some kind of plug-in or an emulator. But the details were right. That block letter courier font, perfect for ASCII art. Flashing block cursor, throwing back to the days before GUIs.

Gold text on a black background, though. That looked familiar. In fact, Charlie hadn't seen that since he last logged into PolyMath, the old bulletin board he used to haunt way back in the day...

This did look like the old PolyMath site. Except it didn't have the old PolyMath interface. Used to show an ASCII art image of a book opening and all kinds of languages and sciences would pour out of it. Even then the design was a holdover from the days of Internet yore.

PolyMath was just what it sounded like — a site for would-be polymaths. A place for students of dozens of disciplines to compare notes. They had chat rooms for just about every interest, and debates (and the occasional flame war) were nightly occurrences. Charlie sometimes thought he learned more just lurking on that site than he ever did in high school.

Instead of the book image, though, the website in front of Charlie went through an ASCII art depiction of the solar system in motion, then resolved down to a single question in the middle of the screen.

Which is more important? A) Fathering children. B) Advancing science.

No text box. No check box. This looked like the kind of setup where Charlie would push either 'A' or 'B' and the webpage would move on to the next question.

Charlie pressed 'C.' Nothing happened. He did it again. He tried 'Enter' next, but again, nothing.

"What if I don't think it's A or B? What if I think it's A and B? What if I want to explain my answer?"

Charlie sighed.

Charlie started trying keyboard shortcuts. Anything he could think of from the half-dozen operating systems he'd either played with or used seriously, trying to find his way from the browser to the desktop, or maybe the file system. Heck, Charlie would have settled for a list of programs he could run.

But none of the keyboard shortcuts made a difference. Not even ones that should have forced a reboot.

He considered not answering, but that would have been as bad as refusing to come in the first place. This was their game and their rules, and if the Greenies wanted Charlie to answer a bunch of strange questions, then Charlie felt obligated to answer them.

He shook his head and pressed 'A,' but he wasn't sure he believed in his answer.

Question one melted into question two.

Which is a better way for society to handle its murderers? A) Lifetime imprisonment. B) Death penalty.

"Oh, come on. You've got to give me a 'C' option here. At least give me a None of the Above. Something."

No response. Not that Charlie was really expecting one.

"Fine," Charlie grumbled, and pressed 'A.'

Which is more damaging to a society? A) Racism. B) Sexism.

Charlie leaned down and thumped his head on the table repeatedly. What the hell kind of question was that? How can it possibly be either / or when both issues had already caused so very many problems in the United States alone?

And who the hell was Charlie to answer that question on behalf of the whole human race? Charlie was a man. And white. Both racism and sexism were things he could talk about, but not things he had to live through.

If anything, Charlie was much more likely to accidentally perpetrate them than suffer from them. So who the hell was he to say which was worse?

A detail began to twist in Charlie's gut. The question wasn't which was worse. The question was which was more damaging to society.

Racism led to riots and fights. Entire segments of society being feared and hated because of a weird us-them psychological division. Reduced chances at education and opportunity. Hazards to life and limb.

Sexism didn't lead to riots. But it also led to reduced opportunities and weird legal snafus over things like abortion.

Wait. Sexism affected half of *all people*. Racism affected large groups, but in terms of percentages....

That twist in Charlie's gut knotted further. Could he really boil this issue down to numbers? Was he sure the damage done by sexism outweighed slavery? Jim Crow law? "Voter registration" acts?

Wait. The question was "a society," not "the United States." Charlie had only been thinking in terms of American history, not world history. But Charlie wasn't here as a citizen of the United States, but of the human race.

Lots of ills had been committed in terms of nationalism and racism, but Charlie kept coming back to the fact that sexism affected half the planet.

Charlie squeezed his eyes closed and pressed 'B,' hating himself the entire time.

Another question popped up.

28

A-Day-Plus-One. Nine-Oh-Seven A.M. Lounge Local Time

Brice might not have understood the sociological and zoological implications of an elephant who had killed its own kind, but he couldn't just stand by and let a helpless animal get slaughtered. Not when he could do something about it.

But what could he do?

No way he could fight off a single hyena, much less a pack. And if lions showed up? Forget it. All Brice could do was hide up here in a tree that couldn't ... couldn't quite ... support his weight.

The elephant trumpeted again, growing almost frantic in its struggles, but for all the shifting of its body it couldn't move. Brice could see what held it now. And he thought it was in fact something like quicksand. Some patch of dark, oily ground where the grass wasn't growing. It sloshed like thick, viscous liquid with every thrash of the elephant's legs.

The elephant had no purchase. Nothing to use as leverage to free itself.

Brice thought about the tree he was in. Swaying under his weight, and Brice wasn't even moving. His stomach lurched and sweat broke out on his forehead. He had to close his eyes and breathe until the impending vertigo faded.

The tree might bend far enough...

No. This was stupid. This had to be the stupidest, most dangerous idea Brice had considered since he was young and single, convinced of his own immortality.

This was just plain foolish. Chances were, all Brice would accomplish would be breaking a bunch of bones and functionally offering himself up to the hyenas when they came back.

No. There had to be another way. There were the corpses of the other elephants. Maybe Brice could...

What? Brice would be lucky to be able to shift even one of those massive legs, much less the head. And even if he could, would the living elephant be willing and able to use an elephant corpse to escape?

No. Brice knew what he had to do.

"Stupid, stupid, stupid," Brice chanted at himself as he climbed higher in the tree. The acacia protested by dropping more leaves and swaying hard enough to make Brice queasy. He hoped he didn't lose his scrambled eggs and bacon.

Brice pulled off his now-soaked tee shirt, grimacing against the smell of the gory scene nearby. He tied his shirt around the top of the core of the trunk, where most of the thicker branches grew, then tied the short sleeves around his own wrists, pulling the cotton tight with his teeth.

Brice wondered briefly if his pasty, dumpy body could get sunburnt when there was no sun.

He puffed out a breath and jumped, gripping tight to his tee shirt. His weight against the strength of the trunk. As the pressure hit, Brice's fingers, wrists, elbows, shoulders, and hips immediately told him this was a bad idea.

The trunk began to bow. But not nearly far enough.

Brice swung his feet back, and then forward hard. The tree followed. Back and forth. Back and forth. The elephant was watching him now. Curious, but still frightened enough to trumpet at him.

Then his head began to spin, and his gut with it.

It would have been just Brice's luck to have this work, only to have the freed elephant trample him. The most poetic ending to his life he could think of. He tried to imagine how he would have reported it on *Weeknightly*, to distract himself from the growing pains in his gripping fingers and straining shoulders, the spinning in his head and gut as he swung back and forth. Back and forth.

Brice DePaul died as he lived. Half naked and trampled by an elephant.

Weirdly his gut settled down and his head stopped spinning. As though his old fear of heights got overwhelmed and quit.

Brice's feet could almost touch the ground now at the far points of each swing. The trunk groaned harder with each pass. He'd lost all control of direction though. He had enough sideways momentum that there was no true pendulum-like back and forth. But as long as he didn't gore himself on elephant tusks, the exact direction of each swing didn't matter. All he needed to do was work hard enough to snap the trunk like an oversized twig. Then he could—

Brice heard a hyena giggle. Then another.

The elephant trumpeted again, louder and longer than anything Brice had heard yet. His eyes squeezed tight against the pain in his ears, sharper even than the hell his joints were giving him.

Too loud. Brice couldn't hear anything now but a ringing sound. But still he kept throwing his legs forward and back, straining the tree more and more.

He could see hyenas now. Three ... no, four of them, spread out. But all along the same side. That meant more had to be around behind him.

Brice was surrounded, and he was doing nothing but swinging his body like a fool. Hoping he could ... what? Break the trunk? And still retain enough strength in his arms to bring it to the elephant? And hope the elephant could get out of whatever held it before the hyenas ate him for his trouble?

"Stupid, stupid, stupid," chanted Brice, fear making his voice squeaky.

Crap, now he was headed down straight at the elephant. Branches cracking and snapping against the great, reddish-brown beast as it swung its massive head to meet him.

"*Stupid!*" Brice managed one more time, squeezing his eyes shut and praying for a quick, merciful death.

Blurp.

Brice descended into the viscous quagmire feet first, inches from the bloody tusks.

Knee deep and going.

Waist deep and going.

Chest deep now in the sandy, oily stuff that smelled like cat litter filled with motor oil.

Brice opened his eyes and saw hyenas approaching.

The elephant's trunk grabbed the tree.

Brice submerged into the quagmire, barely squeezing his eyes and mouth shut before he went under completely. He could feel the pumping of the elephant's legs next to him, churning the viscous substance.

And moving.

It was working. The elephant was pulling itself out.

Brice's lungs screamed at him for air. The world flashed red behind his closed eyes. He tried to climb up the branches after the elephant, but his wrists were tied to the tree trunk, and the branches all around him were too weak to help.

The elephant must have broken the tree trunk. It might get out, but Brice would drown here, tied to the top of a submerged acacia tree.

Stupid, stupid, stupid.

Brice kicked his legs, determined to surface. Praying for at least one more breath. The elephant wasn't even close to him now. It had to be pulling itself out onto the ground. But Brice was getting nowhere. He might as well have been kicking air.

Brice's lungs begged, pleaded with him for air. A muddy, oily taste slipped past the seal of his lips. His heart pounded like the bass of his son's music. His blood roared past his ears.

Movement! Brice was coming up. And up. His face broke through the surface and he gasped so loud he could hear it even over the elephant trumpeting a challenge at the hyenas.

But Brice was still going. Up past his waist now. He blinked his eyes, but by the time he could see past the morass of residue his feet were clearing the quagmire.

The acacia tree was springing back. But he could see the cracks in its trunk. Hear more forming as the exhausted elephant began stumbling away.

Brice flew up into the air.

The trunk snapped beneath him.

And a golden glow surrounded him.

29

A-DAY-PLUS-ONE. EIGHT-THIRTY-FOUR A.M. LOUNGE LOCAL TIME

Laura's jaw dropped open, and her arms hung down loosely at her sides. She barely held on to her slashing rock.

The scene before her was so similar, so much like what had happened to her those eight short years ago. The frogs and the crickets, singing like it was their last night on earth. The shine of a full moon overhead. Black oaks and hickories and other trees around her, with so little underbrush this might have been so near that campsite she remembered from Wayne National Forest. The cool night breeze. That gray and white boulder with the jagged ridge.

The heavy-set creeper with all that black hair and beard, looking just as he did that night. Thick jeans torn at the knees. Suspenders and a long john shirt. Ankle high black leather work boots. Tanned like he spent every day of his life outdoors.

A young girl victim with long blond hair. Coltish still, just starting to fill out her pink, spaghetti-strap top — now torn to reveal her pale skin and white bra — and form-fitting blue jeans.

So very much the same.

And yet it was ending so differently.

Laura remembered all too well how it ended last time.

This time, the victim had a stun gun and the presence of mind to use it.

The creeper lay face down on the forest floor, shaking and smelling as though he wet his pants. The victim clutched her top with one hand, shaking just as much as her attacker as she gripped her stun gun tight. Like she considered hitting him with it again.

"Are you…" Laura's words died when the girl looked up at her.

Laura's rapid pulse skipped. This girl had the same blue eyes Laura saw in the mirror every morning.

The girl stammered, then stamped her foot to get words out. "T-t-thank you."

"Don't thank me," said Laura, amazed that any words came out at all. "You did that yourself."

"Bastard." The girl spat at the man, her nose wrinkled and lips pulled in as though he smelled even worse than Laura thought he did. The girl's elbows pulled in close, forearms pressed against her body. Her knees together as though afraid to be separated.

"Well," said Laura, "it's—"

The girl reached down and zapped him again. The creeper's body locked tight. So rigid it shook. Laura could see a touch of foam at the edge of his lips.

The creeper definitely wasn't going anywhere anytime soon.

Laura felt shaky herself. Adrenaline still pulsed through her system, but nothing to spend it on now. She had to force her breathing to slow down before she got a head rush and risked passing out.

"We should tie him up," Laura said.

"You have rope?" The girl's expression plainly added, "dumbass."

"No." Laura made the word slow. Tried to slip into one of her action hero characters. Someone smooth and cool, who could handle this better than she felt like she could. "But he's got suspenders. We can hogtie him. Throw his boots away too, so if he gets free he can't run."

"Yeah," said the girl, with realization dawning in her voice. "Then he's all ours."

That tone pulled Laura out of her acting exercises. Forced her to stay Laura, not one of her characters.

"Ours?" she said. "You mean for the police?"

"Fuck the police," said the girl. "What are they going to do? Slap this guy on the wrist and make him pick up trash on the side of the road for six months? Then send him back home so he can do this again? Find another girl to victimize?"

"No. We caught him this time. He'll pay."

"Oh, he'll pay all right." The girl rolled the unconscious creeper over, and the urine smell wafted out strong from the dark stain at his crotch. She undid the clips of his suspenders and yanked them free. "I can think of some great uses for that rock you have there."

Laura felt a wave of cold through her guts. Numbing her insides, even as she still felt the embers of rage shaking her hands and knees. This was him. She'd recognize him anywhere. Especially the little details that stood out so plain now. Little details that never made it into her police report. That tiny vertical scar just under his left eye. The blue tattoo ink, barely visible past his beard on the right side of his neck.

This was the same man. The same man who attacked Laura. The same man the police refused to chase.

"Come help me," said the girl, seeming to have forgotten the way her top fell open now that she had a purpose. "Between the two of us, we can make this bastard pay."

"That's not right."

Automatic words coming out of Laura's mouth. Civilized words. But a voice in the back of her head tried to get her attention. And its ideas weren't so civilized.

"Right?" The girl had the suspenders in her hands now, and snapped them tight. "*Right?* You know what this guy just tried to do to me. And don't tell me he hasn't done it before. Don't you stand there with that look in your eye and try to tell me he didn't do the same thing to you."

Laura couldn't say anything. Laura was raised to be a good citizen. To pay her taxes and obey all the important laws. To let the police handle the bad men. Like that stalker she had last year. The police took care of it. The police...

The police took care of everything except the time she needed them the most.

Everything except the creeper.

"He did, didn't he?" The girl's voice was quiet now. Sympathetic. "Don't hide from it. Tell the truth. If it wasn't him it was someone else. Wasn't it? And you didn't have a stun gun."

"We should call the rangers. Turn him over to the authorities. We have—"

"*We have this bastard at our mercy.*" Fire in the girl's familiar eyes now. So like the fire that made Laura shake. "Come on. Help me."

The girl rolled the creeper back onto his belly, put her foot on his wide ass and started yanking at his boots.

"No," said Laura, dropping her rock. "You need to untie his laces first. Work boots like those go too high up the ankle to yank off."

Together Laura and the girl got the creeper out of his boots and tied his ankles to his wrists. The black suspenders had a lot of stretch to them, too much for quick, clean tying. So they had to loop and loop those suspenders around his wrists and ankles, tying them again every third loop.

By the time they were done, the skin of his hands and feet was pale and blotchy from lack of blood. They probably tied him too tightly, but Laura didn't care. She and the girl were both kneeling in their jeans, looking at one another across the unconscious creeper.

The creeper uttered a low groan, shifting slightly.

"He's going to wake up soon," said Laura.

"Grab his socks," said the girl. "They're heavy wool. Make a good gag."

"He's not going anywhere," said Laura. "We should get—"

"He might have friends. What if he calls out to them?"

Laura grabbed those sour-smelling, sweaty socks and shoved

them into the creeper's mouth. Just as she finished, his eyes blinked open. He got his first real look at Laura.

And Laura saw no sign of recognition in those eyes. He didn't even remember her. All the years of suffering she'd endured, and he didn't even remember her. She was just another girl to him.

Laura scrambled for her rock.

"Yes!" said the girl. She pulled the creeper's hair, lifting his head to he could see what Laura was doing. "She's got a sharp, sharp rock with your name on it. Maybe she'll fuck you with it. You'd like that, wouldn't you? You rapist bastard."

Laura stopped, one hand on her tapering rock. Was this what she wanted? To hurt him the way he hurt her? She looked over at the creeper, saw the fear in his eyes. This time she was the strong one and he the helpless one.

Laura could do anything she wanted to him, and he couldn't stop her.

Laura dropped the rock.

"No." Laura stood straight and spoke loudly over the battling emotions in her own psyche. She wrapped her arms around her belly. "No payback and no torture. That's his way. Not ours."

"Ours?" said the girl.

"Be better than him," said Laura, voice steady now. Confidence back in her step as she walked over to the stun gun, forgotten in the haste to tie up the creeper. She lifted the weapon. "We put him out again with this. And we get the rangers."

Laura puffed out a sigh. "And we call our shrink, first thing Monday."

"*Our?*" The girl sounded outraged. As much fire in that one word as anything Laura had said or felt all day.

"Yes," said Laura. She walked over and knelt beside the girl. She stroked the girl's cheek with her free hand. "Our."

"So we're not going to do anything at all to this bastard?"

"Well, I do think it's in our best interests to knock him out again."

Laura shoved the stun gun into the creeper's wet groin and

emptied the batteries firing it off. And she could not deny taking some pleasure in the lock-limbed tremors the creeper endured.

When the stun gun clicked empty she dropped it and turned to hug the girl...

...and the golden glow took Laura away.

30

Charlie sat in the roller chair in the dimly lit room, sweating through his tee shirt and jeans. His loafers kept jouncing his knees nonstop, shaking him all the way up.

These questions were the worst. He had answered more than two hundred now. Every one of them some kind of moral dilemma worthy of a national conversation. A debate. Possibly political action.

Instead his choices were always 'A' or 'B.' 'A' or 'B.'

Cold. Sterile. Distant.

Charlie's skin was burning now. Feverish. And his stomach rumbled as though he'd been here answering questions for days. Laughter over breakfast felt like a distant dream.

And the questions weren't numbered. The gold text on the web page interface merely melted from one question into the next, as soon as he selected his answer.

Charlie devoutly wished for a slice of that pepperoni pizza he kidded himself that he could still smell. Or maybe something from the soda machine. He no longer cared what. Cola or lemon-lime, caffeinated or not. Anything wet and vaguely cool. Anything to splash through his dry mouth and throat. Anything he could use as an excuse to turn away from this computer with its damned, endless list of questions.

Which would go further to reducing street crime? A) Fair and balanced laws. B) Fair and balanced enforcement.

Which fosters stronger family units? A) Polygamous people forced into monogamy. B) Monogamous people forced into polygamy.

Which would go further to reduce racism and sexism? A) Equal representation in government. B) Equal representation in media.

Charlie was getting to the point that he could barely remember his answers anymore. He hated every answer. And he hated every question. And he was starting to really hate the Greenies for putting him through this. At some point he started typing "You guys suck" before selecting his answer, in hopes that they were receiving his test results through captured keyboard strokes.

He knew it wasn't likely. But still. They should have at least had the decency to offer him an option 'C' once in a while.

Charlie's feelings toward his fellow humans weren't all that charitable right now either. Having to answer these questions reminded him just exactly how messed up the human race was. Maybe the whole of the universe would be better off in the long run if humans never left their own planet. Just stayed here until they killed themselves off or until the sun went nova.

Charlie felt as though he might still be in the shower when the sun went nova. These questions made him feel as though he might never really get clean again.

Of course, that assumed he wasn't right here in this very chair, answering yet more questions for the Greenies.

His one consolation — the only faint light at the end of this dark tunnel — was that at least Charlie wasn't the only one. Sure, he was the only one in this ridiculous dim room that looked like a reject from a LAN party. But the others all had to be taking the same test, didn't they? Surely the Greenies wouldn't put the whole onus of answering these questions on one white man.

No. They were all probably here in the room even, separated by the inability to leave the handful of tables and computers around them. Just the way Charlie was. This was probably the same room as the lounge and the cafeteria. As soon as Charlie reached the last of these endless questions, the lights would come on and he would see the door to his suite or something.

The gold glow that "brought him here" probably didn't actually teleport him that time. It probably just transformed the room around him.

That thought gave Charlie hope as he turned his eyes back to the monitor to see the next question.

Which solution to overpopulation produces a stronger society? A) Legalized cannibalism. B) Mandatory sterilization below a given economic threshold.

Charlie stared at the question. He read it and reread it, trying to make more sense out of what he was reading. Finally he came to the conclusion that his reading skills had not failed him. That he was indeed reading a question about choosing between cannibalism and mandatory sterilization, under the excuse of producing a "stronger society."

As Charlie saw it, there was only one answer to that question.

He reached out and turned off the computer and monitor. No hum or whine from a hard drive closed off without warning — which was odd — but the monitor crackled a momentary static charge.

And then Charlie was alone in that room full of computers, his eyes adjusting to the loss of light from the monitor.

"Are you sure you want to do that?"

Kyna's voice — actually Kyna's emulation of the voice of the actress who played Shireen on *Two Friends No Waiting* — coming from Charlie's right.

He didn't look at her.

"All the questions were ridiculous." He spun his chair a hundred-eighty degrees, facing the three computers that had been behind him, but still not looking at Kyna. "But that last one ... that last one was too far over the top."

"One of your group has already passed the current round of testing. And one of your group has failed. Are you sure you want to risk—"

"If those questions are indicative of your people's attitudes, maybe we're better off without you."

Big words, but Charlie's heart was thumping hard in his chest.

"Why won't you look at me?" Curiosity in Kyna's voice now, not judgment.

"Because that shape, that look... It's a lie. Just like Mynack's look. Just like our rooms, and the lounge, and the cafeteria. Hell, everything since that flying saucer. All some kind of calculated image."

"So what do you think I look like?"

Charlie couldn't help but glance at Kyna now. Still green-skinned and wearing a skimpy silver spacesuit with knee-high boots, she stood with one hip resting against the edge of a brown table, her arms crossed under the swell of what on a human woman would have been breasts.

"Either your true form is some kind of angelic shape of pure energy, or a tentacled horror. Which I think you are depends on when you ask me."

Kyna chuckled softly. "Let me guess. The more irritated you are with us, the slimier and more betentacled I get?"

"Is betentacled even a word?"

Kyna shrugged, eyebrows high.

"Just the opposite," said Charlie, looking down at his borrowed brown loafers. "When I'm mad at you guys, I remind myself that you might be so super-evolved that you're beyond our ability to really understand. At the same time, whenever I find myself thinking something like, 'oh, this is cool,' I remind myself that this might all be a *To Serve Man* kind of setup."

"You think we came here to eat you?"

"You're the ones asking about cannibalism."

Kyna said nothing for a moment. Charlie just stared at his loafers. Brown suede. Little tan leather laces. Good leather soles. More comfortable than Charlie would have—

"Are you sure you're not going to answer any more questions on the computer? You risk failing, and possibly dragging down your whole group."

"There's nothing you can learn from my answers, when you're not asking good questions."

"You'd be surprised," said Kyna.

And the gold glow enveloped them both.

PART III

TESTS AND DECISIONS

31

A-Day-Plus-One. One-Oh-Eight P.M. Lounge Local Time

Charlie blinked his heavy eyelids open. Dim room. Too-soft white cotton pillow beneath his head. Bed then. Good.

Wait. Charlie's pillowcases were pale blue, and flannel. But these were white. And not flannel. Why?

He tried to sit up, but his eyelids weren't the only things that felt heavy. His arms, his legs, his head. In fact, the whole of his body felt pretty certain that the best thing Charlie could do right now was close his eyes again and drift back to sleep...

Wait. Sleep?

Charlie wrestled his arms out of the white cotton sheets and stretched. He knew where he was now. The bedroom of the suite the Greenies provided him, tucked away in his king-sized bed as though he hadn't already had breakfast and taken that eternal test...

What time was it? What day?

One-oh-nine according to the red digits of the alarm clock on his blonde wood nightstand. One of two nightstands, actually. A matched set, like the brass table lamps with mauve shades that adorned them both.

The whole suite looked as though it could have been plucked out of almost any convention hotel Charlie had ever stayed in. Thin tan carpeting. Textured walls the color of mocha, with black-and-white pictures of train tracks or empty platforms or switching stations. Floral potpourri smell, as from some kind of plug-in air freshener, tucked away out of sight somewhere.

Opposite the bed, a dark brown chest of drawers (empty) with a cabinet that housed a flat screen television with Blu-ray player. Brown wood doors led to a bathroom and the gigantic walk-in closet that went way beyond any hotel Charlie had ever set foot in.

And down at the other end of the room, the part that Charlie tried not to think about. The drapes. Mauve like the lampshades, those drapes did not cover windows or a sliding glass door. Instead, they covered floor-to-ceiling panels that shed light proportionate to the time of day. Right now he could see their bright midday glow around the edges of the curtains.

Charlie sat up, still wearing his Golf Academy video game tee shirt. He remembered now. Kyna teleported him to the front room of his suite, and Charlie felt so overwhelmed and exhausted he crawled into bed without taking off anything but his loafers.

Had he gotten that tired answering questions? Charlie couldn't remember. For that matter, he couldn't really remember the questions themselves. Only that they were egregious, and that he finally refused to answer any more of them.

Charlie rubbed sleep out of his eyes, and hoped he'd made the right decision. His limbs still dragged as he threw back the cream-colored bedspread and got to his feet. His shirt stuck to him like he'd been sweating.

Charlie peeled off his clothes and took a long hot shower in a bathroom with more than enough space and counter for two people. He scrubbed and scrubbed, trying to get rid of the psychic residue of answering so many questions that he was sure he hated, without quite remembering what they were.

When he finally felt clean enough, he wandered into the clothing store that masqueraded as a walk-in closet and dug out fresh underwear and another pair of loose jeans, black this time. To go with the jeans he found a black shirt featuring the Misfits skull, and completed the look with white socks and black sneakers. He brushed out his brown curls, and decided he was presentable.

He wandered back through his suite's social room — complete with enough chair and couch space for at least ten people, shelves of books and movies, and a wall-mounted sixty-inch plasma that would have been perfect for the next super bowl — and steadied himself with his hand on the knob of the white door. Would it be the cafeteria still, from breakfast? Something else entirely?

Charlie opened the door.

The lounge again, little kitchen off to his left, pinball machines and game tables past the facing distressed leather sectional couches. Sky blue ceilings and grass-green plush carpeting.

Right now, Jesse and Dubba J were playing an animated game of foosball, complete with trash talk and loud clacking as they twisted handles to knock the mini-soccer ball back and forth. And Brice and Alita sat facing each other on the couches, talking across the coffee table.

Brice must have showered too. He'd changed into a pale blue polo shirt with a pair of tan slacks. But Alita still had on the same pink top and red corduroy pants. The test must not have made her sweat as much.

"Hey, Charlie," said Brice with a smile, while Alita waved at him over her shoulder. "Not the last to arrive for once."

"Come join us," added Alita.

"Just let me grab a drink." Charlie wandered onto the hardwood flooring of the kitchen and dug around inside the huge, brushed steel refrigerator. Eggs and cheeses and meats and fruits and vegetables and at least three varieties each of butter and yogurt.

Finally he found a red and orange can of Diet Eruption Cola and popped the top as he wandered back over to sit beside Brice.

"No sign of Laura yet?" Charlie said, taking a sip.

"Was that the last one?" said Alita.

Charlie shook his head as he swallowed, and Alita rolled over the back of the couch, heading for the kitchen.

"Not yet," said Brice. "I was just wondering if someone needs to knock on her door and check on her. Some of this morning's tests have been pretty intense so far."

"Stupidest questions I could have imagined," said Charlie, shaking his head. "Can't really remember them though. Do you remember yours?"

"Questions?" Brice shared a glance with Alita as she resumed her seat on the facing couch, legs folded under her.

"Yeah," said Charlie. "Didn't they make you answer a bunch of strange moral dilemmas?" A wave of anger washed through Charlie as a few details surfaced. "A or B. I remember that much. Didn't matter what the question was or how complicated the issue might have really been, they always wanted a choice between A and B."

"Lady or the tiger kind of stuff?" said Alita.

"Worse." Charlie squeezed his eyes tight, trying to grasp what felt so elusive inside his head. "I think ... the breaking point for me ... was something like choosing between ... cannibalism and mandatory sterilization."

"What?" said Brice and Alita at the same time, both with eyebrows heading for the ceiling.

"That's what I mean." Charlie opened his eyes and took a long breath. "Stupid things like that."

"How did you answer that one?" said Brice.

"I didn't." Charlie sipped at his cola. "I shut off the computer and said I was done with that crap. Kyna showed up, and when I stuck to my guns she brought me back here."

"Mine was nothing like that," said Brice. "They sent me to the African savannah, I think. I had to save an albino elephant from both a quagmire and a pack of hyenas."

"I was back home in *Agua de Dios*," said Alita, "where I grew up. I had to moderate disputes among four — *four* — generations of Lunas." Alita started grumbling in Spanish, then chugged about half of her Diet Eruption Cola.

"What about those two?" said Charlie, pointing with his thumb at the enthusiastic foosball players.

"Jesse said his had to do with his early days in Hollywood, but wouldn't give any more details than that."

"More than Dubba J would say," added Alita. "He just said he didn't want to talk about it." Alita leaned forward, one supporting hand on her knee. "Whatever it was, he didn't like it. He got pale when I asked. Shook his head like he could shake out the memory."

"I know I got back so exhausted I fell asleep fully clothed, and still needed a long shower before I could feel clean again." Charlie tapped one finger against his soda can for a high, metallic note. "So this was clearly stressful for all of us, but in different ways."

All three of them turned and looked at Laura's door. In the silence of the moment, Dubba J whooped at scoring a goal.

"One of us should check on her," said Charlie.

"I'll do it," said Brice. He started to stand, but Alita waved him back down.

"Nothing personal, Brice," she said, "but I think Laura might need to talk to a woman."

"Hang on a sec." Charlie hopped to his feet and ran into the kitchen. He grabbed a cup of cherry yogurt, a spoon, and a napkin, and brought them back to hand to Alita.

Alita blinked at his choice, then gave Charlie an expectant look.

"It's her favorite flavor," said Charlie, trying not to blush at how this must have looked. "She mentioned it in an interview."

Alita didn't say anything, though Charlie could see her fighting down a smile as she nodded and took the offering toward Laura's door.

"She'll probably be hungry," said Brice in a soothing voice. He reached up and clapped Charlie on the shoulder. "It's a good thought."

But Charlie's eyes were on Alita, now at Laura's door.

She knocked.

32

A-Day-Plus-One. One-Twenty-Six P.M. Lounge Local Time

Laura sat huddled on the hardwood floor of the front room of her suite, knees tucked up to her chin and her arms clutching her legs in tight. Her back was wedged into a corner, between a red-and-gold Louis XVI couch and the pale, flowery wallpaper.

The collar of her red plaid felt shirt was up, protecting her neck. Dried tears and ruined makeup made a mess of her eyes and cheeks. Trail of snot under her nose.

None of that mattered.

A test. That had been a test. The aliens had sent Laura back to the worst moment of her life for a test.

She didn't beat the creeper. He was still out there somewhere.

She didn't save her younger self. What happened to her still happened.

Her skin felt hot. Not flushed. Feverish. She pressed her forehead against her knees, eyes shut. Breaths coming slow in, held for a four count, slow out, held for a four count. Just the way she was taught. Best way for her to stave off the panic attacks when they threatened.

Little routines. All Laura could count on to hold herself together when her stomach tied itself in knots and her knuckles clenched tight. All that kept her from wrecking the pretty room. Shattering the expensive mirror with its gold leaf.

But none of this was real either.

Probably just another test. Mynack and Kyna were probably sitting somewhere watching her on a monitor. *How will she react to that scene?*

Directors. The same everywhere. This was just another shoot, like any other. Only more personal this time. Too personal. How dare they—

Someone knocked on her door.

Laura snorted. Of course this was when the A.D. came knocking. Next shot must be ready.

No one cared what Laura was going through, only that she be in character and hit her marks for as long as the light held out. *Look pretty for the camera, Laura. I know your character's a badass, Laura, but she really needs to be rescued in this scene. This slow bikini shot is vital to establishing character, Laura.*

Tell the director about trauma, and all he'd say was *Use it!*

The knock came again. Words she couldn't make out. A soft voice. Feminine. Her hair stylist?

No. This wasn't a shoot. She was getting confused.

"Alita?" said Laura. Then she realized that her rough whisper wouldn't carry to the door, much less beyond it.

All of Laura's muscles complained when she stood. Every one of them. How long had she been like that?

She walked gingerly across the creaky cherry wood floor, still in her sneakers. She puffed out one more breath before opening the door a crack.

Alita stood just on the threshold, and her expression went from smiling to shocked and worried in an instant.

"*Pobrecita,*" she said, pushing through the doorway to take Laura in her arms. In the same movement, Alita kicked the door shut behind her.

Laura didn't know Alita. Not really. And Alita stood a good half-foot shorter than Laura, which should have made the moment awkward. But Laura couldn't help herself. There was something so comforting in the pure expression of sympathy and compassion. Laura tucked her face into Alita's shoulder and started crying again.

"Shhhh," said Alita, cooing soft words in Spanish that Laura didn't understand, but comprehension didn't seem to matter.

Something began to unclench in Laura's gut and the tears became a torrent. Probably ruining Alita's pretty top, but she didn't seem to mind. She just held Laura, and stroked her back, and kept saying soft things in Spanish that sounded comforting, whatever they meant. Even Alita's subtle perfume helped, citrus and floral, like a tea shop Laura liked down in Santa Barbara.

Finally Laura stopped crying again. She pulled back, an embarrassed smile spreading across her face.

"No." Alita held up a hand and stilled Laura with a confidence that Laura envied in that moment. "No apologies. No excuses. Now, Charlie was good enough to fetch you a cup of cherry yogurt, which I dropped on the carpet outside that door. It's still sealed, so I'm going to get it for you, along with a fresh spoon, a napkin, and something hot to drink. You want tea, coffee or coco?"

"Tea's fine. Green tea if they have it."

"All right. You go wash your face. You'll feel better. I'm going to be right back, and then you and I are going to sit on that couch and talk about whatever you want to talk about. And if you don't want to talk, I'll just sit with you. Okay?"

"Yeah," said Laura with a shaky little nod.

And then Alita was out the door, and Laura wandered back through the bedroom and into the huge, luxury bathroom with its eight-direction mist shower, spa bath tub big enough for six, and everywhere Brazilian marble that was mostly blue, but with swirls of purple, gold, and other colors throughout. Laura scrubbed her face with scented, herbal soap and a fluffy washcloth that probably cost more than the first dress she ever bought herself.

The hot water and the simple cleansing act did their job though. After she dried her face, Laura looked at herself in the mirror. She'd scrubbed enough that even without makeup she couldn't tell she'd been crying.

People magazine shot her that way once. Without makeup. Just to "demonstrate the purity of her beauty."

All Laura saw was a scared girl who just happened to be a good enough actress to convince the world she had her shit together.

"He's gone," she said. The old mantra coming back past her lips. "He can't hurt you here."

Laura shook out her hands, then her arms. She bounced on her toes, rolled her hips, rolled her neck. Shifted her jaw back and forth. She swung her hands up and slowly bent backwards. Not far enough to touch the floor right now, just enough to let herself hang there for a moment, before swinging her upper body in a slow circle.

One more deep breath, then she walked back into her sitting room. Alita was waiting for her. The cup of yogurt open and spoon in it, next to their steaming white porcelain cups of green tea.

No coasters on the Louis XVI table, but the white veined marble wouldn't care, much less the gilt edging and legs. If any of it were real, it would have cost a fortune.

"Much better," said Alita, smiling up at Laura. "You and me, we have a lot in common. Raised ourselves up on our talent. Faced down the bullshit that plagues our gender in the entertainment fields. Bet we both have stories to tell, stories we don't tell because they're just the price of getting where we are today. And I'm guessing the Greenies made you face something like that."

Laura shook her head and sat next to Alita on the stiff, black cushions of the expensive couch. Enough gold leaf on it, too, to feed a family of four for a month.

"That's what they did to me," said Alita, holding her cup in both her hands and looking off into the distance. "I left a lot behind when I left *Agua de Dios*. Family, mostly. I send them money, but it's not the same."

Alita sipped her tea, and Laura started toying with her yogurt, stirring it in the plastic cup even though it was already mixed. Barely remembering to spoon any of it into her mouth as she listened.

"I swear the Greenies made me deal with two years' worth of problems in two hours. All personal stuff. All things that needed me, not my money. Hard to hear. Problems that made me question how I could ever have left my family for something as selfish as a career."

And suddenly Laura was telling Alita everything. The creeper, when she was fourteen. The aftermath. The skeezy detective who wouldn't press the search. The years of therapy. The bad moments when Laura was sure she heard him in her house, coming for her.

And finally how the Greenies made her go through that all again, feel it all coming back fresh as an open wound. Facing down the creeper with what might have been her fourteen-year-old self and a stun gun.

"But," said Alita, voice soft, "you got him this time."

"*That wasn't real!*" Laura threw the yogurt at the fancy fucking mirror. "That wasn't the creeper. That girl wasn't me. I probably wasn't even in Wayne National Forest. This was all some sick fucking test. They're jerking us around."

Laura sat there, panting for breath through her open mouth. Her brow down and jaw forward. Anger sped through her system, reddened the edges of her vision. Serve the Greenies right if she wrecked their expensive suite.

Then she drew a deep, deep breath. So deep a breath her nostrils had to flare wide. So deep some of the air had to come in through her mouth. Her lungs filled just as full as they could get. So did her diaphragm. She inhaled so deeply her body felt like a balloon ready to pop.

Eyes closed, Laura held that breath and counted to four. Each heartbeat resonated through her chest.

Then she blew that breath back out through pursed lips. Slow and smooth and steady until her lungs emptied and her diaphragm emptied and her torso curled forward.

Laura sat back up, slowly, and looked at Alita, who sipped at her tea as though Laura had done the most normal thing in the world.

"Better?" said Alita.

"Yeah. You see my problem though."

"What *I* see is a survivor. And a strong one. Don't let these Gree-nies break you." Alita finished her tea and set down the cup. "Now, don't tell the others anything else you don't want to say. Anyone tries to pressure you, they answer to me. And if you want to talk with me some more later, my door is always open."

Laura's next words came out quiet. Not much more than a whis-per. But they had to. Any louder and they would have dragged tears out with them.

"Thank you."

Alita stood up. "But right now I think you and I need to get the others together to talk about these 'tests.'"

33

Brice looked around at the gathered people here in "the lounge." His fellow humans, sharing the crucible of these tests with him.

Charlie next to him on the leather sectional. Seemed like a nice enough kid, if somehow even more out of his element than the rest of them. Which sounded ridiculous to Brice, since as far as he knew, none of them had ever been tested by aliens before.

On the other side of Brice, draped across the chaise longue, sat Jesse. He maintained a pretense of calm, but Brice noticed the way his eyes kept glancing at Laura. Concerned.

Laura sat as far from Jesse as she could get and still be part of the conversation. She sat cross-legged, tucked into the corner of the other couch's chaise longue. She looked like she'd come through the worst of it.

Heck, Brice had almost died, and he was starting to think he got off light, compared to her.

Protectively close to Laura sat Alita, shoes on the plush carpeting for once. The entire time Laura told what little she'd been willing to share, Alita had been leveling a stare at the men as though daring them to say the wrong thing.

No one had been stupid enough to say a word.

On the other side of Alita and giving the women space sat Dubba J. Even he didn't seem quite so much his gregarious self during the conversation. No crossed legs or sweeping arms this time. Like Alita, both feet on the carpet. Unlike Alita, he drummed his fingers on his thighs past the edges of his cargo shorts.

Another tub of popcorn sat on the table between the couches. Jesse's idea. No one had touched it, despite its salty, buttery, cheesy tempting smell.

Everyone was dressed for summer, even though they had no access to the outside. They could have been anywhere. Certainly wouldn't have been a challenge to maintain this crisp, sixty-eight degree temperature.

"Thank you for sharing that, Laura," Brice finally said into the silence, though Laura hadn't shared anything close to details. But he was sure she had her reasons, and that faraway look in her eye made it clear that whatever she'd been through had been horrible. "The Greenies made you relive the worst experience of your life. And you've all heard what Charlie, Alita and I—"

"Did we?" said Jesse, looking at Charlie again. "Did we hear what the great Evansessence really experienced for his test?"

"Yeah," said Charlie with a shrug. "Is it my fault they made me answer a bunch of stupid questions?"

"And you don't remember the questions?"

"Not really." Sour cast to Charlie's face now as he thought about it. "There were so many, and they just kept coming. They were all vague, morality choices. Pick A or B, when neither option is any damn good and they both oversimplify the problem and the solution."

Charlie shrugged again.

"Every one of us had to do something of some kind of personal importance. Even Brice and his elephant."

"I almost died," said Brice. "What's your point?"

"My point is, everyone had to do something deep and meaningful except him. Answer a bunch of questions? I don't buy it."

"Does sound a little weak," said Dubba J.

"I didn't pick it," said Charlie, "and I can tell you that sitting there, feeling like every answer is some great statement about the people and attitudes of the human race made it feel like a pretty damned big deal. I was sweating and stressing so bad I thought I'd have a heart attack."

"So they went for our weak spots," said Brice. "Look at it that way and Charlie's test makes more sense than mine."

"You had to risk your life to save not another human being," said Jesse, "but a trapped animal. I see it. And Laura had to confront the guy who—"

"*SHUT YOUR FUCKING MOUTH!*"

Those words ripped out of Laura's throat. Not a scream or a shout, exactly, but some kind of feral challenge. And Brice was sure that if Jesse said the wrong thing right now, Laura would tear his throat out.

And from the look on Alita's face, she was more than willing to help do it.

When Laura had said she had to save her past self from something horrible, Brice imagined at least a dozen possibilities. He didn't like to think about what he imagined now.

The silence held for a long moment. A silence so profound that Brice could actually hear a faint hum from the refrigerator in the background, and perhaps even a hint of rumble from the air conditioner, wherever it was.

"I'm sorry," said Jesse, looking down. "I wasn't thinking."

"You never think," said Laura, voice low and threatening. "Ever. You just fucking do."

"So, Jesse," said Brice, "for all your finger-pointing at Charlie, I can't help but notice that you haven't told us what the Greenies did to you. Only that it had something to do with your early days in Hollywood."

"I'm not proud of it." Jesse's turn to look off into the distance. "I didn't want to be one more unemployed actor waiting tables in L.A., so I ... I sold drugs. Just pot and coke. Things that I thought would help me get into the right parties." Jesse shrugged, the barest movement of his shoulders. "Got me into the wrong parties. The wrong element. Caused a lot of troubles in the early days."

Jesse shook his head and glanced at Laura, then focused on Brice.

"The Greenies made me ... well, let's just say it involved some of my old clients and I wish I could have been sitting in a room answering fucking questions." Jesse sat back. "If that's what he really did."

"Just leave him alone, man," said Dubba J, sounding as tired as any of them. "He didn't choose how they tested him, and I bet they picked a way that hit him as hard as yours hit you."

"Not two minutes ago you agreed it sounded weak."

Dubba J threw one shoulder up in a half shrug.

"Well what did *you* do then?"

Dubba J stuffed a big handful of popcorn in his mouth, but if he hoped that would shift the attention from him, he was out of luck. Each of the other five watched as he crunched and chewed and finally swallowed.

Dubba J looked around at the others, then said, "Fine. My sister died when I was eight. Hit by a car." He snorted, but not like it was funny. "Chased *my* basketball into the street. Little kid chasing a ball. Never saw the car. But I did. Some rusty brown Dodge coupe from the Stone Age. But it did the job on her. And the Greenies..."

Dubba J blasted out a sigh like he was trying to blow lights off the ceiling.

"The Greenies sent me back to make a choice. My sister or another little girl."

"It wasn't real," said Laura. "Wasn't your sister. Wasn't the car."

"*Sure fucking felt real.*" Dubba J stopped himself from whatever he was going to say next. Instead he dug a leather thong out of his pocket and started trying back his cloud of dreadlocks. When he finished, he continued.

"Maybe it wasn't Juliet, but it sure looked and sounded like her. I believed it was her. And past that, what really matters? Might as well have been her. Might as well have been another real little girl. Might as well have been a real choice I made, because it sure felt real when I made it."

"It wasn't real," Laura said again, but soft this time. More to herself than to Dubba J.

"Maybe the Greenies goal is to give us all PTSD," said Brice, reaching for the joke by reflex. Not that his words got more than a half-hearted exhalation from anyone.

"'One has already failed,'" said Charlie. Everyone dragged themselves out of whatever they were thinking to look at Charlie. "Kyna said that to me when I told her I wasn't going to answer any more of these ridiculous questions. 'One has already succeeded, and one has already failed.'"

"You don't remember the questions you answered," said Jesse, "but you remember your Greenie girlfriend's cryptic bullshit?"

"Just came back to me now," said Charlie.

"Well you can all stop wondering," said Jesse, stretching, "because the failure was me. I'm not sure exactly what the Greenies wanted from me, but I can guaran-damn-tee you it wasn't what they got."

"You're sure?" asked Brice. "Because that sounds like the kind of half-truth people use to lead you—"

"I'm sure." Jesse stood up. "Now if you'll excuse me, I'd like a nap before they—"

"Actually," said Mynack, appearing beside Jesse, "I'm afraid it's time for the next test."

"No," said Charlie.

34

Charlie's heart was going a mile a minute, pounding so loud that the only other sound he could hear was the blood rushing past his ears. He could feel his pulse in every part of his body, especially this throat.

But Charlie stood and faced Mynack right there in the Greenies' lounge. The others stared at him, even Jesse, who stood next to Mynack beside the leather sectional.

"We're exhausted. We need rest, and we need to eat. Something more than that." Charlie pointed to the bowl of cheesy buttered popcorn in the middle of the coffee table. "Give us until tomorrow."

Mynack watched Charlie, patience in those odd yellow eyes, but Charlie had nothing more he wanted to say.

Finally, Mynack spoke.

"I'm afraid that's not the way this works. You must all be tested, in the right way and at the right time. If any of you wish to exclude yourselves, you may opt to fail this portion of the test, but make sure you understand that such a decision would have consequences."

"Everybody slow down," said Brice, raising his hands. "No one is refusing anything. I think we're all just a little punchy after that earlier round of tests. You have to admit, they were pretty intense for us."

Mynack said nothing.

"Wait," said Charlie, an idea dawning. "I ... I get the feeling I got off light this morning. From the sound of the other tests, anyway. So how about we make a deal? How about I handle this round of tests for everyone? No one is failing or refusing. It's just that pass or fail, the whole thing is on my shoulders for this round. Then everyone else can rest and eat and recover from their intense experiences."

Mynack said nothing.

"Could we do that?" said Brice. "Could we opt to have one of our number represent us all for one round?"

"This has never been done before," said Kyna, from somewhere behind Charlie. "But there's nothing in the rules that prevent it."

Mynack said nothing.

Charlie's heart slowed a bit from its rapid run, but it felt now as though every beat were twice as strong as it needed to be. His fingers started twitching, eager for a decision one way or the other. This was crazy. Charlie knew it was crazy. But guilt gnawed at his stomach that somehow he had been spared the worst of the testing.

"Will you guys let me do this?" said Charlie, addressing not the Greenies now, but his fellow humans. "You need a break. And you need it more than I do."

Alita nodded, then Brice, then Dubba J. Laura furrowed her brow, but nodded. Finally Jesse looked away, then nodded as well.

"They're willing," said Charlie, "and so am I. None of them are withdrawing or failing. I'm just standing in for them in addition to taking my own part of the test. We're all willing to play it this way, if you guys will agree."

"Very well," said Mynack. "The rest of you may return to your rooms to rest. Kyna and I will require a moment alone with Charlie 'Evansessence' Evans before the next test begins."

The others all stood and started filing toward their rooms. But before Laura left, she stepped close to Charlie. So close he could smell the herbal soap she used to bathe with.

Laura put one hand on the back of Charlie's head and kissed him. Soft and sincere and all too brief. Not much more than a deliberate press of her perfect lips against his, but Charlie's heart was speeding again.

She looked Charlie in the eye, proximity lending even more intimacy to the moment.

"Thank you," she whispered.

And then she was gone, walking toward her door and Charlie was left alone with the two Greenies.

Charlie had no idea what they might have had in mind, but just then he felt like he could handle anything.

35

Charlie stood there in the lounge, a light perspiration starting on his forehead and the tingle of Laura's quick kiss still lingering on his lips. He wanted to focus on that. To fix that kiss in his memory so he would remember it in full detail when he someday told his children and grandchildren the tale of how he and five celebrities were tested by aliens.

But Mynack stared at Charlie. Those yellow, alien eyes considering, or maybe probing. Was that it? Could Mynack read their minds? Was that what he was doing whenever he stood statue still like that and stared as though he had an infinity of time stretching out before him?

Or maybe Mynack was just waiting for Kyna to join him. Because she was padding softly around the back of one of the leather sectionals to stand beside Mynack at the other end of the coffee table from Charlie.

The whole moment suddenly felt entirely surreal to Charlie. Like he had come to lucidity mid-dream because his mind formed some connection amid all the general strangeness.

It was the smell of the popcorn. The cheesy, salty popcorn. Just the way Charlie used to eat it when he stayed up late on Friday or Saturday nights in high school, watching old science fiction movies and the voluptuous television hostess who mocked them at every commercial break.

Charlie felt like he should be waking up on his parents' big, cushy couch to find Shadow, his old black lab, digging into the popcorn, and a commercial for some Laura Jefferson movie on the screen leading back into tonight's B-movie masterpiece.

But Charlie didn't wake up. Instead Mynack and Kyna still stood side-by-side here in the lounge. Him taller, her curvier. Both with the oversized craniums, silver spacesuits, and green skin. Both watching Charlie. Perhaps waiting for him to make the next move.

If so, then he might as well ask again the question he considered too important to ignore.

"Why the green skinned, silver spacesuit look?" said Charlie. "Why go for the old B-movie stereotype? Plenty of old movies had aliens look like humans with maybe an odd facial feature or a pair of antennae. For that matter, you could have gone with any alien race from *Star Trek* or *Babylon 5* or any number of other options. But you went with the green skin and silver spacesuits, complete with flying saucer. I don't get it."

Kyna opened her mouth to speak, but Mynack raised a finger and she stilled.

"Why do you think?" said Mynack.

"I don't know. You were worried about trademark or copyright infringement or something?"

Kyna almost smiled. Charlie was sure of it. But she said nothing, and neither did Mynack.

"That wasn't a guess, was it? It was a question." Charlie ran his fingers through his hair. His perspiration had dried on his forehead by now. "If I guess right, will you tell me?"

"Consider it part of the test," said Mynack.

That was enough to make Charlie shift from foot to foot, suddenly feeling as though he'd been standing still too long. His stomach quivered, and he wondered if he should have asked for the chance to eat something before they started him on ... whatever he'd just volunteered for.

But Charlie couldn't quite call himself an idiot. Not when he could still feel a little of the tingle from Laura's kiss.

Charlie took a deep breath and let it out slowly.

"All right," he said, and ran his hands through his hair again. "All right. Why would you choose this look instead of any other alien look?" He tugged at his tee-shirt. "If you came out looking like Vulcans, we'd all expect Mr. Spock. If you looked like Yoda, backwards you'd have to talk. And you'd have to do that little snickering laugh like Frank Oz."

Charlie scratched the back of his neck. Tugged at the collar of his shirt. Maybe he should have chosen one a size larger. Did they have a size larger? Or were all the clothes sized what the Greenies thought was the right size for him?

"But it might look even more like a publicity stunt." Charlie felt realization raise his eyebrows. "Wait. It's not just that. It would be obvious, blatant manipulation. No one would believe that you really look like that. Everyone would figure you were trying to play up to us. But I can't be the only one who doesn't believe this is your real appearance. So that can't be the whole reason..."

Mynack only stared back, patience in those yellow eyes. Kyna, though. Charlie would have sworn he saw encouragement in her orange eyes.

"But this look is old. Out of fashion. Goes back to the early science fiction writers, I think, if not just the old SF movies. 'Little green men from Mars' is still something you might hear people say."

Charlie rubbed his chin. Slapped himself lightly on one cheek.

"The Grays! That's it. Lots of people either know or believe that the Grays have been visiting our world for years. You aren't trying to hide that. If anything, you left the implication hanging that maybe *you* have been to this planet before. Only not to abduct and probe people. Implying maybe there's truth in some of those old stories or movies. That maybe the writers or producers or directors had seen you, or read references to you, and worked you into their stories."

Charlie felt confidence now as he pointed at Mynack.

"This look doesn't just scratch a memory itch for people, or give them an antiquated enough referent to relax them a little bit. It implies to us all that you guys have been to our planet before, and that we've met you, and that we lived to tell the tale. And that tale wasn't a horror story. Sometimes there were good aliens in those old books and movies after all."

"Is that your answer?" said Mynack.

"Yes."

"And you are certain this is not simply our native appearance?"

"Positive," Charlie said with a firm nod.

"Very well then," said Mynack, turning to face Kyna.

"Wait," said Charlie. "Am I right?"

A golden glow surrounded Charlie, and the lounge around him faded away.

36

Brice had a movie on the television, but he wasn't watching it. To be honest, he wasn't even sure what movie he'd put on. He'd just grabbed one at random from the bookcase overflowing with Blu-ray discs, put it in the player, and turned on the sixty-inch, wall-mounted flatscreen.

Bigger television than he bothered with at home, but then the whole suite was something fancier than he would have paid for himself. Maybe if Laetitia were with him and it was a special occasion, but on his own? Never. The place reminded him of that Four Seasons penthouse he got to enjoy for a whole weekend in London once because the Duchess of Kent wanted to meet him.

Like that place, this suite was decorated in browns and tans, with lots of comfortable furniture and puffy carpeting that felt like he was walking on air. Air scented by spring fresh potpourri in little wooden bowls around the suite. Live plants in every corner, ferns and rubber trees. Only the bookshelves didn't fit the image. Two of them, eight feet tall by four feet wide. One filled with novels and the other with movies.

Well, the bookshelves *and* the bizarre light panels on the other side of the curtains down at the far end of the room. But Brice didn't want to think about those.

And novels would have required concentration. All Brice had wanted when he came back into his suite was rest. He still felt more than a little spent from his morning in the African savannah — complete with near-death experience — and losing himself in a movie seemed like the way to go.

Brice forced himself to notice what was on the screen. Vivacious brunette Vivian Holt in a business suit and glasses, having a heated argument with brown-haired leading man Bradford Collins, also suited and matching her glare for glare.

If someone could have bottled the sheer sex appeal on that screen, they could have made billions.

The movie was a romantic comedy, of course. By the end their characters would be happily married and probably terrorizing the business world with their combined charisma or something like that.

The kind of movie Brice pretended to let Laetitia drag him to. That was their little game. He was as much a sucker for these movies as she was, but he hadn't admitted it until their fifth date. Happy endings. People falling in love. How could anyone not like that?

Sitting there on the couch, Brice smiled. He wondered what Laetitia was doing right now.

Worrying about him, probably. Not sleeping any better than he was. The anxiety of the unknown.

Brice's smile faded. Worrying about her worrying about him wouldn't help either of them. He just had to get through the tests as intact as possible and get back to her. That was what mattered. This was just another little obstacle to overcome on their way to their own happy ending.

But it wasn't just that he was worried about her. He didn't want to tell Laetitia about the savannah. About the trapped elephant, the hyenas, and Brice's near drowning in the quagmire. He didn't want to tell her just how close he came to dying today.

He didn't want to tell her those things, but he would. A promise was a promise. And they hadn't been married for more than twenty-five years without keeping their promises to one another.

But guilt scraped at the back of Brice's neck all the same. Hard as it would be to tell Laetitia about the savannah, he would have a harder time telling her about right now. About this minute. About how he was resting and recovering in his fancy suite in perfect safety while he let a kid — and Charlie was a kid, even if he *was* old enough to drink — take Brice's test for him.

Laetitia would approve. Brice knew that. It meant more time that Brice was safe. A greater chance of him making it back alive. Brice wasn't a kid anymore, and that little escapade in the savannah probably pushed him even more than he realized.

He should probably be taking ibuprofen or aspirin or something. Shouldn't he have a couple of sore muscles at least? God knew it felt strenuous enough at the time...

But still. It hadn't been the emotional roller coaster that the others had been on.

And the Greenies probably wouldn't throw another physical test at him again so soon. They would have to know his limits. Or at least have a good idea of them. After all, if the Greenies really wanted to help humans, they had to be rooting for Brice's little group to succeed. Deliberately pushing them beyond their limits wouldn't be a test. It would be torture.

That would make the Greenies no better, as a species, than little kids burning ants with a magnifying glass or tearing the wings off of flies. Brice couldn't afford to believe that was even a possibility.

Besides, if that were the case, wouldn't they have taken someone more important than Brice? Yeah, he had fans, but wouldn't the evil child find more satisfaction in burning the queen of the anthill than just another ant? If torture was what the Greenies were after, wouldn't they have chosen world leaders for their prey?

No. The Greenies were sincere. They had to be. That meant Brice and the others probably didn't really need this break. Or maybe the others did. God knew Laura looked like she needed a break. Sounded like it too. But Brice?

Brice should be out there with Charlie. Brice had no business lying here, watching Vivian Holt slap Bradford Collins and storm out of a room. Brice could have split the six tests in two. Each of them handling three instead of making Charlie handle all six. It wasn't fair. It wasn't reasonable.

Brice sat up, his loafers cushing into the soft carpet.

Damn it, what had Brice been thinking? Agreeing to this in the first place? He had to contact Mynack. Get the Greenies to split the tests. Give him half and Charlie half.

But that line of thought seemed to burn out the last of whatever adrenaline might have been flowing through Brice's system. Because when he went to stand up he got a head rush, that sideways feeling accompanied by his whole field of vision going red.

And then Brice was lying back on the couch, his whole body gratefully sinking into the soft, sand-colored cushions.

Muscles relaxing. Eyes relaxing. Breaths getting slower and deeper.

The last thing Brice remembered before he lost consciousness was the sound of Vivian Holt saying, "I'll get him to the negotiating table and whip his tight little ass!"

37

Charlie had known many days when he felt like a rat in a maze. Most of them in high school, taking standardized tests. Each question on the Scan-Tron card was a choice point.

The worst part about those mazes was that even when he got through them — finished the test — he didn't know how he did until much later. Would he get cheese? A food pellet? Or just find nothing waiting for him?

He may have had a *sense* of how he did on those tests, nevertheless he had to wait weeks or months to find out *for sure.*

Charlie paused and looked up at the high walls around him. Just like the flooring under his sneakers. Stones in irregular sizes, mostly grays but also browns and whites. Fitted together tight and bonded with mortar.

A literal freaking maze.

The moment the golden glow had faded, Charlie had found himself shivering against the chill of a cool breeze, and surrounded by what he had first thought were the walls of some great castle. Except that there was no ceiling. Just high walls — at least fifty feet — and much higher clouds, varying between storm gray and black.

Threatening. The image wasn't lost on Charlie. In fact, he felt like someone had pulled him out of an old B-grade SF film and dropped him into something produced by Hammer. Any minute now Christopher Lee would spring out at him in evening wear to drain his blood.

Yeah, that's just what Charlie needed to think about right now, when he couldn't see the next turn or the last one. And the air smelled musty, like the kind of old dirt Dracula would keep in his coffin.

Charlie rubbed the back of his neck and kept going.

So far he'd been consistent, taking every left-hand turn since he left the center. He'd read somewhere that this was an old Phoenician trick to avoid getting lost in a maze. Didn't seem to be doing him much good though. He couldn't tell one part of the maze from another. For all he knew, he'd been walking in circles.

If only there'd been torches burning in sconces on the wall, like a proper castle. Instead of the same sourceless dimness he dealt with in that weird computer room this morning. Charlie could have taken a torch with him. Maybe singed some mortar at each corner to make sure he never started retracing his—

What was that?

Charlie stopped still, pressing his arms in to minimize his shivering and holding his breath.

Just barely in the distance, coming from up ahead, he heard a woman's voice.

"Help."

The woman sounded familiar. Charlie couldn't quite place her voice though.

"Help," she called again.

"Coming!" yelled Charlie, but before he could start forward, he heard a second voice. Also faint. This one from behind him.

A man's voice this time. "Help."

Wait. Charlie recognized that voice. He heard it several nights a week when he watched *Weeknightly*. That was Brice.

The woman's voice snapped into place then. Alita.

Brice and Alita, both needed Charlie's help. But they were too far away. He could barely hear them now. If he went to help one, he'd never be able to...

Oh.

So that was the next test. Would Charlie help Brice or Alita? The woman or the man? No idea what the problem was, just that they both needed help. Go after one and lose the ability to find the other.

Heck, it probably wasn't even a real test. Mynack had sent the others off to rest. They were probably all safe in their rooms right now. This was probably just another illusion of some sort. Maybe Mynack imitating Brice and Kyna imitating Alita. After all, both had proven that they could mimic specific human voices, Mynack sounding like a sportscaster and Kyna like a sit-com star.

Then a wave of cold passed through Charlie that had nothing to do with the wind.

Brice had nearly gotten himself killed helping that elephant this morning. And Laura, well, Charlie didn't know exactly what Laura had dealt with, but it was clearly bad news.

What if by "resting" Mynack meant that the other five would all be part of the test, but unable to participate? Unable to affect the outcome. Only able to call for help...

What if both Brice and Alita were really in danger right now?

What if only Charlie could save them, and he had to choose which?

How could he possibly make that choice?

Charlie dropped down to his knees on the cold stone floor. He looked up at the clouds, but it was the Greenies he addressed.

"You guys are fucking evil. If you are really threatening these people's lives for a test, then you're truly fucking evil and the Grays can't possibly be any worse."

Charlie shook his head. He could still hear them both. Alita and Brice, both crying for help, voices straining as though about to give out. Alita was younger. Fitter. Brice ... was a man. Brice was married. Alita ... Charlie didn't know. She'd been married once, he knew, to a rapper. But Charlie didn't think she was married now.

Both of them had kids.

Charlie hung his head.

Parents. Charlie hadn't even thought about his parents since this whole alien thing happened. His mom and dad must have heard that he was one of the "lucky" few chosen to represent humanity. *Mom must be tearing her hair out...*

The cries for help came again. Agitated. Desperate. Begging Charlie to stop his recriminations and get moving.

Brice was a father. Alita was a mother. Charlie'd grown up with two parents, but ... but he couldn't imagine growing up without a mother. He'd never be able to force that on anyone. He wouldn't wish for anyone to grow up without a father either, but the choice was clear. And if felt just like one of the questions he might have answered this morning.

Which child grows up healthier and happier? A) The child who grows up without a mother. B) The child who grows up without a father.

Charlie gritted his teeth and chose B. He started running down the corridor, glad he was wearing sneakers this time, not loafers.

He could hear Alita a little more clearly now. Brice a little more faintly.

Charlie tried not to think about that. Just pushed his feet faster.

Left. Right. Left. Right. Sneakers slapping.

He abandoned his little left-hand-wall game when he heard Alita's voice coming straight ahead of him at a three-way junction.

Down that hall. Follow the long, slow curve to the right. Sweating now. Panting for breath. Shirt sticking to his chest. Jeans sticking to his thighs, pulling and chafing.

But Alita's voice grew louder. And louder.

Finally, Charlie finished the curve and there she stood. Alita Luna. Chained to the wall at her wrists and ankles. Clad in an orange prison jumpsuit, torn across the mid-section to reveal her flat belly.

"Are you all right?" said Charlie, eyes darting around for a key, perhaps dangling from a hook. "Are you hurt? Do you know where the key is?"

"Help," she cried again, her voice fading as a golden glow surrounded her and took her away.

38

A-Day-Plus-One. Four-Fifty-Eight P.M. Lounge Local Time

Laura awoke deep within the heavenly padding of this luxuri-
ously oversized bed. California king, the design was called. Boring
name, but what it meant was that when Laura lay in the middle of
the mattress, she felt as though she had an acre of room to roll
around in every direction. Deep pillow top. Marvelously soft sage
green sheets. Dark green comforter that felt just right tucked under
her neck.

Of all the things these aliens had done to make her feel at home
in her little suite, the bed was far and away the best touch. Most of
the décor just felt like the kind of high-end hotel people booked her
into when they were trying to impress her. Or sleep with her. But this
bed, this bed was delightful.

Laura stretched and rolled around a little, sheets caressing
her skin.

She felt better. Meditation to clear her head, then a nap without
an alarm always did the trick to help her put behind her what she
thought of as her "episodes."

She was a famous actress now, right? Famous actresses didn't get
"panic attacks" or "fits." They had "episodes." Episodes were colorful.

Made good press. Panic attacks, that was a phrase journalists used when they wanted to slam someone. Fits were even worse.

Not that anyone knew about her episodes yet. But it was only a matter of time. Especially with Jesse's loose tongue.

Laura heard a knock at her door. A five-rap beat.

Was that what had woken her up?

Laura sighed. This was a break period, provided selflessly by Charlie in perhaps the sweetest gesture Laura had seen in a long time. Maybe ever. She wanted to make the most of it. Sleep some more. Then maybe eat.

But the knock came again.

With an impish smile, Laura rolled her way to the edge of the bed and swung her feet under her just in time to avoid a crash. She grabbed a red silk robe from the bathroom, tied it, and trotted through the bedroom and sitting room to the white door.

Laura opened the door a crack. Alita stood on the other side. Smiling.

"Come on in," said Laura, hiding herself behind the door and opening it just enough to let Alita in. Alita was still in her pink top and red corduroy pants, with pink sneakers added now.

"Either you just mussed up your hair or you've been able to sleep." Alita nodded. "Good."

"I could do with a little more." Laura didn't try to stifle the yawn that came out then.

"I'm sure we all could, but Brice brought up a good point. Chances are, the Greenies are busy testing Charlie."

"He's not back yet?"

Alita shook her head. "Might give us all a little time to talk unobserved. Throw on some clothes and come have something to eat with us."

Laura ran a quick brush through her hair, then threw on some shapeless black slacks, a tan cashmere sweater with long sleeves and a high neck, and a pair of simple black flats. By the time she came out of her room, she could see the others seated around the leather sectionals. Brice, Jesse and Dubba J on one side, Alita on the other.

Alita had her legs curled under her again, and Dubba J had relaxed enough to spread out again, right ankle on his left knee. They were all eating something that smelled heavenly from white ceramic bowls, and sharing a bottle of red wine.

"Who made this wonderful meal?" asked Laura as she took a seat next to Alita. No curling up for Laura though. She sat with her back against the cushions and her shoes on the floor.

Alita smiled and pointed to herself.

Laura applauded, and picked up the bowl that was waiting for her. Rice and black beans, with bits of sausage and pork mixed in. Not her usual, but she found herself digging in with her fork anyway. It smelled like her youth blended with the unknown, including savory spices she couldn't quite place.

This meant Laura's mouth was full when she asked her next question, but she asked it anyway.

"No word about Charlie?"

"No sign," said Brice, "and one of us has been knocking on his door every fifteen minutes since about—"

"*You've* been knocking on his door every fifteen minutes," said Jesse. "*I* was sleeping like a sensible person."

"You don't feel the least bit guilty that Charlie is out there facing who-knows-what on our behalf?"

"It was his choice," said Dubba J.

"He did it so we could rest," said Jesse. "You want him to have done it in vain?"

"I was out like a light," said Alita. "Only woke up a little while ago. And I had the weirdest dream—"

"Me too," said Brice. "Something about a castle."

Alita's eyes rounded wider than the bowl in her hands.

"Dreams are all well and good," said Jesse, "but what do we do about the Greenies?"

"What do you mean?" said Laura. "It's pretty clear that they're holding all the cards here."

"Maybe. Maybe not." Jesse pointed with his fork at Charlie's door. "Charlie threw them a curveball, and they had to go with the pitch."

"Can someone translate that for us non-native speakers?" said Alita.

"He hit them with the unexpected," said Brice, Mets cap back on his head, "and it was the Greenies who had to adjust."

"If they did," said Laura. "We don't know what they're expecting and what they're not. For all we know they chose to hit us with a test at just that time to see which of us would step up so the others could have a break."

"If we assume they're omniscient, then we have no play," said Jesse.

"What kind of play do you want?" said Dubba J, picking up his wine. "Whole idea here is they're testing us. You want to quit and go home, they'll let you. But you fail your part."

Dubba J swirled his wine under his nose with his eyes closed. Just then Laura noted that he held the glass right for red wine — by the stem. The question came out before she could stop it.

"Are you a wine-drinker, Dubba J?"

"What? A brother can't have some culture?"

"I didn't—"

Dubba J started laughing, that percolating, infectious laugh of his. Everyone else smiled, even Laura, after a moment.

"Couldn't resist," said Dubba J. "Yeah, my dad's a big time aficionado. Taught me all about wines. If I ever get enough money, I want to buy him a vineyard."

"Really?" said Jesse in a flat voice, and the gaze he gave Laura was just as flat. "You want to talk about wine?"

"Maybe we should." She shrugged. "Dubba J's right. We're all in this one way or the other. Maybe instead of conspiring against the Greenies, or whatever you want to do, we should take this time and get to know each other a little better."

"I hate wine," said Brice, lips pursed and glaring at his glass like it could bite him. "It goes against every one of my French ancestors, but I just can't stand it. Yet they serve it at every big function I've ever had to go to, and I always have to smile and pretend that this sour grape juice is the best thing ever. Would it kill them to offer a good microbrew?"

Everyone stared at Brice for a moment.

"Cretin," said Dubba J, and everyone was lost in laughter. Even Jesse.

39

A-DAY-PLUS-ONE. FIVE-FORTY-SIX P.M. LOUNGE LOCAL TIME

Charlie had no idea how long he had been stuck in this drafty mess of stone walls under stormy skies, but it had to have been at least as long as he'd spent answering questions this morning.

Which meant this bloody day had already lasted at least two lifetimes, so far as Charlie was concerned. No. Check that. Three lifetimes, because long as the morning seemed, this afternoon seemed even longer. The Greenies had him chasing phantoms. After Alita, it was a choice between Dubba J and Jesse. Then all the others or Laura.

Then it was Laura or Lucy, Charlie's ex-.

Then they got diabolical. Fire one direction, flood the other. Which would Charlie choose? (Flood. He couldn't swim in flames.) Earthquakes or tornadoes? Or at least, that was how he interpreted it when the ground started shaking and cracking in one direction and gale force winds lashed at Charlie from the other. (He chose earthquakes, but he still wasn't sure why.)

Choice after choice. Always 'A' or 'B', and never a choice he liked. But this time he had to run and jump and swim and climb (when tremors had collapsed a wall in front of him) and more.

His legs were exhausted and sore. And he might have pulled something in his left thigh. He'd been dragging his feet now for at least the last fifty turns. Even during the occasional spate of very necessary running (running that now listed because of a limp).

His arms were exhausted. He'd swung over a pit like some kind of video game hero, from one rope to another. Abrading his hands on the rough rope. Screaming in terror the entire time.

Somewhere in there, Charlie had actually stopped sweating. Not because his body didn't need cooling. Not because he no longer felt any stress. God knew Charlie's heart was trying to set some sort of speed record. He figured that he must just have finally exhausted even his sweat glands. Made sense. His mouth was dry too, and his lips stuck to his gums.

Plus, Charlie certainly *smelled* as though he'd used up his body's entire supply of sweat.

And his stomach had finally given up rumbling and complaining some time ago. Apparently even his stomach was too tired to complain about how hungry and thirsty he was.

But now, at least, the end of the maze was finally in sight.

Or at least, Charlie assumed it had to be the end of the maze. He could see a shimmering golden glow, with what looked like the lounge on the other side.

If it really was the lounge, then the rest of the group was safe. He could see all five of them sitting on the distressed leather sectionals, Alita and Laura on one side and the guys on the other. They were all drinking beer and wine, and laughing and talking and generally acting as though they'd been having a very good time.

Something about that scene squeezed a few tears out of Charlie's dehydrated body, but spent as he was he couldn't tell if he felt sorrow at feeling excluded from the party, or joy that they were safe and enjoying themselves.

Didn't matter. Once Charlie reached them, he could have a beer and laugh with them too. And sleep. He could sleep a whole lot. That almost sounded better than socializing.

But then reality set in. Before Charlie could join them he had to reach that golden glow. Before Charlie could reach that golden glow...

...he had to cross a pit of blazing fire. On a stone bridge no wider than his feet.

Charlie dropped down to his knees. He started crying again, but this time his tear ducts couldn't accomplish more than blurring his vision a little. It wasn't fair. It just wasn't fair. Every part of him was shaky with stress and exhaustion. How could they possibly expect Charlie to keep his feet? How could they possibly expect him to take slow, measured steps with orange flames licking at his shoes? And after they kept him running all this time?

The hot air smelled like sulfur. These might have been the fires of Hell itself. Even fifteen feet or so back from the blaze, the heat was toasting his skin. Crossing it, there was no way he'd avoid a burn. Assuming he even managed to not fall in and suffer the worst possible death Charlie could imagine.

Maybe this was a trick. Maybe there was some way around the pit.

Charlie edged up close enough that the heat got uncomfortable. He crouched low to see if maybe there was a secret, wider beam hidden from where he'd been standing. Transparent maybe. But there was nothing except the dancing flames, all too eager to feast on Charlie's flesh. He looked around the edges of the fire pit too — standing for a better view — but still, nothing. No higher, safe walkway. Not even handholds and footholds that might promise more stability. Or at least some variation in muscle-work.

The only way across was that narrow, narrow bridge over unforgiving fire. Charlie couldn't even see what the flames were burning down below him. He could only see the swirls of red, yellow and orange. Hear the crackling, the snapping like hungry jaws.

No. This couldn't be right. This had to be choice 'A', didn't it? Didn't there have to be some choice 'B' around here somewhere? That was the format the Greenies had set up. Why would they abandon it now?

Then again, given the other choices Charlie had made that day, maybe the 'B' option would be even worse. Maybe he should just forget it and...

No. The choice had to be here. Somewhere. The choice couldn't be simply staying in the maze and not returning to the lounge. That was no choice at all. Sure, Charlie was at a dead end, but if he back-tracked behind him...

...where did the maze go?

Behind Charlie now was a solid wall, fitted together out of the same gray, white and brown stones as all the other walls, even to the point of mortar sealing the cracks. But that wall hadn't been there a moment ago.

The Greenies had cut Charlie off from the rest of the maze.

Even hunting for another exit was no longer an option.

"Your maze is broken," Charlie said to the clouds above, his voice dry and raspy. "I'm supposed to get a choice 'B' somewhere, but all I can see is 'A.'" Charlie pointed to the bridge and the fire pit. "You can't say I'm making a choice if I only have one option. And don't pretend staying here is an option. Starving to death isn't..."

Charlie looked down at the flames again.

Maybe that was the other choice. Burning alive was just about the worst way to die that Charlie could imagine. But what if the other option was starving to death? How could that possibly be any better?

Which is better? A) Starve to death alone in safety. B) Risk burning alive to seek food and companionship?

Charlie finally understood why Mynack never showed up to answer his questions. If Mynack showed his face right now, Charlie would punch him. Right in that long, skinny nose.

"I've said it before, and I'm sure I'll say it again. Your choices suck and I hate you people."

Charlie walked up to the edge of the fire pit. The "bridge" was about four inches wide and about fifteen feet long. He couldn't see any support for the bridge. That was bad. A straight bridge — no arch — with nothing underneath it for support? How could he trust it to hold his weight? The mortar between the stones had to have dried out. That bridge was probably ready to crumble if so much as a butterfly alighted it.

Charlie's stomach started puckering again. His skin was still dry though. Chalky. Not good. Way too dehydrated. That couldn't be good for his balance.

Charlie slapped himself across both cheeks. The bridge was here, so it had to hold. A bridge that collapsed was no test at all. Had to have a steel core or something. Or maybe the mortar was some kind of special Greenie nanotech or ... something.

Something.

And that bridge wasn't getting any wider.

Charlie turned sideways to the bridge. He bent his knees, spread his feet, and stretched out his arms like he was some surfer from Santa Cruz. His legs already started shaking, especially the left leg with its pulled muscle. Charlie shook his head. Slapped himself again.

He drew a deep breath, then started across.

He didn't lift his feet. He just slid them along, his left foot first, moving across stones so hot he could feel them through the rubber soles of his sneaker. A few inches at a time. One foot, then the other foot.

Then both feet were on the little bridge. The heat was intense. Searing. His body hairs rose in the hot air. His shirt ballooned out. Charlie felt like he was being barbecued, and his body managed to find a little water left in his system to shunt out of his pores as sweat. Maybe stolen from his tear ducts, because his eyes weren't watering.

And he still had fifteen feet to go. Charlie kept his eyes on the lounge. Tried to keep his thoughts there too, instead of focusing on the inferno below him. Dubba J gestured wildly, telling some story that almost made him spill his wine. Everyone was laughing.

Next step. Keep the feet sliding. Reach the lounge. Reach the party.

Charlie didn't get halfway across the bridge before a golden glow surrounded him, spiriting him away.

40

Brice separated himself from the group while Jesse was telling a story about the first commercial he ever booked. Laura's idea of the five of them getting to know each other better was a good one. Everyone was sharing stories and jokes, and the general sense of camaraderie around those distressed leather sectionals had grown by leaps and bounds. Much better than the earlier animosity, first between Laura and Jesse, and then blossoming into girls against boys.

Or at least, that was how it seemed to be devolving after that morning test.

The second bottle of wine had helped too. Or maybe it was the third. Brice had lost track of their chosen beverage after he switched to beer. Turned out the Greenies stocked that little kitchen area with some dark beer from Oregon that could give Guinness a run for their money. Rich and full and subtle. Everything people said of good wines, but Brice never believed about anything other than a good stout.

Somewhere in there, Alita had dug out a vegetable tray and a mixed cookie platter, and the late afternoon was turning into a proper party.

A proper party missing an important guest, which was why Brice padded across the grass green carpet to knock on Charlie's door again. Surely the Greenies didn't intend to hold onto the boy all night. Not that it was easy to keep track of time here. Sure there was a clock on the wall — red digits proclaiming that it had just turned six o'clock — but that bright blue ceiling gave the sense of a high summer sky, as though the day would never end.

Here was hoping that Charlie's day had finally ended.

Brice knocked, three strong thumps on the white door. He counted to ten, while behind him Jesse whistled a Doppler like a falling bomb that ended in an eruption of laughter from the group.

Brice knocked again.

"...second..."

The voice was muffled. And tired. Had to be Charlie.

Sure enough, the door jerked open, and there stood Charlie. His brown curls plastered to his scalp. His black Misfits tee-shirt stuck to his chest where it didn't hang, waterlogged, past his waist. His shoulders hung down, his head forward, and he looked as though he might collapse where he stood. He also smelled like a high school locker room.

Brice wrapped Charlie in a bear hug before the poor boy could say a word. Charlie didn't hug back. His arms hung limp at his sides, but that didn't deter Brice for a moment.

"Thank God you're safe," he said. "I was so worried about you. I should have helped. I shouldn't have taken the break. I'm sorry I—"

"Don't." Charlie's voice was so hoarse Brice might not have heard the word if he weren't crushing the boy in a hug. "'salright."

Behind Brice, the laughter stopped.

"Charlie!" said Laura, and from the sound of things the whole group got up to descend on them.

Brice let the poor boy go, but kept his hands on Charlie's shoulders, looking deep into his sleepy eyes.

"Are you all right?" asked Brice, voice a little too loud. "Do you need anything?"

"Sleep. Food. Shower."

Alita and Laura slipped around Brice to hug Charlie, but Jesse and Dubba J seemed content to wait behind Brice.

"I..." Charlie only just got that word out before he collapsed, Laura and Alita now struggling with his weight.

"'Scuse me, Brice," said Dubba J, stepping past. "I think I'll be more help now."

Dubba J scooped up Charlie like a toddler in his strong arms and carried him over to a reddish couch that didn't look long enough for Charlie to stretch out on. In fact, Brice frowned as he looked around the rest of the front room of Charlie's suite. The little place the Greenies gave him could have been plucked out of any moderate chain hotel. Not nearly as nice as what they gave Brice.

"He'd be more comfortable on his bed," said Jesse.

"This boy is every inch as sweaty as he smells," said Dubba J. "He's not going to want to spoil his bed like this. Trust me."

Dubba J eased Charlie onto the couch, then adjusted the cushions to make him comfortable. Just then Alita came out of the bedroom carrying a blue fuzzy blanket. When had she gone into Charlie's bedroom? She draped it across Charlie and tucked him in.

"Don't think he'll be too warm?" said Dubba J.

"He'll get the chills when his sweat gels," she said. "Wish he could have taken a shower before he collapsed."

"Well," said Brice, "we've done all we can for him for now. Let's go back into the lounge and let him sleep."

"He should have food," said Laura. She turned and strode toward the kitchen, returning a moment later with a tall glass of water and a small, white plate, loaded with vegetables and cookies from the party trays.

"Okay, now," said Brice. "I think that's everything we can do besides let him rest. I know we all want to know what happened to him, but the boy needs his sleep."

Dubba J started laughing.

"What?"

Dubba J clapped Brice on the shoulder. "When did you adopt him?"

41

A-DAY-PLUS-ONE. NINE-TWENTY-SEVEN P.M. LOUNGE LOCAL TIME

Laura sat alone in the lounge, black flats on the floor and her feet curled underneath her on the creaky leather cushion. She had a Smokey Dalton mystery novel in her hand, but she was only half-reading it. Mostly it was an excuse to sit out here while the others retreated into their rooms to make sure they all got a good night's sleep before whatever the Greenies had in store for them for tomorrow.

Laura should have been sleeping too. Probably. Alita had told her so, and Laura had to admit that she felt the languorous ache of exhaustion pull at her. But she wasn't ready. She needed to see Charlie. To know that he had come through his afternoon ordeal intact.

Alita had picked up on that, even though Laura hadn't said anything. Pointed out that Charlie might sleep through the night.

But Laura didn't think so. If anything, he would be too hungry. He hadn't had dinner, and from the way he looked when he got back, he'd burned a whole lot of calories. Way more than he'd get back from the little plate she'd left him.

Besides. Alita had been there when Laura needed someone to

talk to. Laura had every intention of being there for Charlie, in case he needed that now.

Before her on the coffee table sat a glass of water and a plate with three toll house chocolate chip cookies on it. Laura hadn't had any yet, despite the ravings of the others about their quality. For some reason she wanted to wait. As though the cookies felt celebratory, somehow, and she needed to know that she had something to celebrate.

She was just starting to wonder if Charlie might sleep through the night after all when his door opened. He was barefoot, wearing black and blue plaid pajamas, and he favored his left leg with not quite a limp. Definitely had a shower. His brown curls looked as though he'd rubbed them dry for ten minutes and still couldn't get them to behave.

Laura found herself smiling at that.

"Hey," she said, and Charlie jumped, wincing as he did.

"Hey," he said, his voice still hoarse. He cleared his throat and tried again. Didn't help much. "Do you know if there's any dinner left?"

"Alita left some for you in the crock pot." Laura got up and followed him to the kitchen. "How are you feeling?"

"Tired. Sore."

"Do you want to talk about it?" Laura pulled a stool out from under the breakfast bar and sat while Charlie filled a bowl with black beans, rice, sausage and pork, then dug around in the fridge for one of Brice's beers.

"I was in a freaking video game or something," he said. "Running through a maze, trying to save..." Charlie twisted his lips to one side, set down his bowl and popped off the cap of his beer bottle. He leaned back against the counter and frowned at Laura. "I don't know what I was trying to save. They kept making it look and sound like you guys were in jeopardy, but you were all here the whole time, weren't you?"

Laura's turn to frown.

"I think so. I know we were later in the afternoon. Brice got us all together to talk. But early on, we were all sleeping. And Brice and Alita talked about some kind of dream involving a castle—"

"The maze walls looked like a castle!" Charlie swigged from his beer, then grabbed his food and sat next to Laura at the breakfast bar.

Well, not quite next to Laura. He left an empty stool between them, which Laura found amusing. But the tale he told her wasn't funny at all. A whole day of stress and strain, running from rescue to rescue at first, and then simply fleeing one form of disaster and into another. Always making choices, and from the way Charlie described it, every choice was bad.

Not that Laura followed the whole thing, though she tried to. She gave Charlie her full attention. But his tale was just this side of a ramble, and his words all but blended together at times.

But that was all right. Laura knew she just needed to be there and listen. That was what she had needed from Alita earlier, and Laura was sure it was all Charlie needed from her now.

By the time he finished, Charlie had emptied his beer and not touched his food. And either the beer was stronger than it seemed when Brice was drinking it, or Charlie was in no shape to be drinking, because he was swaying on his stool and had the first hints of a drunken flush high on his throat.

Laura reached over and pushed his bowl at him to remind him to eat. She got up and went to the cabinet for a glass for him.

"So you were saying you felt like it was the same kind of test they gave you this morning, only physical instead of intellectual?" She filled the glass with water.

Charlie nodded, mouth half-full as he said, "Visheral." He swallowed. "Yeah."

"What are they going to do tomorrow, then, do you think?" She set the water glass in front of Charlie and reclaimed her seat. "Spiritual?"

Laura meant that as a joke, but instead of smiling, Charlie sucked his lips into a line, as though he considered her words seriously. He shook his head.

"Seems like just the sort of thing these sadistic bastards would do." He pointed at Laura with a forkful of black beans and rice. "Which creates a stronger society? A) Monotheistic autocracy. B) Polytheistic anarchy?"

Laura shuddered. "No option 'C'?"

"Never!"

The word came out of Charlie's mouth so harsh and rough Laura felt a chill crawl up her spine and nestle between her shoulder blades. Anger in his eyes, as dark as his beer as he continued.

"Offering an option 'C' might be reasonable. Might invite complex thought, or maybe even discourse. The Greenies aren't interested in complex thought or discourse. They aren't interested in real opinions or real perspectives. All they want is to make us run through their little mazes for them. And maybe they'll give us cheese when we finish. Or maybe they'll give us a pellet. Or maybe, just maybe, we'll make it all the way through to the end only to find out *they never intended to give us any damn thing at all.*"

"Do you believe that?" A woman's voice, but Laura didn't ask that question. She looked over her shoulder and saw Kyna standing only a few steps away.

"Yes I do," said Charlie, spinning on the stool to face the alien woman, his food once more forgotten behind him. "These tests are ridiculous oversimplifications. There's no way you could learn anything meaningful from them. Would I rather risk immolation or drowning? Just what the hell kind of test was that?"

Kyna hesitated, but her next words came out subdued.

"I can't answer questions about the tests, I'm afraid. But that wasn't what I meant. Do you really believe this is all for nothing?"

"You're dangling a big carrot in front of us. And we're charging after it like we're trying to win the Kentucky Derby. But we don't have a shred of proof that you guys have any intention of doing what you promised. No look at what we're working toward? No testimonials from other planets?" Charlie pushed his head forward and shook it slowly. "No. Nothing but your word."

The anger radiating off of Charlie echoed the fury Laura had felt earlier. She began to feel those embers rekindling inside her. Looking for release. And a Greenie was right here.

No. Better to run back to her room and hide. Better to turn away from this conversation. Anything to keep from letting out the truth. From revealing the person behind the actress.

Glimpses of the woman behind Laura Jefferson were fine. When she was at ease. Having fun. But this kind of truth was for people who could be vulnerable. People with nothing to lose.

Laura moved to stand, but stopped herself.

There were no paparazzi here. No reporters. Only Charlie. Laura felt she could trust him. And the Greenie. Kyna. No point in hiding from the Greenies. They watched everything. They'd already seen Laura at her worst.

But she couldn't talk just yet. So Kyna filled the silence.

"Why else would we do this? All we want to do is help people."

That was too much. Laura didn't have to look for the right words. They boiled out of her.

"*If what you did to me today was help, your whole planet can fuck off.*"

Charlie and Kyna were both staring at Laura now, Charlie's jaw slack but Kyna's eyes that inscrutable patience she shared with Mynack.

"You made me believe I was back there. That I was facing that bastard. Saving another girl from what he did to me. But it was all a lie. There's no catharsis. No happy ending. That *bastard* is still out there preying on young girls."

Laura stood up now, anger perfecting her posture beyond any acting technique. Adrenaline beat through her veins, but she held it back to a rumble in her voice.

"But you guys could find him, couldn't you. Like you found all of us. You and Mynack and whoever else you have working behind the scenes. You could be doing actual good for the human race right now by putting a stop to people like that bastard. But no. You'd rather sit here, comfy and happy, observing your little chosen rats running through their maze."

Laura stepped up to those patient orange eyes and spat her next words right into Kyna's face.

"Who the fuck are you to judge anyone?"

Kyna vanished in a flash of gold.

Laura's nostrils flared in a deep breath, easing out anger as she released it. She did that twice more until she felt like she had control of herself again.

She looked back over her shoulder at Charlie, who was blinking like he couldn't believe what he'd just seen.

Laura smiled at him. "Goodnight, Charlie. Sleep tight."

She was already walking back toward her room before she heard Charlie say, "'Night."

She stopped to pick up her plate of cookies though. Laura felt she'd earned them.

42

A-Day-Plus-Two. Eight-Thirty-Three A.M. Lounge Local Time

Working at home as a freelancer had made Charlie more than a little casual about the clothes he wore. Tee shirts were a daily choice, and sweat pants were practically his uniform.

It hadn't started that way. When he started freelancing full time after college, he made himself dress in business casual every day. "Look successful, be successful." That sort of thing. But over time the motto began to slip out of his daily usage. Then came the realization that there was little difference between jeans and cargo pants for office work.

The degradation from there became a simple matter of economics. His office casual clothes were all dirty. Charlie could have washed them, but they came to just over a full load, which would have meant all but wasting a second load. And money was tight. Much better to wait until he had two full loads. No one would care if he wore tee shirts sometimes. It wasn't as though he had co-workers to complain.

Then sometimes became every time. And jeans became sweats. Before he knew it, Charlie just threw on whatever clean clothes came first to hand in the morning. That was how he had lived for some time now.

So for Charlie, the weirdest thing about this morning was the realization that he had to think about what he was going to wear for the day ahead. And he wasn't even going on a date.

He ended up in blue jeans — tighter than his usual loose preference, after the way his jeans had tugged and slipped on him yesterday — good running shoes, and a plain gray tee shirt and hoodie. That should prepare him for just about anything the Greenies could throw at him.

So when Charlie finally stepped outside his room into the cafeteria — because apparently lounging was for afternoon and evening, but morning was for breakfast buffets and eating around a bench table in closer quarters — he wasn't surprised to see he was not the only one who dressed for practicality.

Laura smiled at him from the breakfast bar, her plate full of melons and fruits, with two buttered English muffins and a pair of hardboiled eggs. She wore another felt shirt, green plaid this time, over a pale green tee shirt that matched the narrow stripes in the plaid. She too wore jeans and sneakers, though the latter were lime green high-tops.

Charlie was struck again by just how beautiful this woman really was, even without Hollywood makeup or tailoring.

She was apparently on better terms with Jesse this morning, because he stood next to her at the breakfast bar and neither one of them looked upset about it. He was in army camo pants with rugged-looking combat boots. He wore the matching camo shirt open over a tan tank top. He looked like a poster for a military romance movie. *An Officer and a Gentleman II*. His plate had a scattering of fruit, but six slices of rye toast and some scrambled eggs with what looked like cheddar.

The others were already seated at the table. One of them had filled carafes with ice water and orange juice, and all six spots had a glass of each waiting.

Brice's half-full plate was a mess of egg yolk and toast crust, with a stack of bacon still ready for his attention. Brice smiled and saluted Charlie with a glass of orange juice. Brice had his Mets hat on again, but he was wearing a dark blue, short-sleeved button up shirt with loose jeans and a brown belt.

Alita waved her spoon from her spot across from Brice at one end of the table. She had a bowl of yogurt and granola she picked at between bites of kiwi, pineapple and strawberry from her plate. She wore an orange flannel shirt with the sleeves rolled up to the elbows and the top two buttons open, and simple black jeans. Gorgeous and understated.

Dubba J sat beside Brice, in the center of the table. Dubba J wore cargo shorts, but his white shirt had buttons and pockets this morning, despite its short sleeves. And he had a gray hoodie on the bench next to him. Whatever breakfast he chose was already finished. Nothing on his plate but remainder fruit juice and crumbs.

"Last to arrive again," said Jesse as he reclaimed his seat on the other side of Dubba J. But Jesse smiled as he said it, for once.

"Not sure we're recognize Charlie if he came out first," said Brice. "Maybe have to check his room for pods."

That made Alita frown. "Could we be invaded by aliens while in the care of different aliens? That doesn't seem fair somehow."

The others debated that issue while Charlie shoveled food on his plate. He used their conversation to cover a quiet question to Laura as she added milk to her coffee at the end of the breakfast buffet.

"How are you doing this morning?"

"Excellent," she said with another smile and no attempt to be quiet. "Slept like the dead. Must have found some catharsis yesterday after all."

She preceded Charlie to the table, where he found himself sitting between Laura and Alita. He pulled in a bit as he ate, to avoid accidentally bumping either of them.

Meanwhile, Dubba J teased Jesse about the camouflage outfit, and Brice munched his bacon and watched Charlie intently. Finally, Brice said, "I notice you're limping a little. Are you all right?"

"Pulled something in the back of my thigh," said Charlie, after a swallow of water to wash down some excellent scrambled eggs with fennel and paprika. "Not too bad though."

"That sucks," said Dubba J. "Hamstring pulls can linger. Make sure you walk on it, but don't push it or overstretch it."

Charlie was nodding, with a mouth full of sourdough toast, when Mynack appeared at the end of the table beside Jesse and Alita.

"Good morning," said Mynack.

"Charlie's barely had two bites of food," said Brice, "and Laura hasn't had much more. Please give us a chance to finish eating before you test us."

"Plus we need the social time," said Alita. "None of us got to talk to Charlie after he got back last night. Don't separate us again so soon."

"And he's injured," said Dubba J. "I hope you keep that in mind before you assign the tests today. His physical performance will be hampered."

Charlie was overcome. Here were some of the most famous people on Earth, and they were leaping to defend *him*. His breath caught, and surprise made him slump while his mouth hung open like a fool.

Mynack said nothing, perhaps waiting for any other objections to come forward.

When it became clear that the humans were waiting to see how Mynack responded, he said, "A reasonable question was asked last night, and while you eat I will address it."

Charlie pushed to eat a little faster, and he wasn't the only one. Even Alita set about her yogurt with berries and granola with more urgency.

"It was pointed out," said Mynack, "that you are taking a great deal on faith. Unfortunately, that is as it must be. I could introduce you to others we have helped, but you would have no more reason to trust them than to trust us. And as at least one of you believes we have not shown you our true form, you would have no way of knowing any testimonials came from anyone but — what is the word you use? — ah, yes. Shills."

"To be fair," said Brice, "when you spoke on television you used the same patterns and phrasing as the sportscaster whose voice you've borrowed, Chris Burghoff. But since we've all been *here*, you've kept the voice and gotten more formal with the tone. Kind of lends to the huckster vibe, if you will. A show for the masses, but a different approach behind the scenes."

"Specifics would be nice," said Jesse. "What *exactly* would you be doing for us, and what *is* the implementation plan you referred to earlier?"

"Every sapient species goes through a phase when its skills outstrip its patience. When that happens, long-range consequences are eschewed for immediate benefits. My people remember that phase all too well, because it almost destroyed us."

That concession made Charlie pause in the middle of biting a red delicious apple, juice running from the corners of his mouth. This was the first admission of anything less than perfection he had heard from the Greenies.

"So once we had the capacity," Mynack continued, "we began to seek out other species who were reaching such a state, with a goal of easing them through that choice point. We made some terrible mistakes in our early days, and none worse than helping every species without regard to their psychological and sociological development. We aided species that became terrors in space, and for a time we had much to answer for."

Jesse started to ask a question, but Brice stilled him with a gesture.

"That was why we began the tests. We never again wish to aid a species that will look to other planets and peoples and see only what they can exploit."

Mynack blinked, and Charlie realized he'd never seen those yellow eyes close before, not even for a moment. Charlie shook himself and went back to devouring his breakfast in case the tale ended abruptly.

"But if we waited for every member of a species to be ready for our aid, we would never find any worth saving from themselves. So we tested representatives, and for those species that pass the tests, we handled disbursing the benefits, beginning with an eye toward preservation of the host planet, and continuing through instruction until the species became — in our judgment — independent and ready for rapid space flight. Then we leave them to their own destiny."

"But what are the benefits?" asked Jesse. "And how are they distributed?"

Mynack turned and looked at Brice. Stared at him until pretty soon everyone at the table was staring at Brice too. Finally, he said, "I only know what the men in black told me. 'Food production. Water reclamation and purification. Recycling on a level beyond anything we've imagined. Energy technologies so cheap and efficient they're supposed to make solar and wind look like coal and oil.' That kind of thing."

Mynack nodded.

"And distribution?" said Jesse.

"That must remain our secret for the time being, to avoid the risk of interference."

"Bullshit," said Jesse, in a tone so harsh that Dubba J chuckled. "This just sounds like an excuse for invasion without anyone firing a shot. 'We'll just come in and make things better.' That worked *so well* for the U.S. in the Middle East."

"Well, to be fair," said Brice, "the U.S. was coming in with guns and soldiers. What these guys are doing sounds more like an inter-stellar Peace Corps."

"*Sounds like*," said Jesse. "But—"

"I see that everyone has finished eating," said Mynack. "Then I believe it's time to begin."

And once more a golden glow enveloped Charlie, and when it passed he was once more somewhere else.

PART IV

A NEXUS OF CRISES

43

When the golden glow around Brice faded from his eyes, he found himself standing on a path through a field of wheat. A warm wind rustled the high stalks all around him, filling his nose with their earthy grain smell. High above, trails of white clouds moved swiftly through a royal blue sky.

The path curved in either direction from Brice, as though he stood at the apex of a horseshoe-shaped trail. He looked left and right, but saw no indication of which way he was supposed to go.

"Hardly two paths diverging in the woods," he muttered, looking at the trail floor, "but maybe the road less traveled is the right call here."

Even more stalks of wheat covered the trail, but as Brice looked closer, he saw that they weren't mown down as he had first thought. They were bent down. Each one of them. About an inch up the stalks, something had pressed them flat to the ground and each other, thickly enough that Brice had to work his hand down between stiff resistance to reach the rich, brown soil underneath.

Even weirder, they weren't all bent the same direction. They appeared to have bent from the spot Brice had appeared, the stalks on his right bending away to the right along the curve of the path, and the stalks to his left bending to his left the same way.

No footprints, tears or breaks to indicate that anyone had walked on these stalks before him. So much for taking the road less traveled.

"Fine, then," said Brice, shaking his head. He looked up. "I guess it's a choice between the right hand path and the left hand path. Maybe this isn't what you guys intended, but I'm a good Christian boy and I know a good Christian dilemma when I see one."

Though to himself Brice admitted that he would have felt better about this decision if the right hand path were more difficult to walk. Rockier maybe, or something like that. Still, he started whistling "Bringing in the Sheaves" and began walking. It curved left and left, and a few minutes later another path intersected it, moving away to his right.

Brice kept following the curve to the left. Before long he realized something had changed. The stalks underfoot were pointing toward Brice now, instead of bending away. That slowed him, but he stopped walking entirely when he reached a seam in the trail, where the stalks ahead of him bent away from him again.

"Wait," said Brice. "Did I just walk in a circle?"

No answer but the rustling of stalks in the wind.

"Screw this." Brice pushed straight through the center of the wheat circle toward the side trail he'd passed up. Stiff stalks poked and prodded at him as he made his way through, bits of wheat sticking to his clothes and hair, and getting into his shoes. But he was determined now to be done with this.

When he came to the trail again he did not pause, but began straight down the trail. Short dead-ends branched off at right angles, followed by their longer cousins a few steps later. Then longer curves split off to his left and right, as though the intersection of a much larger circle now...

...in the crops.

Brice stopped walking. He looked up. "A crop circle? You guys are responsible for crop circles too?"

No. We are.

The words appeared in Brice's head, but they weren't his. They didn't sound like him, feel like him, anything. They were high and rough, as though a small frog had managed to croak words directly into Brice's mind.

And the worst part was that those words felt as though they were coming from behind him.

Brice turned.

And there stood what had to be a Gray. No more than four feet tall, if that, its whole body as skinny as a hyperactive child, save for an oversized egg-head that tapered to a narrow chin. Arms at its sides, relaxed, not threatening. Body naked and sexless, with slate gray skin that had the texture and shine of a frog.

Or maybe Brice just had frogs on his mind.

But there was nothing frog-like about those eyes. Huge and glossy black, but smooth. Not segmented like an insect's, but extruding from the skin further than anything *but* an insect, or maybe a lizard. And no eyelids at all. Tiny little slit for a mouth, and if it had more than a slight bump for a nose, Brice couldn't see it.

"That was you, wasn't it?" Brice pointed at the Gray, though he felt silly doing so. "Talking in my head."

Telepathy is how my people communicate. This ... is a less intrusive alternative.

"Speaking into my head isn't telepathy?"

True communication is swift and complete. It would overwhelm you. Risks confusing, panicking you. Not my wish.

Brice was now standing less than arm's length away from the second alien species he'd met this week. "Overwhelming" barely began to cover it. Shock had already begun to chill his skin, in spite of the warm wind.

"I, um, appreciate that," he began, but the alien interrupted.

No time. I diverted your travel. They will find you, recover you, soon. But your committee must know. My people stand ready to offer you everything the Others have, and we will not judge you. No tests. No danger.

"What about the 'tests' you've already done to our people?"

Finished. We need no more. We would have settled for working with your governments, but now that the Others have become involved, we must be more direct.

"You mean the Greenies? Just knowing they're involved means you'd—"

They are coming. Tell your committee. My people are a known, trustworthy alternative. Focus all six of your minds and call out to us, and we will hear you even through the Others' defenses.

"But how do we know..."

The rest of Brice's question was spoken into a spreading aura of gold.

44

Laura tried another door — a real door this time — a heavy exterior door with a stainless steel kick guard along the bottom and a push-bar that should let her outside.

Should. Except that the cold metal push-bar wouldn't push, and the heavy door wouldn't do more than rattle a little. Locked, like the three others she'd tried so far. The three others that had been real doors, anyway. The others had just been props. Fake doors built into sets that didn't need the expense of mundanities like working hinges, knobs, latches, et cetera. "Modern day" sets, that looked like actual living rooms, bedrooms and offices, any one of which might have had real doors.

And that was the worst part about being all alone in a darkened movie studio. The light was dim enough that she couldn't always tell whether she was on a set or backstage.

Laura tried not to think of that as a metaphor for her life.

The place smelled musty, like it hadn't been used in a while. If it had been in use, she would have smelled paint, acetone, latex, sawdust, and that dry smell that comes from running lots of hot lights for way too long. But the musty smell was moist, edging toward mildew. So likely no one had been here in quite some time.

Or at least, no one had shot any scenes here in quite some time. As to whether or not anyone else had been here recently, Laura couldn't shake the feeling that there was someone on the catwalks up above her. Every once in a while she heard some metallic creaking that might have been the place settling.

Then again, it might not. The Greenies had thrown Laura up against the creeper yesterday. Did they plan on some kind of sequel for today?

She kept trying to splice that line of thought out of her head, but it wouldn't stay cut. Her mind returned over and over to the ballast bags full of sand up above her, and the props and lights, and other things that hung precariously from ropes and chains. That spot between her shoulder blades kept twitching with a creepy, exposed sensation. Flipping up the collar of her plaid felt shirt had helped, but she really wanted to find an exit. Or at least a light switch. What little light she had must have come from windows high up, or some kind of intermittent safety lights...

...or just that sourceless lighting the Greenies used everywhere else.

That was something Laura needed to keep in mind. This might look like a movie studio, but it was just a Greenie construct. Everything here was part of their test. This was the maze, and she was the rat.

Which meant that someone had to be on those catwalks. The building might not be real enough to settle. If "real" was the right word. She could see, smell, feel the place around her. She could probably even taste it, but she drew a little comfort from the lingering taste of breakfast pineapple in her mouth, and had no desire to chase it away licking props.

So what did she know then?

The place smelled of disuse. That meant help wasn't coming. Laura was here on her own. The light was dim. That meant there were things they didn't want her to see. Or at least, not see until they felt the time was right. The air was cool, but not cold. Not a factor. And she could hear someone in the background. Someone who didn't want to be heard.

Well that was too bad for them.

Laura put her back to the wall and stilled her steps on the concrete floor beneath her. Right now, whoever was up above her might have known she was there, but slow sneakers on concrete were a hell of a lot more stealthy than any kind of weight on a catwalk.

And in case it *was* the creeper, she needed a weapon. Something to help even the odds. She had nothing on her person, of course, but unless she was mistaken she had just passed through some kind of office set. At least, it had a desk, so it was most likely an office set. That meant it had to have a paperweight or a letter opener, something she could use if violence was the solution to this Greenie problem.

She pushed away from the concrete outer wall toward that set. Every step slow and measured, weight coming down along the outside of her foot, toe to heel. Laura kept her hands out to her sides to make sure she wasn't going to bump into something half-seen in the dimness. Not the time to trip on a rack of lights or boom stand. Bad enough there might be un-taped cables loose on the floor.

She made it from concrete to thin carpeting. Laura smirked. She'd just broken the fourth wall in the reverse direction, coming from the camera area into the set. Darker in here, like the office set had a ceiling instead of extending up into the rafters. Terrible for sound miking. How would they get the boom inside without spoiling—

Laura stopped moving and shook her head. This was not the time for the logistics of a set she wasn't working on. She turned her head slowly from left to right, peering into the deeper darkness. She could make out a few things. Big, heavy desk under a frame on the wall. Probably a green screen "window." Fancy executive chair behind the desk, and two padded wooden chairs for guests in front.

Slow steps. One at a time. She reached the desk. Grainy texture of oak with the bare stickiness of old lacquer. Bent desk lamp with a pull chain, cool like brass. Laura ached to pull the chain. Shed more light. But that would have been telling Mr. Catwalk right where she was. And Mr. Catwalk had gone quiet, like she'd disappeared and he figured out that she knew he was there.

Laura contented herself with darkness. Her fingers found a glass paperweight. Round like a globe, but with a spiral ridge. The spiral made the paperweight almost jagged at the top, and the middle of the globe was hollow. She moved it to the corner of the desk and kept searching. Stapler. Desk blotter. Nothing else.

She started rifling through the drawers. Pens in the center drawer. Pens, pens, pens, and here! A letter opener. Laura eased the drawer closed and was about to turn away, but something nagged at her. The desk had other drawers, two small and one big down the right side. Maybe she'd find something even better.

The bottom drawer was full of file folders (empty) and a fifth of something (half-empty). Probably iced tea pretending to be whisky. The middle drawer was empty. Laura closed her eyes and prayed for a moment — *please let this be a noir P.I. set with a gun in the—*

The top drawer was locked. Laura yanked it a few times, but it didn't want to come. She puffed out a sigh and ran her fingers through her hair to banish the strands that had draped down in front of her face. The key had to be here somewhere.

Laura set the letter opener on the desk and started shoveling pens out of the top drawer, running her hands along the bottom and sides to make sure she didn't miss anything. No key. She pulled the drawer out entirely and checked the bottom. No key.

She gave the bottom two drawers the same treatment. Still no key.

Laura sat in the executive chair, which turned out to be cloth, not leather. And it wobbled as though its springs had seen better days. She ran her hands over the wooden armrests and under the front of the chair. Still no key.

Creaking sound up above. Mr. Catwalk was on the move again. This time, though, Laura had a ceiling between her and him. Even if he had on night vision goggles or something, he still wouldn't be able to see her from above.

The answer had to be in that locked drawer. Why else would the Greenies have locked it? Charlie had made the comparison to a video game, and now Laura wondered if this, too, was a scene out of some game.

She sighed again. She really didn't want to use the letter opener to open the drawer. She might need it as sharp as possible. But if she wanted to find out what the Greenies had locked away, she was out of options.

She didn't need long to pry the drawer open, but now the tip of the letter opener was bent. Inside the drawer she found a flask (also half full). Probably "the good stuff." Then her fingers skated along the cool steel of what she hoped to find — a revolver.

The pistol was big. Bigger than any she had ever fired, and Laura had fired her share and then some: .38s, .380s, .22s, 9mms, even a .357 magnum. But this huge beast was heavier than any of them. Had to be a .45, or maybe a .44 magnum.

Geez. Someone was compensating. This was way too much pistol for most private investigators. This was a gun for hunting elephants. Laura shook her head. Didn't matter. This was supposed to be a film studio. No way the revolver was loaded with anything but blanks.

But blanks could be loud and scary. And at close enough range, even the paper or plastic wadding in the shell would do some damage. Plus, it had a good handle for gripping, and hitting someone with it would be a lot more effective than that stupid paperweight.

With her elephant hunting pistol in one hand and her letter opener in the other, Laura snuck out of the office set. Now she was ready to find Mr. Catwalk.

45

The hoodie had been a mistake. Charlie saw that now. The sneakers too. And probably the jeans. Honestly, if anyone had bothered to *tell* Charlie what he would be doing for his next portion of the test — quite possibly his *last* portion of the test — he would have just stayed in bed and skipped the whole thing.

Instead, Charlie was treading water somewhere in the middle of the ocean. Clear, pale sky above, with nothing more than wisps of cloud. Sun just past mid-day — or maybe just about to reach it, he had no frame of reference for where he was. Distant though. Warm, but not blazing hot. Not that a little heat would have been so bad. The water was cold, and the whipping wind even colder.

Each heavy breath brought the tang of brine, and he tasted salt water every time a wave splashed his face. Which happened so often he felt as though he never stopped blinking his eyes clear, and spitting.

He'd ditched the hoodie almost immediately. The sneakers went some five minutes later, kicked off while his arms worked overtime to keep him above water. But his jeans were heavy. And the ache in his left thigh — hamstring as Dubba J pointed out — was getting worse.

The tee shirt was adding weight too, but Charlie was loath to change up his rhythm just to ditch any extra cloth.

Worse, his breakfast was threatening to cramp his stomach. But that was to be expected. He was always told to wait an hour after eating before going swimming. Not two minutes.

"I've said it before and I'll say it again," grumbled Charlie. "You guys suck."

Well, to be fair, Charlie had bitched and bitched about the "A" or "B" choices the Greenies kept giving him. Maybe it was his fault he was treading water in the middle of nowhere, with no sign of land or a ship in sight. After all, from the look of things, the Greenies had set this one up as the simplest A-B dilemma ever.

Which would make you happier? A) Drown in the ocean immediately. B) Tread water until your limbs give out, and then drown.

Though now that Charlie thought of it that way, this wasn't all that different from any of the other choices he'd had to make as part of these tests. In each case, both options were bad and Charlie was desperate for a third possible outcome. "C."

Of course, in this case, the outcome looked like death any way he sliced it. Nothing to swim to. No ladder to reach for. Just a vast sea, looking as endless as the sky at night.

That couldn't be right though. The Greenies couldn't have put Charlie here with no chance of survival. Could they? No. There had to be some sort of rescue coming. Something. If they'd wanted to just kill him, they could have teleported him into space, or the sun, or just about anywhere else. Heck, they could have teleported him just a mile deeper than he was and that would have done the trick, and then some.

So, no, the Greenies couldn't just be killing him.

And no, Charlie decided, this couldn't be his fault. If the Greenies couldn't handle a little bitching about their tests, then there was no way any sentient beings had ever gone through them before. Because what sane, sensible individual could possibly deal with all this crap and not get a little pissed off?

The blame for Charlie being where he was, dressed the way he was, and doing exactly what he was doing, was entirely on the Greenies, all the way down.

Well, rescue did not appear to be arriving anytime soon, and Charlie wasn't going down without a fight. He started getting a feel for the current, counting out the timing of the waves. Figuring out how to rise with them instead of getting a face full of water every time.

The good news was, that helped. The bad news was that the cramp kept building in his gut. And his arms were getting tired. So were his legs. And that ache in his left hamstring was getting sharper with each passing minute.

What if no rescue was coming after all?

"What kind of test is it if you kill me?"

No answer, of course.

"Come on. At least tell me that much. What can you learn by pointlessly murdering me? How tough the human spirit really is, or some crap like that?"

Nothing but the wind and another face-full of seawater.

And then the cramp hit hard, sharp as a gut-punch. It doubled Charlie forward, dunking him under the water.

He wasn't ready. He got a mouthful of water. Swallowed some. Spat more, clawing back for the surface. Forcing his body straighter, teeth gritted so hard against the pain in his gut and his leg that he felt a fleeting worry his teeth would shatter.

All too soon that might be the least of his problems.

Charlie spun belly up, barely getting his face above the waterline and spewing water like lava out of a volcano. But the air coming back in tasted sweeter than Charlie could have imagined.

This respite was brief. He knew that now. The cramp. The pulled hamstring. And now his limbs as slow and heavy as if they'd been filled with lead.

He was about to die.

But his life didn't flash before his eyes. Instead he thought about all the things he'd never done. Never get to do. Never get to say goodbye to his parents. His friends. Not even Lucy, his ex-, who might try to blame herself for this somehow. Wouldn't be the first time she did something like that.

Never get to hear Laura laugh again.

Panic set in. Charlie started hyperventilating. He dipped under the surface again, but slamming his mouth shut didn't stop or slow his breathing. His diaphragm twitched and his lungs seized, trying for more air through his desperately sealed lips.

The world began to go dark around the edges of his vision. Dimmed on him.

Charlie managed to get his face above water one more time. Just enough for one more breath. But he didn't try to hold it. And he didn't waste it cursing the Greenies for killing him.

Instead, Charlie rasped out one simple thing. "Kyna. Please. Save me."

46

"...you're any better..." Brice's words trailed off as the golden glow around him faded. The wheat field with its crop circle was gone. The Gray was gone. Instead, Brice found himself sitting at one end of the kind of poker table he sometimes saw on the sports channels. Oblong oval of green felt with a black padded rail that had ten drink holders built into the rail (currently filled with unlabeled bottles of water), one for each seat at the table.

The table was spot-lit from above, but Brice could see empty rows of cushy seats, stadium style, in the darkness around the table in all directions. Two walkways for the players, like tunnels leading away under the seats past the ends of the table.

The stands may have been empty, but all the seats at the table were occupied by the kind of people Brice saw on those televised poker shows. Eight men (including Brice) between the ages of twenty and sixty, all in varied casual dress and three wearing sunglasses. Four Caucasians, two African Americans and two Asian Americans. Two women at the table. One a pale blonde in a sparkly red dress at the far end from Brice. The other was Alita, sitting two seats away from Brice, around the end of the table.

Or at least, something that looked like Alita was sitting two seats from Brice. From what Laura said at breakfast, Charlie dealt with phantom doppelgangers of the rest of the — what had the Gray called them? A committee? — while running through a maze yesterday.

Everyone at the table — except the dealer, a man with short blond hair — had a stack of chips in front of him or her, various quantities of red, green and black. Most of them looked about even with the stack Brice found in front of himself, as though they'd only barely started. But the air smelled like they'd been playing for a while, musky colognes getting a bit thick and deodorants wearing thin.

"Alita," said Brice while the dealer called for blinds and dealt everyone at the table a pair of cards, "is that really you?"

"As far as I know," said Alita, glancing at her cards. "Where've you been?"

"Action's to you, new player," said the dealer, looking at Brice.

Brice looked down at his cards. The ten of hearts and the eight of spades. Those cards weren't even good in cribbage, to say nothing of poker.

"I fold," he said.

"Just toss them toward the center of the table," said the young Asian man between Brice and Alita. "Not too hard, though. Just enough to show you're throwing them in."

Brice did.

The young Asian man folded too, but Alita threw in four green chips. A raise. And she took one of her black chips and set it on the back of her cards. So she knew more about what she was doing than Brice did.

Spot by spot around the table, more people either folded their cards or tossed in four green chips. Meanwhile, Brice turned to the man seated to his right, who looked to be about eighty, with gray hair and wrinkles that had more to do with frowning than smiling.

"How long have you been playing?" Brice said.

The man glanced at Brice, then ignored him and watched what

the other players were doing. He already had two green chips in the pot. "The big blind" if Brice recalled the right term. By the time the "action" got back to him, three other players had called Alita. The man grumbled something Brice couldn't hear and tossed in two more green chips.

The dealer set the top card of the deck to one side, face down, then snapped out three cards and flipped them over all at once: the ten of diamonds, the ten of clubs, and the eight of clubs.

"I should have stayed in," said Brice, drawing a couple of quick glances. "I would have had—"

"Will you shut up?" said the old man to Brice's right. "Have some respect for the other players."

Brice saw a little sympathy, but mostly agreement in the brief glances from the strangers at the table. This was not exactly the kind of casual game he played with his staff writers every blue moon or so.

"Maybe you guys better just cash me out."

That got a chuckle or two, but mostly eye-rolls. Alita said, "This is a tournament game, not a cash game. You're playing as long as you have chips."

"But I don't know what I'm doing."

"I think we've all figured that out," said the old man to Brice's right. "So be quiet, kiddo, and let the adults play cards."

Brice stared at the old man, who was pushing six red chips forward.

"Screw this," said Brice, getting up from the table. Alita threw in her cards and jumped up to catch him.

"What are you doing?" she said. "If they put us here to play cards, we play cards."

"I'd just sit there and lose anyway. Why bother playing?"

"Blinds, please," said the dealer. The old man next to Brice's seat pushed two of Brice's green chips forward.

"You're in the hand anyway," said Alita, pointing at what just happened on the table. "Just sit back down and play. So what if you lose?"

"I'm not going to sit there and be insulted for not knowing how to play while handing over my money. Or whoever's money that is."

"Action's to you, Ms. Luna," said the dealer.

"Call," said Alita, without looking. To Brice she said, quietly, "You missed three hands. Where were you?"

"Long story. I'll tell you later. You better get back and play."

"What are you going to do?"

"I'm going to see where those tunnels go."

Brice started to turn away, but Alita hissed to get his attention and he turned back.

"What if we're not playing for money?" she said, words so soft Brice could barely hear them.

"Then it may be something I can't afford to lose. So I decline to play."

"The bet is five hundred to you, Ms. Luna," said the dealer.

Alita looked as though she had something more to say, but turned back to resume her seat and look over the table to see who'd done what.

Brice shook his head, picked a tunnel, and started walking.

47

A-Day-Plus-Two. Ten-Sixteen A.M. Lounge Local Time

Laura stood at the bottom of a set of steel stairs leading up to the catwalks. The smell of grease was thicker here than the usual backdrop and set smells. She must have been near a storage cage for mechanical equipment.

Interesting that this mock-studio had stairs. Some of the older studios — at least, some of the older studios that Laura had seen — only had ladder access to the catwalks. A ladder would have been better. Quieter.

Of course, if there had been a ladder, Mr. Catwalk could have come down to the ground floor without Laura knowing. The chances that he got down these metal stairs without making them creak and squeak the whole way down were pretty slim.

But that was the problem before Laura now. She could walk with a light foot when she wanted too — she'd filmed too many stealthy scenes not to have learned a few things about moving silently — but if the welds holding these stairs in place had any rust, any weak spots, they might shift. Loudly. Then she'd be telling Mr. Catwalk exactly where she was.

Not smart.

And Mr. Catwalk had been silent since Laura left that little office set. She had a vague sense that he might have been around seventy feet from her, back that direction, as of the last time she heard him move. But she wasn't willing to act on that. Too flimsy. He might have realized how much noise he was making.

Maybe he knew a thing or two about stealth too.

On the other hand, there were eight cartridges in the big, heavy pistol in her hand. She could always fire one in that general direction. The blank wouldn't do any damage, but the sound might get him moving. Let her figure out where he was...

...assuming she could hear his immediate movements. Guns were loud. And this was the biggest, baddest hunk of iron Laura had ever held, much less shot. She had to assume its report was going to be proportionately louder than she was used to.

Hell, just firing this beast was probably going to leave her with a sore shoulder. No reason to seek that out when she might not have to use it after all.

Just the thought made her snort. Yeah. Sure she wouldn't. Who was she kidding? The thing might as well have been labeled "Chekhov Act III."

Yesterday it was the creeper. Today it was some mystery man in a darkened movie studio. The Greenies seemed to be getting off on the hot-chick-fighting-big-men thing. Maybe Joss Whedon was writing their scenarios?

That got a smirk out of her. Couldn't be the case anyway. Joss would have given her some hot guy to trade quips with as part of the buildup to the inevitable big kiss...

Laura spliced that line of thought out of her head. This wasn't a shoot. There was no script. And aliens were calling the shots, not Joss. For some reason they wanted to match her up with big guys. Maybe they were testing her "pluck," or something equally demeaning if she let herself think about it.

Or maybe their "tests" were just some kind of voyeuristic fetish.

Laura puffed out a breath, then winced at how loud it sounded in her ears and tapped the cold pistol against her forehead in admonishment. She moved to the edge of the stairs against the wall and began a slow ascent, her breaths shallow. Each leg moving slowly and steadily, lifting one sneaker to a stair, easing her weight down onto it, pausing for just a hair, then starting the next leg. She leaned her shoulder against the wall, for a third point of stability. She kept a good grip on the pistol in her right hand, but she held it low. Thing had to weigh more than five pounds. No reason to tire her arm holding it up before she had to. In her left hand she still held her bent-tipped letter opener.

A letter opener with a bent tip and a pistol armed with blanks. Not exactly the recipe for an action hero.

The stairs seemed to stretch on forever, but they probably didn't take her more than forty feet up before she finally reached the catwalk. Steel mesh, no doubt coated with thick black paint, or plastic, or whatever it was exactly that covered catwalks. It still gave when she stepped on it. Just a little. Just enough to creak, even under her modest weight. Not much of a sound the way she eased her step down, but still. Enough.

Enough that Mr. Catwalk heard her. Laura could hear him on the move again. Her direction. He was trying to be quiet, but he was too heavy on the mesh. Little squeaks and creaks coming closer. Little squeaks and creaks that slowed, slowed, stopped.

Laura crouched where she was. Put her letter opener hand under her gun hand, ready to add stability when she raised up. Her heart was pumping faster now. She'd kept it steady enough on the stairs, but now, here, crouched with a gun in her hand and a strange man out there somewhere all too close, now her heart was setting a beat fast enough for some composer to build an action theme around.

In the silence of the moment, it sounded impossibly loud.

Her eyes strained into the darkness. She could barely make out the stretch of mesh between herself and Mr. Catwalk. Off the edge to each side and over the sets below she could see racks holding currently useless lights. A couple of small things swinging that were probably bags of sand.

There.

She could just barely see a big shape moving in the blackness. Crouched low. Massive. Not like the creeper was massive, but body builder massive. This wasn't a second shot at the creeper. This was some stranger stalking her, with murderous intent, or maybe worse.

Laura raised up her pistol. She took aim for the center of mass...

...and stopped. This wasn't a movie. She wasn't playing one of her action heroines. She couldn't just pull the trigger on some stranger in the dark.

"Stop where you are," she said, voice as loud and resonant as her training could make it, "I have a gun."

"Laura?"

"Dubba J?" Laura lowered her gun and sank down, sitting against the wall. Her heart still beat double-time, but the release gave her a head rush that threatened to black her out. She started breathing as slowly and deeply as she could manage.

"Thank God!" he said, hustling over to her and setting off such a cacophony that she wondered how she'd ever had trouble telling where he was. He slid down to sit cross-legged facing her, dropping a crowbar to rattle on the mesh beside him when he did. "I thought ... never mind."

"I thought ... you were the guy ... who attacked me once." Laura couldn't seem to get enough air. And she felt really hot, all flushed through the face. Was this just letting go of stress?

"I ... well ... let's just say I thought something similar."

Laura blinked at Dubba J. She couldn't really get a good look at him in the dim light, but something in his voice sounded familiar. Maybe they had more in common than she thought.

"Was this the test?" she said, her breath finally back under control, and her flush starting to recede. "Think they just wanted to see if we'd try to kill each other?"

"You're the one with the gun."

"Yeah, this thing just has blanks in it anyway. But you could crack my head open with that crowbar."

"You sure about that?"

"You'd split my skull like a melon!"

"No, about the blanks."

Laura shrugged, but he probably couldn't see it.

"I found it in the top desk of the set for some noir P.I.'s office." She dropped the gun on the catwalk between them, just to hear the loud thump and creak. "No way a movie set gun has bullets in it."

"Did you check?" Dubba J picked up the pistol. "Whoa, this thing has enough firepower to shoot through a moose. Lengthwise."

"Doesn't matter now," she said. "Obviously I didn't pull the trigger."

Dubba J popped out the cylinder and pulled out a cartridge. "Catch," he said and tossed the cartridge to her. She missed in the darkness, and it got caught in the folds of her shirt.

She dug it out and ran her fingers over it, from the round base to the snub-nosed lead tip of the very real bullet.

"Oh, God," she said, cold shock settling over her, just as she and Dubba J were limned in gold, and vanished.

48

A-Day-Plus-Two. Ten-Eighteen A.M. Lounge Local Time

Brice wasn't sure exactly how long he'd been walking down this dark tunnel, but he *was* sure he wasn't getting anywhere. Nothing had changed. Still vague white light in the distance, as though the tunnel had an end. Yellowish-white light behind him, and if he listened carefully enough, he could hear the sounds of people calling and raising, and the clicking of chips, in the distance.

He'd been walking too long to still be able to hear any of that. He was sure of that much too.

Same thin, gray carpet — or at least it looked gray in the low light where he was. Smell of carpet cleaner and stale cigarettes, with just a soupcon of alcohol underlying it. When Brice thought about how long he'd been walking, he decided that at least the undersmell should have changed.

Brice stopped and looked up at the low, black ceiling, which probably should have had lights inset along the way, but looked as though no one had bothered with that level of safety. Definitely not a real casino. Bright lights and noise were the backdrop of a proper casino. Everyone knew that, even guys like Brice, who'd been to Atlantic City all of once, and decided it was a bad idea right then.

Staking money on a game of chance. Why were people willing to do that, when they weren't willing to bet on themselves? They'd rather throw money away on a chance of instantaneous wealth rather than invest in their futures? Their interests? Their...

Brice shook his head with a wistful smile. If only Laetitia were here to tease him about his favorite rant. She'd let him finish, then kiss him and confide that she felt the same way, but it was those other people's money and no one had any business telling them what to do with it. Not even her "brilliant husband."

He missed her so much he ached. It had been five years since he was last apart from her for this long, and he had no intention of ever separating from her for so long again.

But first he had to get back to her. And that meant finishing this test. If it was a test. It sure didn't feel like a test. It was just a freaking poker game. And besides...

Brice looked up again. "How is a poker game a test, guys? Seriously. Trying to find out how bad I am at cards? Here's a hint — *I don't care that I'm bad at cards.* Stupid card games don't mean a thing to me. So if you're trying to find out if I'd be willing to take Alita's money, let's settle that right now."

Brice pointed back toward the game.

"Alita knows what she's doing. I don't. Alita obviously plays poker more than once every blue moon. I don't. Alita might be good enough to take down the rest of your ringers, or whatever they are. I'm not."

Brice spread his arms wide.

"So you want to know what I do in that poker game? I lose. There's your answer. Might as well take me back."

No golden glow.

"So how real do you want to get here? If I run back there and flip over the table, are your construct players going to kick my ass?"

Nothing.

It was a false threat anyway. Brice knew he could never have thrown over that poker table. Not faster than they could have stopped him. That thing had looked so stable it might have weighed a hundred pounds. And all those chips must have made it even heavier.

"I'm not a gambler. If you were trying to get to 'the real me' or something, you would have been better off making me renegotiate my contract. That always gets real pretty darn quick."

Nothing.

Brice turned back toward the poker game, and there stood Mynack.

Brice got a sudden cold feeling of exposure across his neck and down his spine. Mynack effectively had him trapped. Pinned between the poker game and the distant white light that didn't seem to be reachable. Separated from Alita, and everyone else.

Brice immediately tried to dismiss the sensation. The Greenies had full control here. They could have him alone anytime they wanted.

But the feeling wouldn't fade.

"In all the centuries I have overseen these tests," said Mynack, "never has a transportation been delayed."

"Maybe you guys are having technical problems. I know that I can't ever seem to get through a show without at least one. I remember this one time—"

"If there were a "technical problem" in your transportation, you would be dead."

"Maybe," said Brice, heart pounding as his tongue ran ahead of his brain. It tended to do that in times of stress. "Or this could have been what the kids these days call 'lag.' It affects online games all the time, when too many users are making demands of a server at the same time, slows the whole processor down, and..."

Mynack's amber eyes had that look of eternal patience again.

"...and it's a ... technical issue, but it's not. You know?" Brice had to rub his neck now. Every word fell from his lips as lamely as the alibi of a thief caught on camera.

"I assure you that was not the case."

"Well, I don't know what you want me to say. I mean, you guys are handling all the logistics, and the whole point of the exercise is just how far ahead of us your technology is, so it's not as though I could help you troubleshoot—"

"Brice DePaul, do you wish to represent to me that travel from your breakfast table to the poker table appeared instantaneous to you, and that you neither noticed any delay, nor arrived at any intermediary place where you might have passed time?"

Up until this moment, Brice had thought of Mynack's patience as that of a stone wall. Or maybe a mountain. Endless and utterly absent any concern. But now, this time, Brice realized that there was indeed some quality tucked away inside the core of that serene waiting.

But Brice could not tell if it was the compassionate patience of a saint, or the malevolent patience of the Devil.

"I arrived in a wheat field. A crop circle." Brice blew out a deep breath. "I talked to a Gray."

Mynack said nothing. Brice tried to match that silence against the backdrop of the poker game in the distance. But Brice broke first.

"The Gray, he said his people could give us everything yours are offering, and that there wouldn't be any more tests. That his people had done all the testing they needed to do."

"Did you accept his offer?"

"He — or maybe it was a she, I don't know — asked me to take it to my committee, and told me how to reach him if we want to take him up on it."

"Why tell me? Why not lie?"

The comedian in Brice gave him a dozen flippant answers that his tongue longed to voice while he blinked in confusion, but Brice clamped down on all of them. Instead he stepped up to Mynack and looked him dead in those amber eyes.

"I want to believe you're telling us the truth about all of this. Maybe you're not. Maybe this is just all some kind of sick joke. But I know this much. I'm not going to be the first one to start telling lies. If I catch you in one, all bets are off. But as long as I think you're playing us straight, I'll play fair."

"Suppose the only way to win is to cheat. Would you lie then?"

Brice snorted softly.

"Don't watch my show, do you? Everything I do. Everything I am. That's all predicated on my integrity. I slam both our political parties when they're wrong, and I'll lay the smack down on the mainstream media for the same reasons. And when I'm wrong, I own up to it." Brice raised his index finger. "If I cross that line even once, I'm no better that the people I make fun of."

Brice shook his head and looked off toward the poker game. "I'd rather lose than cheat."

"And if I think you're lying?"

Brice looked Mynack in the eye.

"I can't control what you think. Call me a failure and send me home if you want. Tell the whole world I lied to you if it makes you feel better. I'm not a kid anymore. I know who I am."

Brice ran his eyes up and down Mynack's silver spacesuit.

"And I don't need some reject from a B-movie to tell me."

A golden glow surrounded Brice, and he vanished.

49

As consciousness returned, the first thing Charlie noticed was a smell. Floral. Not roses though ... rhododendrons? Didn't quite match the citrus taste on the air, but still. With every breath his nose filled with that spicy, almost apple scent of rhododendrons.

He tried opening his eyes, but that was a bad idea. They slammed closed immediately against the bright white light on the other side of his eyelids.

He squeezed them shut tighter. Even the afterimage felt too intense.

Sunlight wasn't that white. But the flash he'd seen didn't have the blue tinge of fluorescence either. Where was he?

As he wondered that, Charlie realized that he was lying down, not floating in the ocean still. Underneath him didn't feel like a bed or pillows or a couch though. More like ... a massage table with extra padding. Maybe a stiff futon of some sort. A slight rise under his head where a pillow would go, but not that oval shape like a massage table would have.

Charlie raised his hand and shaded his eyes, maybe an inch or two above his skin. He started blinking his lids open, then eased his hand away when he felt like he could handle it. He expected to find himself staring up at a light bulb, but there was no bulb. No ceiling either, for that matter. He seemed to be under a pale blue sky without a sun. But it was bright, brighter than high summer back in San Jose.

Not as warm as that though. In fact, the air was a breezeless kind of cool, which was a surprise, given that he was...

...dry. His shirt, his jeans, his skin. All dry. But not salty dry like he'd been pulled unconscious out of the ocean and left to lie until he awoke. His clothes were fresh and his skin was clean. Even his brown curls felt soft under his fingers.

Charlie sat up on the silvery futon. It was supported by a single chrome pylon under the center, that extended down about a meter into dark green grass. The grass looked freshly mown to ankle height, though any leavings had already been raked, bagged, and carted away.

The grass stretched out in every direction, but Charlie saw no sign of those rhododendrons. In fact, he saw no sign of anything else until he looked behind himself and saw Kyna, still in her silver space-suit, sitting on her knees, with her knee-high silver boots beneath her on the grass. Watching him.

"Where am I?" he said, surprised at how smooth his voice sounded. No rough wear and tear from his morning's activities.

"My room. Feeling better?"

"Yes." Charlie hopped to his feet. No fatigue in his arms or legs. He rolled his shoulders, neck and hips. He bent to touch his toes. No pain. Not anywhere. Not even in his hamstring. Not so much as stiffness in his biceps. "Completely better. Was that all just... Wait." Charlie looked around at the sky and grassy field. "Your *room*?"

"Yes." Her smile was small and cryptic, but Charlie would have sworn she was pleased. "It can look many ways, but I've been favoring this one lately. Your planet is quite beautiful."

"Thank you." Charlie frowned as he sat cross-legged, opposite her. The grass was as cushy as any throw pillow he'd ever sat on. "So was that all just illusion this morning?"

"No. You were in a specific spot in your Pacific Ocean. One where no cargo liners or pleasure cruises would have passed you today, and where you would not be attacked by any local fauna. A nearby warm current ensured that you would not freeze."

"What was that supposed to test?"

Kyna said nothing, but the smile did not vanish entirely from her orange eyes.

"You're not allowed to answer questions about the test," Charlie said with a sigh. "You did rescue me though. Does that mean I failed?"

Kyna's eyes settled into that seemingly eternal patience she shared with Mynack.

"Which is a question about the test." Charlie looked off at the horizon that had to be an illusion. "Well, now I understand why I couldn't leave that computer room."

"Oh?"

"You called this a room, so it has walls. But I wonder what would happen if I picked a direction and started wandering. I bet my body would find the wall — because it's there somewhere — but my eyes wouldn't see it and my skin wouldn't feel it. I'd just keep walking and not getting anywhere. Wouldn't I?"

Charlie looked at Kyna, who showed no sign of intending to answer him.

"Not even that, huh? Well, could you at least tell me why I'm here and not back in my room or in the lounge?"

"You asked me to save you."

"I didn't want to die." Charlie stopped his next words and puffed out a slow breath. "You mean I didn't just drown *expecting* you to rescue me. And I didn't manage to save myself, though you kind of stacked the odds against me. Would you guys have let me drown?"

No response.

"Which is a question about the test." Charlie spat toward that horizon. "Talking to you is damned difficult, you know."

"I'm sorry about that. Past tests have proven that answering questions only muddies the results. Why did you call me and not Mynack?"

"You're the one who's shown up before when I've had problems. At my apartment. In that computer room. I figured you were maybe assigned to me as a caseworker or something."

"No other reason?"

Charlie looked at Kyna again. Still that patience in her eyes, but maybe, just maybe, he could see something more underneath it. Something that looked familiar.

Something maybe he'd seen in a girl's eyes before.

Charlie looked away.

"Kyna, I don't know quite how to tell you this, but I'm not kidding when I tell you that I don't believe that's your true appearance. And you can't sit here in a room that looks like a field more perfect than any I've ever seen, that smells like rhododendrons without a single blossom in sight — you can't sit there in the middle of all this and tell me I don't have good reason to wonder what you really look like."

"But you have no particular reason to wonder what this room really looks like? Or your suite? Or the lounge?"

"None of those things has an agenda. You and Mynack do. For all I know, part of the test is whether or not you could seduce me. And I can admit that out loud, knowing you aren't going to tell me one way or the other anyway. So let me make this clear. I'm not one of those xenophile guys. I never fantasized about green-skinned alien lovers or Twi'lek dancing girls. I like humans. All races, creeds and religions, but human."

Charlie shrugged. He knew his words sounded harsh, but if the Greenies seemed to be after anything, it was honesty. Better to be clear now than to leave doubt.

"Maybe if I believed that was your real appearance, and that we were biologically compatible which is a whole new level of complication I don't even want to think about — maybe then I could see you as a woman, just from a different culture. But every conversation with you and Mynack just drives home for me that you guys may have less in common with me than dolphins do."

"Are you saying—"

"I'm saying I could imagine being friends with a dolphin, but I couldn't imagine anything more than that."

"I understand." Simple words, but no emotion in those orange eyes except that perpetual, seemingly inexhaustible patience.

A golden glow surrounded Charlie and took him away.

50

A-Day-Plus-Two. Eleven Fifty A.M. Lounge Local Time

Back in the lounge kitchen, Laura drank strong coffee with milk and more sugar than usual while Alita told her all about the strangest game of Texas Hold'em she'd ever played.

"...and I started seeing resemblances to people I know. This rude old guy started reminding me of my uncle Miguel. A young Chinese guy reminded me of Jerry, my first boyfriend. It was like I was taking money from people I knew."

"And how was that?" The coffee was good. Rich. And it warmed Laura all the way down to her belly. That was important right now. Staying warm. She'd almost shot someone this morning. Every time she thought about it a whole new wave of cold washed over her.

She'd almost shot Dubba J. Dubba J, who right now was playing pinball with Brice somewhere on the other side of the room. Dubba J with that big smile and infectious laugh. And Laura almost put two or three big holes in him.

That gun she found was made for killing elephants or something, not wounding human beings.

"Weird," continued Alita, "but not too bad. I mean, you sit down at the table and you take your chances. If you can't afford to lose, don't play." She shrugged, her orange flannel shirt sliding around her shoulders with the movement. "Well, not too bad until it was down to me and this girl in a red spangled fuck-me dress."

"Trying to distract the boys at the table?" Laura could still feel the handle in her hand, the weight of the pistol, her finger on the trigger.

"Of course." Alita rolled her eyes. "Worked too. Most of the guys spent more time watching her cleavage than how she played. Honestly, I don't know why Brice got so stressed out. This was hardly a table of pros."

"So what happened?" Laura shivered and held her cup with both hands.

"Came down to me and her, and I was having a bad run of cards. My stack dwindling. But then I realized something — she wasn't protecting her hand. If I leaned back, I could see what she had when she checked it."

"What did you do?"

Alita smiled. "Tightened up and took her to the cleaners." She held up a fist and Laura bumped it. "It's all part of the game. If she wanted to show me her cards, who was I to argue?"

Laura smiled, but she could tell it didn't come out right because the humor leaked out of Alita's eyes. "You didn't shoot him."

Laura looked into the milk chocolate color of her doctored coffee.

"I almost did. My finger was on the trigger. I was already letting a breath out slow, like I do at the range."

"But you didn't."

"But I almost—"

"*Almost* shooting somebody is like being *almost* pregnant. Does. Not. Count." Alita snapped her fingers to get Laura to look up. "Do you hear me?"

Across the room came the sound of Dubba J's laughter. Laura smiled. "Doesn't sound like he has PTSD, does it."

"No, but I'm getting worried about you. That thing yesterday, now this today. You have a therapist, right?"

Laura nodded.

"Good. Don't hold back in your next session. You need to clear this out before—"

"Yes, yes, I know." Laura smacked her half-full cup down on the counter hard enough to crack it and slosh coffee over the side. "I need to clear it all out before filming starts. I need to get all the Laura out of the way so I can be whoever they need me to be."

"Hey." Alita reached out and squeezed Laura's shoulder. "I was going to say you need to clear this out before it eats you up from the inside."

Laura grabbed her in a hug, tears squeezing their way out of her eyes, and Alita wasted no time in holding her just as tight.

"Miss your mom, don't you?" said Alita.

Laura just nodded against Alita's shoulder and sniffled until she got past the worst of the moment. Then she eased back from the hug and leaned back against the counter, hugging her stomach.

"I talk to my mom just about every day. At least, every day I can."

"I'm not quite that good," said Alita. "I call mine every week or two. I know what you mean though. Being here, away from our support, is a rough way to go through all this."

Laura nodded, and blew her nose on a paper towel.

"But hey," said Alita with a smile that did not quite hide the shine in her eyes. "We've got each other. And the boys aren't too bad."

Laura raised an eyebrow.

"Well, all right, Jesse aside." Alita rolled her lips in and then back out. "I have to say, though, that he really does sound sorry about whatever happened between—"

"He always sounds sorry. And he always does it again. That is *over*."

The change in topic helped though. Irritation with Jesse might not be as useful as full-blown anger was, but it was better than recriminations over something that even Laura had to admit she didn't do, however close she came to pulling the trigger.

"Come on." Alita gestured toward the game tables with a flourish. "No reason the boys should have all the fun. Let's play some foosball."

Laura wrinkled her nose. "How about air hockey?"

Alita gave an exasperated snort. "You are so white I'm surprised you don't glow in the dark."

"My skin *has* been described as 'luminescent.'"

Laura barely got the words out before she started laughing. Alita joined her, and they walked off toward the game tables.

51

A-Day-Plus-Two. Twelve-Twenty-Nine p.m. Lounge Local Time

"Here you go," said Dubba J, walking in from the kitchen carrying a plate full of sandwiches in one hand, and a stack of sandwich plates in the other. "Grilled gruyere and mahon on rye, with just the right amount of butter and salt and a few spices I will take to my grave."

"Gourmet grilled cheese?" said Charlie. He was stretched out on the comfort of one chaise longue while Alita and Laura lounged on the rest of the couch. Across the coffee table Brice looked half-asleep, tucked deep into the cushions with his Mets cap low over his eyes.

"You've had the rest." Dubba J smiled, setting the plates on the coffee table. "Now try the best." He took three for himself before plopping down next to Brice hard enough to rouse him.

Alita, Laura and Brice were quick to offer thanks and grab a sandwich or two for themselves — well, only Brice grabbed two — but Charlie stayed reclining where he was, staring at the mock blue sky ceiling above him.

The four diners tucked into their sandwiches, with appreciative sounds coming from Alita and Laura, and an absolute moan of pleasure from Brice.

"Eat something, Charlie," said Alita.

"I'm not hungry." And it was true, he wasn't. Though he should have been after all that exertion this morning. But his legs weren't sore, his arms weren't tired, and his stomach, it seemed, wasn't empty. "But they do smell good."

"If your coarse palate can't handle the exquisite combination of flavors," said Dubba J, "I'll understand, but at least *try* one."

"How's your hamstring?" asked Brice. His tone wasn't sharp, but still Charlie felt the older man's keen attention.

"We said we weren't going to talk about our morning until Jesse got here."

Everyone got quiet at that, as though they'd heard more in Charlie's words than he remembered saying. To distract them he sat up and took a sandwich. He wasn't sure he could take more than a bite, but still...

...that one bite convinced him he would finish the sandwich. The cheese was rich, with an undercurrent Charlie couldn't place, set off perfectly by the sharpness of the rye and accented by the butter and salt.

The silence that followed felt more companionable as they finished their sandwiches, washing them down with water (Alita and Laura), Diet Eruption Cola (Brice and Charlie), or iced tea (Dubba J).

They were just finishing the final bites when the door to Jesse's room opened.

Jesse strolled in, and Laura scoffed.

"Ungh," she said. "You're disgusting."

Whatever she saw, Charlie couldn't see. Jesse looked just the way he had this morning. Camo pants, combat boots, tan tank top. The camo shirt was gone, but otherwise nothing looked different. Except maybe the grin on his face...

"Jealous?" said Jesse. If anything his grin got wider.

"Just feeling the need for another battery of STD tests. I can't believe I ever let you touch me."

Alita was the next to scoff, but Dubba J grinned and called Jesse a dog. Brice just shook his head with a smile that might have been humor and might have been exasperation. Charlie mostly felt suspicious about the relatively short list of potential partners available, but he couldn't keep himself from glancing over at Laura. If she actually was jealous, he couldn't tell. She looked uncomfortable, like she wanted a shower.

"Couple of sandwiches keeping warm for you in the oven," said Dubba J.

Jesse retrieved them, added a glass of water, and started eating before he reached the couch. But despite a full mouth full of bread and cheese he tried to say something.

Brice cut him off.

"All right. We're all here, so why don't we talk about the events of this morning. Dubba J, you want to go first?"

Dubba J and Laura told the tale of feeling hunted in an abandoned movie studio, and how close they came to killing each other. It sounded awful for both of them, but Charlie decided it must have been worse for Laura. Dubba J seemed like himself, but Laura was more reserved than she had been this morning. Though Charlie had to admit that it might have been his imagination.

Alita went next, telling the story of how she won a poker tournament, going into more technical detail than Charlie could even hope to follow. But when she got to the end and was telling how she beat her final opponent, Brice asked a question.

"So you won by cheating?"

His words echoed for a moment as everyone turned to look at him. No sounds at all except Jesse's chewing.

"I wouldn't say I cheated," Alita said, one eyebrow high and posture defiant. "It's her job to protect her cards, and if she was more worried about her cleavage than her game—"

"You could have told her what she was doing," said Brice. "You could have not looked."

"This coming from the guy who didn't have the guts to play?" She was leaning forward on the couch now, her feet on the carpet instead of underneath her. "It's a game of skill, and handling your cards is a skill."

"I'm sorry." Brice raised his hands in surrender, though Charlie kind of agreed with him that it sounded like cheating. "I'm sorry. It's just ... here. Let me tell you about my morning and ... no. I should go last. Mine's a doozy."

"All right," said Alita. "But I wasn't cheating."

"I'll go next," said Jesse, and his tone alone was enough to make Laura roll her eyes. "I was marching through the desert, and I came to an oasis."

Jesse smiled and looked off in the distance.

"Pretty as a picture it was. Deep blue lagoon. Date palms swaying in the hot desert wind. And a big khaki canvas tent, with—"

"Let me guess," said Laura. "A brothel?"

"Nope." Jesse actually looked troubled for a moment. "It was a hospital of some sort. Wounded people convalescing on cots. IV drips. The works. Doctors and nurses in tan fatigues, but I didn't recognize their insignia, and they didn't speak any language I understood."

"Would you recognize Arabic?" said Brice. "I speak some."

"They didn't look Middle Eastern. Skin was that deep, African black that looks almost purple. Anyway, I was just settling down with some water after my long hike, when these three guys with AK-47s burst in dragging a fourth guy. Wounded. Damn near lost half his left leg and their field tourniquet was wearing through."

"Same uniforms?" said Dubba J.

"No. Theirs were almost our own military's olive drab, but cut different and again, different insignia. Anyway, the uniform difference was a problem because the men and the doctors were yelling back and forth and finally the soldiers started raising their guns."

"What did you do?" said Alita.

"Tried to talk everyone down, but no one was paying me any attention. No surprise. I probably sounded scared shitless, because God knows I was." Jesse sipped some water. "The doctors and nurses started working on the wounded guy, and one of the AK guys went out to stand watch."

Charlie wondered what he would have done, and couldn't

imagine himself interfering either. Everywhere across the world, "interfering" was the least loved kind of American.

"The soldier on watch came in a few minutes later. Incoming hostiles. All three readied their rifles, and the doctors and nurses looked terrified. I managed to glance out through the flap — it was a freaking third army. Blue uniforms and completely different insignia. When one of the doctors saw that, he pointed me to a seam in the rear of the tent and said the only word I'd understood since I got there: 'run.'"

"Did you?" said Charlie.

"I couldn't." He chuckled humorlessly and shook his head. "I mean, I should have, shouldn't I? I was beyond frightened, and I may have shot hundreds of people in action films, but in real life? Never anything but a target."

Jesse shrugged.

"But I couldn't just save my own hide and let a bunch of doctors, nurses and wounded die. I mean, aren't there rules of war against hitting hospitals?"

"Wow, you really never do watch my show," said Brice. "Rules of war don't really mean anything once the shooting starts. Maybe once in a while, but you can't count on it."

"Yeah, well, I found a Colt .45, and crouched behind a foot locker. My heart was beating faster than when I've done my own stunts. I kept thinking over and over, 'this is stupid. I'm going to die.' But I held that pistol steady and waited for the shooting to start."

"Did you have to shoot anyone?" said Brice, and Charlie was impressed at the simplicity of his tone. No judgment. No excess sympathy. Just words.

"Didn't have a chance." Jesse grinned sheepishly. "First bullet punched me in the shoulder and I dropped like a fly. Woke up on a futon in a grassy field. With Kyna. I think you guys have already guessed the rest."

"How long were you hiking?" said Charlie.

"That's your question?" said Jesse. "Not 'how was she?' Not 'was everything *compatible*?'"

"I need to know." Charlie had an idea of how long he'd been floating, but not precisely. And he was unconscious for a while. Overall, between his appearance in the water and his waking up in Kyna's room wasn't more than...

"An hour. Hour and a half maybe." Jesse shrugged. "Why?"

"I was ... floating in the ocean. Basically, treading water until I couldn't anymore. Then I started to drown. I begged Kyna to save me, and I woke up on a futon in a grassy field."

"Ewww," said Laura. "Not you too. Are guys just genetically programmed to fuck anything that spreads its legs?"

"I didn't," Charlie said over whatever rejoinder Jesse tried to voice. "I never touched her. I swear."

"You don't know what you missed then," said Jesse, "because let me tell you—"

"Please don't," said Alita, one hand raised. "What happened, Charlie?"

"Kyna didn't throw off her clothes or anything. I just ... thought I saw that look in her eye, like I've seen a few times before."

Both Dubba J and Jesse tried to say something there, but Brice shushed them.

"I told her I wasn't interested in anything more than friendship. I mean, I don't even think that's what she really looks like."

"If not, it's a damned convincing illusion," said Jesse.

"Anyway," continued Charlie, "she accepted that and I found myself back in my room."

"See Laura," said Alita, "I told you there are still good guys in the world."

A look passed between Alita and Laura that Charlie couldn't interpret, but he didn't have time to puzzle it through.

"You guys are missing part of the point though. Time-wise, I must have been in Kyna's room with her at the same time that Jesse was. If it was the same Kyna."

"Meaning what?" said Jesse, eyes narrowed in suspicion.

"Meaning either the Greenies can be in two places at once, or one of us wasn't talking to Kyna."

"Problem is," said Brice, "it could be either and we'd never know it."

"Whatever," said Jesse. "I just pulled off the ultimate Captain Kirk and none of you are going to tell me otherwise." He slapped his forehead. "I should have torn my shirt!"

"I'm actually feeling a little left out that she didn't try to seduce me too," said Dubba J.

"Maybe if Laura had shot you," said Charlie.

"Can we talk about something other than sex with aliens?" said Laura. "Because if not I'm—"

"I met the Grays," said Brice.

52

A-Day-Plus-Two. One-Oh-Three P.M. Lounge Local Time

Brice definitely had everyone's attention now. Even Laura settled back down onto her place on the couch, and the others were leaning forward intently. But Charlie looked awfully comfortable with that left leg. That little fact started connecting pieces in Brice's head, but he needed more information before he could voice them.

"Before we get to me, though," said Brice, "Charlie, you didn't explain about your leg."

"Oh, when I woke up not-dead I was fresh and clean like I'd had a good sleep and a shower. And a meal, for that matter, since I wasn't hungry either." Charlie gave Jesse a curious look. "In fact, I'm surprised you were hungry."

"I worked up an appetite."

"Let's get back to the Grays," said Laura.

"But your leg was healed?" said Brice.

"Completely," said Charlie. "Didn't even have any sore or tired muscles after all that treading water."

That made the pieces click into place. But how to tell the others?

"Dubba J," said Brice, "when you went to make sandwiches, did you look in the fridge and choose from the kinds of cheese they had there?"

"No, I just hoped they had gruyere and mahon. They're a great combination."

"And when I went for dark beer last night, that was what they had." Brice looked at the others, but he wasn't sure they were catching his point. "Seems to me that we've been getting a lot of little demonstrations of exactly what Greenie tech can do."

"So let's test that," said Charlie. He leaned over and whispered something in Laura's ear, then went into the kitchen. He returned with a plate of brownies kept fresh with cling wrap. He looked at Laura.

"He said he would see if they had any brownies."

"But you didn't say it out loud," said Brice, "to minimize the chances of their hearing you."

"You think they can't hear us whisper?" said Jesse, taking a brownie.

"Moot point," said Dubba J. "I didn't announce the kinds of cheese I wanted, but neither of those were in the fridge last night."

"We already know the Greenie tech's supposed to be amazing," said Alita. "Tell us about the Grays."

"I will. I just want us all to be clear of what evidence we've seen of what the Greenies can do. *Let it go, Jesse.* That kitchen isn't just stocked, it has whatever we're looking for. And from what happened to Charlie and Jesse, even bi-location is on the table as a possibility. We're all agreed?"

Everyone nodded, though some with more enthusiasm and others with more curiosity.

"Their tech is subtle too," said Charlie. "No one's been cleaning our rooms, but I'm betting yours are all as spotless as mine. And there's no linen closet, but my towels and washcloths are always fresh. *And where the hell are the lights in this room?* Everything's clear, but nothing has a shadow."

Charlie held one hand just above the other and both hands were perfectly, gently illuminated.

"All right," said Brice, "I think Charlie's observations finish the main point here. They've been showing us their tech without drawing our attention to it, to start giving us some idea of what we can look forward to. We need to keep that in mind, because another player's entered the game."

Brice looked around at the other five again to make sure he had their attention. Then he told them about the wheat field and the crop circle and the Gray. Then about his talk with Mynack after he left the poker room down an interminable hallway.

"That was why I asked you about cheating," Brice said to Alita. "Willingness to cheat might have been the test."

"Or it might have been *your* test," Alita said, pointing at him for emphasis. "We have no reason to assume we got the same test just because we were sent to the same place."

Laura and Dubba J looked at each other, but didn't say anything. They didn't have to. Brice was pretty sure they'd been given the same test in the same place, so if lying was the point of his and Alita's test, she might not have passed.

"What were you thinking?" said Jesse. "Telling the Greenies about the Grays."

"If he hadn't," said Charlie, "he would have told them right now. Better to be clear and up front."

"Wait," said Laura, holding up both hands. "Wouldn't the Grays know that? Why would they think they could keep it a secret?"

"They might not have tried to," said Brice with a sigh. "I've been thinking about this a lot since I got back, and it seems to me that the Grays knew the Greenies would figure out a) that my teleport had been interrupted, and b) by whom. So secrecy couldn't have been the issue. The issue had to have been whether we would choose the Greenies or the Grays, because it may just be the case that they can't interfere with our choice."

"What exactly is the choice?" Charlie shrugged helplessly. "The Grays have already been dealing with our governments for years. And the Greenies, they never actually asked if we want their help, just whether or not we were good enough to receive it."

That thought seemed to unsettle everyone into silence.

"That's as may be," said Brice. "But here's the situation as we know it. The Grays are already here and working with our governments. The Greenies want to circumvent the government and bring their aid straight to the people. And if we're going to go any further, I think we need to decide right now which way we want to go."

"Fuck the Man," said Dubba J. "Governments always favor the rich and privileged. If Greenie tech will make sure everyone eats, has shelter, and equal access to medicine I'll fuck Kyna *and* Mynack to make it happen."

"I still say it sounds like an invasion force," said Jesse. "They'll have to be down here on the planet with us, living with us and enforcing their system of 'distribution'" He accented that word with finger quotes. "In other words, they make up the rules and we have to follow them. Conquered by aliens without a shot fired. At least with the Grays we're still our own people."

"Charlie?" said Brice.

Charlie furrowed his brow and let out a slow sigh. "I don't know yet."

Jesse started to speak, but Brice cut him off. "Fair enough. We'll come back to you. Laura?"

"The Grays performed medical experiments on us. The Greenies have been putting us through psychological torture that the Geneva Convention would condemn."

She ran her fingers through her hair and straightened her posture as she thought, head tilting at an angle that showed off her cheekbones and throat. Brice wondered if she even knew she'd done it.

"The Grays say they're done with their testing," she said finally. "The Greenies aren't, and I, for one, don't want to endure any more of it. So I say Grays."

"How do we know that drone technology didn't come from the Grays?" said Alita. "I mean, from what you were saying, Brice, most of our biggest tech advances since the 50s can be traced back to the Grays. Yeah, the internet and modern computers are awesome, but have things improved for the human race in that time? Or have we just had faster and more effective ways of abusing each other?"

Alita shook her head. "I vote Greenies. I may hate their tests, but the improved food processing, recycling and so forth sound a lot better to me than newer, better drones."

Brice sighed.

"I'm not exactly the biggest historian in the world," he said, "but there's a trend that dates back hundreds or thousands of years and if there's ever been a major exception, I haven't heard of it."

Brice looked around at the others, then realized it was his television pause and gave them a chagrined shrug.

"Those who have power will fight to keep it. They won't just hand it back. And secret power? Well, there's a reason we fear secret societies — the only thing worse than people holding power over us is finding out that power is held by some secret cabal with no answering body."

"Who watches the watchmen?" said Laura.

"Exactly." Brice shook his head. "I don't like the Greenies. I don't like the front they're showing us, and I don't like the tests we've been given. Though, to be honest, I think I've gotten off lightest. Maybe because I'm the oldest. I don't know."

"And you'll never know," said Charlie, "because they won't answer questions about the tests."

"Exactly. More secrecy." Brice shook his head harder. "But the Grays, that secret is entrenched and our government has a whole hidden branch devoted to preserving it. Just for finding out about them, the men in black will be watching my communications for the rest of my life."

Brice suddenly looked up at the others.

"You guys too. I just realized that. They'll assume I told you, especially once I ditched their bug."

"I find it best to assume the government is always listening," said Dubba J. "That way I won't be shocked when I find out they are."

"More secrecy," Brice said. "More secret power. No. I can't support the Grays handing over more to our governments, when they've already shown us how they'll use it. So I guess I vote Greenie."

Brice looked over at Charlie. "So I guess it's up to you. If you vote Greenie, we have a majority. If you vote Gray, we have to debate this more."

"No," said Charlie, standing up, knees jittery. "No. We can't do it that way."

"Voting's the American way," said Jesse. "And since we have six people, any majority is a two-thirds majority by definition."

"When the Colonies voted for independence," said Brice, realization dawning, "it had to be unanimous. Is that what you're saying?"

"You said the Grays needed all six of us to try to contact them." Charlie shook his index finger like he had a point at the end of it he needed to shake off. "I think they need it to be unanimous. And it makes sense. If *six* human beings can't come together on a decision, what chance do we really have as a people?"

"All right then," said Brice with a sigh. "Robert's Rules of Order. I'll act as chair to moderate. The issue before us is which alien race we want to work with. To start, I'll—"

"No," said Charlie.

"You don't have the floor," said Jesse.

"*No*," said Charlie again. "No simple rhetoric. No public pressure. We've all heard what each other has to say."

"We haven't heard from you yet," said Laura.

"I haven't decided. And I don't want to be pressured into making a snap decision."

"All right," said Brice. "We'll adjourn to our chambers ... sorry. We'll go back to our rooms to think. One person at a time can approach another to discuss this. No ganging up. No pressure. All right? We'll get together again in the morning and vote."

Everyone nodded, though Charlie was the only one who looked eager about it. No, eager wasn't quite the right word. Charlie looked troubled. Nervous. But Brice understood that. This was the biggest decision the boy had ever made. Possibly the biggest decision ever made in the history of the human race.

Rushing into it would be a bad move. Though Brice had to admit, rushing into it sounded very human indeed.

53

Charlie lay flopped on the maroon couch in his suite's sitting room, staring at the textured beige ceiling and waiting for the inevitable knock to come. He was thirsty, and his stomach kept telling him that what he needed most in this world right now was a glass of milk and two brownies.

No way he was leaving his room right now though. He wouldn't dare venture forth until both sides had sent their emissaries to persuade him to their point of view.

That would be a problem. Because Charlie was not feeling very well-disposed toward either of the two alien races right then, but he had a pretty good notion that abstaining would not be an acceptable vote option.

He needed to think. He thought best while writing, but the one thing the Greenies hadn't provided him was a computer. Sure, he could probably have dug up a pen and paper somewhere, but for Charlie typing would have been better. Some of his most popular essays had been written in thirty minutes of frenzied typing as his fingers tried to keep up with his brain.

Handwriting just didn't work for him the same way.

So Charlie defaulted to his old system, the one that went back to just about the onset of puberty — staring at the ceiling and listening to music.

He hadn't been able to find an .mp3 player or any CDs, but he did eventually find music stations on the television channels. Two dozen channels, but nowhere he could just pick an album or an artist and leave them on repeat. So far he'd tried the blues, R&B, and classic rock, and all had failed to become the kind of wallpaper that really let his mind wander.

So it was time to bring out the big guns: classical.

Charlie was just browsing through the channels for a good classical station when someone knocked on his door. He turned off the television and dragged himself to his feet. Best not to prolong this.

When he opened the door, Dubba J was waiting on the other side, big smile on his face.

"How can you smile about this?" said Charlie, stepping aside and gesturing him in. "This is like voting in the worst presidential race ever, with ... with ... with nuclear war hanging over our heads."

Dubba J snickered and sat in the big maroon chair, elbows on his wide-spread knees. "Are you kidding me? I get a vote in this race. A full sixth of the decision in the hands of one brother." He rubbed his hands together. "I bet whole states are pissing themselves in fear about what this black man might do."

Charlie couldn't tell if it was the words or the tone that made him chuckle.

"And that's kind of the point I want to make here. Leaving aside for the moment your unfortunate European heritage, you and I have more in common with each other than either of us do with the others. To whit — we ain't rich."

"I thought your family—"

"My family comes from that endangered species known as the middle class, and I'm betting yours does too."

Charlie nodded.

"Which means that we are not part of the class that's going to benefit from whatever the Grays can give us. That'll be the one percent. Maybe the one percent of the one percent." Dubba J pointed at Charlie. "And you know this."

"Well, yeah, *our* government has problems it's a long way from solving, but as these advances leak into other countries…"

Dubba J laughed hard enough to bounce his dreads around his shoulders. Loud and sudden, the sound knocked Charlie's line of thought right out of his head, rather than dragging him along into its hilarity.

"Other countries are no better." Dubba J frowned. "Well, some are, but most of them are just as bad as ours, or thereabouts. And the ones that are worse are ones we wouldn't want to be compared to anyway."

"Still—"

"Still nothing." Dubba J smacked his palms on his knees. "America damn near invented the Internet, but we're probably fifteenth in percentage of people with broadband. Maybe worse. Our roads are crap. Our bridges rusted. And don't get me started on dams and levees. The United States doesn't care about infrastructure. And in case you missed the memo, 'infrastructure' is just another word for the common people."

Charlie was reeling now. The sheer passion behind Dubba J's tirade was overwhelming. He needed a moment just to swallow, let alone respond.

"So you're saying we need the Greenies."

"I'm saying people the world over are freezing in the winter, sweltering in the summer, and starving year-round. Go to any city or — hell — any town or village, and you'll find people who need medical help who aren't getting it. People who don't even have a bed to lie on or a roof over their heads. Vote with the Grays and that won't change. Vote with the Greenies and it will."

"I hadn't thought of it that way."

A smile touched the edges of Dubba J's lips though it never really formed. But the look in his eyes wasn't humor. If anything, he looked a little sad.

"Of course not. You never had to." He stood up. "I'll let you think now. I gotta go talk to Jesse."

Charlie watched Dubba J walk out the door, waving when Dubba J smiled before closing it behind him.

Charlie sighed. Dubba J made some very good points.

But something bothered Charlie about the Greenies. Something he couldn't quite put a finger on...

54

Charlie sat on his couch and stared at the lone remaining brownie on his plate, surrounded as it was by the crumbs of its fellows. Rich, moist, everything it was supposed to be. It tempted him to devour it in two bites as he had its two brothers.

Not more than a few minutes after Dubba J had left, Charlie decided there was no way he could do this kind of heavy thinking without chocolate. He snuck out into the lounge for three brownies and a tall glass of milk.

The milk was gone now. As were two of the brownies. The last one, well, rich as it was, eating it without something to wash it down would not have been his choice.

But did he want to brave the lounge for more milk? Any minute now, someone — probably Laura, he hoped it would be Laura — would come to try to explain to Charlie why the Grays were the right way to vote.

Charlie wasn't sure about that. Dubba J had been pretty darn convincing. But Charlie still didn't quite trust the Greenies either, and he knew that hearing out both sides without his mind made up was the right way to go.

And right now, thinking about that brownie was a lot more distracting than just about anything else Charlie could think of.

He picked up the glass and started for his suite's bathroom.

Someone knocked on the door.

Charlie sighed and set down his glass. But he was smiling when he opened the door to find…

…Jesse.

"Sorry," said Jesse. "I'm sure you were hoping for *someone else*, but Laura and Alita have been locked up in Laura's room arguing pretty much since the group split up."

Charlie stepped aside and let Jesse in. Jesse started talking even before he perched on the edge of the chair's cushion.

"Just as well that it's me, really. There's something else I wanted to talk to you about. But that can wait until we tackle the business at hand. Agreed?"

"Sure," said Charlie, who found himself mirroring the way Jesse sat and forced himself to ease back and cross his legs.

"Charlie, I'm all for equality. I'm a firm believer in giving everyone free and safe access to the same basic resources needed for life. And goodness knows I spend a lot of my time campaigning for better recycling."

"I hear a 'but' coming."

Jesse smiled. "Sorry. I was pontificating, wasn't I? It's an occupational hazard. You'd be amazed how many speeches Laura and I have to give on an annual basis."

He brushed off his chest as though dusting a suit instead of a tan tank top.

"But here's the thing. For all the talk about 'distribution,' not one of us really knows how the Greenies work. Mynack keeps promising that *everyone* will get access as they ease in their technologies."

"You have to admit, that does seem like the only way to make sure humans don't fuck it up."

"But that's just it. There's no way they can do this without fundamentally changing the underpinnings of our societies. The social structure would begin and end with them. The Greenie way of doing things. And you remember what Brice said about power?"

"Yeah, that people don't give power up once they've got it."

"Well, once those Greenies are situated all over the planet with the power to decide who gets their tech, what makes you think they'll give it up?" Jesse clapped his hands together and said, "There you go, humans. There are all the things we've promised you. Now we'll just get back on our spaceships and leave you in peace."

"Well, they did say that was what they'd—"

"And if they just one day announced they were done and leaving? How do you think people would react?"

Charlie thought about that. "People won't want them to go."

"*Exactly*. We'll be like housecats, turning to them for our next meal and expecting them to clean our litter box. We may strut around and pretend we're fierce hunters like our ancestors, but we'll never actually hunt anything more dangerous than a moving dot of light. And the minute something scary happens? We'll go running to them. Forever. Is that what you want?"

"But with the Grays—"

"With the Grays we get the tech and handle it ourselves. Yeah, it's going to our governments, and yeah, I get it, our governments have problems. But damn it, they're *our* problems. We made them ourselves, and we'll clean them up ourselves. And we'll have a whole lot of fancy tech to help us do it."

Charlie had to look away from Jesse's charisma, and the moment he did Jesse shook himself and sat back on the chair.

"Sorry if I got kind of intense there. It's just that this is a big decision and I don't want to see us fuck it up."

"Here's the thing though," said Charlie, gazing at the black screen of his currently-off television. "All these tech advances, but are we ready for them sociologically? Can we, as a people, handle them? What if we *need* the guidance of—"

"Of a non-human psyche? Are you saying we should try to adapt to a completely alien psychology and sociology? Because that's what we'll get with the Greenies, following their rules and doing things their way."

Jesse looked around the sitting room.

"We've seen what their rules are like. Is this how you want to live your life?"

"This is the testing though. It's not what things would be like if we worked with the Greenies full time."

"You sure about that?" Jesse stood up. "Are you absolutely sure about that? Because if you vote for the Greenies tomorrow, you better be."

Charlie wasn't sure what to say then, and Jesse moved over to the door. He paused with his hand on the doorknob and sighed. Charlie was about to ask what was wrong when Jesse turned back and gave him a look that wasn't intense at all. If anything, there was a touch of pity to it.

"Look," he said. "I hate to bring this up when we already have weighty decisions on our shoulders, but this may be the only time I can talk to you alone without drawing attention."

Jesse's nostrils flared in a deep breath.

"Do yourself a favor. Forget Laura."

The reflexive protest didn't make it past Charlie's lips before Jesse held up a hand to still him.

"Don't bother. We can all tell. I think Alita's even on your side, though she should know better. *Let me talk.*"

Jesse gazed hard at the restless Charlie until he stilled in his place on the couch and nodded.

"This isn't a jealous ex- talking. This is a guy who likes you enough that he doesn't want to see you get hurt. What you imagine with Laura right now isn't what you're going to get. Imagine getting your picture taken everywhere you go and every one of those pictures getting plastered all over the Internet. Imagine guys hitting on your girlfriend right in front of you. Hot guys who make you self-conscious about your looks. A never-ending stream of them. Guys sneering at you and talking shit about you — threatening you even — just because you're with her. Your clients won't be immune to this either.

They'll want to meet her, or have her sign a dozen things, or have her appear at their kid's party. And they'll pressure *you* to make it happen."

Charlie wanted to object, to stop Jesse's words, but a cold knot in his stomach made him sit still and listen.

"Yeah, there are the upsides. She's so beautiful even I ache sometimes when I look at her. And when her attention is focused on you you'll feel like the most important man in the world. But how are you going to feel when she's away for weeks at a time on a shoot? When her co-star is someone like me? When she has to do love scenes with that co-star? When the tabloids see them at lunch and claim they're hooking up? Will you trust her or confront her or bury your head in the sand? And what are you going to do when she has a bout of insecurity about her looks or her talent? Or when she has panic attacks about her past? Or her future?"

Jesse let out one more slow sigh and looked around the suite again.

"When we get back from all this, you're going to get your fifteen minutes. Use them. Find the girl of your dreams, some hottie who shares your interests and doesn't keep a high profile. Don't waste this chance chasing a fantasy."

Jesse turned and left without another word.

Charlie stared at the last brownie on his plate, but he'd lost his appetite.

55

A-DAY-PLUS-THREE. SEVEN-FORTY-SEVEN A.M. LOUNGE LOCAL TIME

Brice stared at himself in his closet mirror. Adjusted the red tie with silver stripes. Smoothed his hands down the crisp white shirt that smelled dry-cleaner fresh. The shirt had perfect creases. His gray-blue slacks were a light wool that he knew from experience would stand up to the hot lights of his show. This was the same kind of suit he wore on the air. Double-stitched. Italian cut. Expensive. Most days he thought of it as "the monkey suit" or his "business clothes."

Right now it was armor.

He slipped on the matching jacket and buttoned the single button. His black leather shoes gleamed while his black leather belt was simple enough to not draw attention.

He dusted off his shoulders, though they didn't need it. He had to do something though, to quell the trembling of nerves in his stomach. Besides. He didn't look quite right for the show. That would have required makeup, and a stylist to make his graying hair behave in ways he could never get from it.

But this would have to do. Someone had to moderate this mess and get these people to agree on a course of action. And Brice

DePaul, host of *Weeknightly with Brice DePaul*, had a much better shot than the sloppy Mets fan he'd been around the others for the last couple of days.

He checked his breath. Mint toothpaste fresh.

"Deep breath, Brice," he encouraged himself. "Nothing to this game."

He inhaled until he felt as though he'd filled every part of his body with air, leaning back, tilting his head back, and sweeping his arms out wide as he did. He held that breath for a three-count, then exhaled just as smoothly, letting his body lean forward until his fingers brushed the thick carpet and his head dangled and his body felt entirely empty of air.

Then he did it again. And one more time for good measure. He shook his jaw back and forth, then waggled his tongue all around, then said "wow" over and over moving his lips as much as possible.

Finally he completed his private ritual with the words his mentor Kerry Dearborn said to him before his first show: "Knock 'em dead, kid."

Brice turned and strutted through his elaborate suite to the door to the main room. He knew he had his work cut out for him. Two hours yesterday trying to moderate between Laura and Alita had accomplished nothing. Two more of his own arguing with Jesse about priorities and solving society's problems and the role of aliens and alien technology in both.

So far as Brice could tell, not one member of this "committee" had shifted his or her opinion a single iota. Not even Charlie, whom both Dubba J and Jesse believed they'd persuaded to their side. Which meant neither was right.

Someone had to take charge. No. That wasn't quite right. Someone had to be the adult here. And as far as Brice could tell, he was the only one in a position to do it.

He opened the door to the main room and found the cafeteria. Disappointment edged at him. For some reason he'd expected the Greenies to do something special for today. They had to know that today was the day that this "committee" had to choose.

Brice stopped two steps onto the bronze-veined white marble floor. What if the Greenies didn't know? Or rather, didn't care? What if they planned to just continue the tests as normal? How would that change everyone's position?

Brice snorted. Didn't matter. The Greenies didn't take them until after breakfast, more or less, and by then he hoped to reach a consensus.

And while he was wishing, he wanted an all-expense-paid trip around the world with Laetitia to celebrate his coming retirement.

At the breakfast buffet he filled his plate with scrambled eggs with extra shredded cheddar, plenty of bacon, and just enough fruit that he'd be able to tell Laetitia he ate fruit with breakfast. He smiled as he spooned pineapple, kiwi and Crenshaw melon onto his plate. Laetitia wouldn't be fooled for a minute. She knew how he ate when she wasn't around.

Still, that was a good thing. If she would have believed him, the lie wouldn't have been fun.

He filled a glass with orange juice, but when it came time to sit at the table, he set his place at the head. Might as well get things started in the right direction.

By eight o'clock the others had started filing in, all in the sort of casual clothes that they could wear whether the Greenies sent them off to work at computers or run through the woods. Jeans, sneakers, and cotton shirts with short sleeves, and from the look of things, sports bras for the women.

"Expecting a camera crew?" Jesse asked Brice once everyone was seated.

Brice picked up his empty water glass and tapped its base against the teak table like a gavel.

"I hereby call this meeting of the Alien Committee to order. We may be pressed for time by our hosts, and so we will dispense with the reading of the minutes and open the floor to discussion. As this is a breakfast meeting, we will forego the need to stand while you have the floor, and you may all continue to eat while we discuss the matter at hand. Questions?"

Brice swept his eyes across the other five, and to his shock they were playing along. Eating, yes, but paying attention. He forged ahead.

"This committee was originally assembled to prove the human race fit for an alliance with the aliens known to us as the Greenies, which alliance represents a boon to our race in technological and environmental gains. However, the aliens known to us as the Grays have contacted us offering a similar alliance, though with different terms. Either way, humanity stands to benefit, and the issue before this committee is to determine which alliance would benefit the human race the most. The chair will now hear arguments."

Alita and Laura both raised their hands, but Alita was a little faster.

"The chair recognizes Alita Luna."

"I grew up in a small town in Colombia. And let me tell you, whatever deal the Grays have with our governments, their advances are not 'trickling down' beyond the superpowers. Travel outside of the United States and you can see poverty that makes our housing projects look like palaces. The system the Grays have in place for distribution helps only the rich and powerful. The people who really need assistance get only what they already have. Nothing. The Greenies will change that. We need their help."

"Thank you, Delegate Luna. The chair recognizes Laura Jefferson."

"What exactly is the Greenie idea of help? We don't really know. The last time we asked Mynack, he made Brice answer for him, and then only nodded. He never actually said, 'yes, Brice has it right.' How can you take someone's word when they don't give it? We can't get anything like specific answers out of him, and Kyna is even more tight-lipped. If we go with the Greenies, we're taking a whole lot on faith."

Laura shook her head, and with her hair tied back her thick ponytail whipped back and forth.

"The current deal with the Grays is not ideal," she continued. "But they've shown they can work with us. For all we know, they'll let us change the terms. Find a path more equitable than the current system. And we know they're reliable because the United States has been dealing with them through decades of presidents and cabinets, from both our political parties. And anyone that can work with *both* the Democrats and Republicans is someone who can be very reasonable. We're better off with the Grays."

Back and forth the arguments went, Jesse and Laura on one side, and Alita and Dubba J on the other. Neither seeming to yield to the arguments of the other, and Charlie not saying a word while the arguments got more heated, and Brice was finally obliged to use his water-glass-gavel to keep order.

It was just after one such occasion that he said, "There's still one delegate we haven't heard from, and the chair does not wish to see his opinion lost behind the charisma of the other delegates. The chair recognizes Charlie Evans."

Everyone turned and looked at Charlie. He swallowed visibly, and Brice felt a knot of guilt in his stomach for putting the boy on the spot.

Finally Charlie sucked in a deep breath, and said, "I think we should say no to both of them."

Charlie actually took a bite of his bacon then, as though he felt saying that was sufficient. Brice wasn't having it.

"The chair asks Delegate Evans to elaborate."

Charlie guzzled some water, then cleared his throat.

"The problem is you're both right. The wealth gap is worse today than at any time in history. I can't believe that the controlled distribution of Gray technology — and the advances we've probably made of our own based on it — aren't responsible for that. That has to stop. But the Greenie answer, that has its problems too. If they come down to earth and start saying who gets what when, well, that pretty much means they're in charge and we're their subjects. In fact, if not in name."

Brice could feel a smile try to work its way onto his lips and fought it down like a crude joke coming to mind during an interview with a sitting President.

"Both options kind of suck for the human race, but who says we need them? Sure, they're telling us that, but why should we believe *them*? We evolved out of apes without their help. Built up whole civilizations, conquered the seas, conquered the skies. And we're supposed to believe what? We've hit our ceiling? We'll never get off this rock without outside help?"

Charlie slammed his fist down on the table hard enough to startle everyone, including himself. But he continued.

"Fuck their shortcuts. The price tag is too high. We're human beings. We can do it ourselves."

Against Robert's Rules of Order Brice started a slow clap, but Dubba J said, "Fuck yes!" and went straight to a standing ovation. The others joined, and Charlie's face turned so red it looked ready to pop.

"Is that your group's final decision?" said Mynack, appearing at the far end of the table from Brice.

"One moment," said Brice, tapping his water-glass-gavel for order. "The chair calls the question. Delegate Evans has proposed that this committee decline the current offers of alliance from both the Greenies and the Grays. All in favor, say aye."

To Brice's amazement, everyone agreed: aye.

"I'm sorry, Mynack," said Brice, "but while we appreciate the offer of advancements, we are unwilling to yield our sovereignty and identity as a people to get them."

Mynack smiled. "Congratulations, you just passed the test."

56

"What?" Charlie stared slack-jawed at Mynack, while the others at the table all made sounds as shocked as his own.

But Mynack was smiling. And instead of patience in his yellow eyes Charlie saw something that looked like pleasure. Kyna appeared next to Mynack now, with an absolute grin on her face and orange eyes shining.

"The tests," Mynack said, "are not kind. I apologize for that. They are never the same for any two societies, but they have a common element. They place the chosen representatives under intense pressure. Force them to make choices they don't like. How you handle them shows us who you are beyond anything we could determine from simple interviews."

"When we deal with people who aren't ready," said Kyna, "they can't hide that during the tests. Their true nature comes out."

"Which reminds me, Laura Jefferson," said Mynack. "The man from your past is currently incarcerated. He was caught for the same crime two years ago, charged with multiple counts, convicted, and stands to serve a long sentence."

Laura narrowed her eyes at Mynack, but nodded with something like satisfaction.

"Point of order," said Brice, but Charlie got there first.

"But we said no."

"No," said Mynack, still smiling, "you declined an offer that would have had us sending many of our people down to your planet for decades. An offer that, as you put it, would have robbed your entire race of its sovereignty and identity. Well put, by the way."

"Thanks," said Brice. "There is a reason I have a talk show."

"So now let us give you our counteroffer. Which is, in fact, the only offer that would result in your getting our help."

"You six work with us," said Kyna. "We help you examine the state of your planet and resources and together we agree on the priorities and timelines."

"But distribution," continued Mynack, "we leave to you."

"You mean us humans?" said Charlie.

"I mean you six."

A hush fell over the table, but Laura broke it.

"We could form an international nonprofit." She glanced around at the other five. "With our contacts we could raise the money like *that*." She snapped her fingers. "And we even have someone here at the table who can write the promotional material."

Laura smiled at Charlie, and he felt heat rise up his neck and cheeks.

"All right," said Brice, "I'll bite. But there are six of us, and a board of directors should have an odd number to break tie votes."

Kyna cleared her throat.

"While we have no interest in undermining your identity or sovereignty, we do need a say in how things go, to make sure the priorities we agree to stay in focus. We're not going to just give you technological advancements and instruction and walk away."

"Perfect then," said Laura. "There's our tiebreaker."

"You?" said Jesse, looking at Kyna.

"Me," she confirmed. "But don't worry, I don't have any personal expectations of you, Jesse."

Charlie wasn't sure, but the set to Jesse's mouth and eyes then looked somewhere between disappointed and moderately insulted.

"I already see one problem though," said Alita. "People are going to try to interfere and redirect the benefits. Governments, corporations, strongmen, anybody with guns..."

"We will make it very clear," said Mynack, "that at the first sign of interference the aid will vanish."

"That'll help, but it won't be enough," said Brice. "They'll infiltrate our volunteers. Bribes, theft, all those tools of corruption will come out full-force."

"No, they won't," said Charlie, feeling a smile stretch broadly on his face. "Not when the alien tech is probably easily traced by other alien tech. And as for guns? Who's going to believe that the Greenies aren't packing lasers or blasters or phasers or something along those lines?"

"The details," said Mynack, "we can begin to work out with you. But only if we have a deal."

Brice tapped his water-glass-gavel on the table again.

"Let the committee vote," he said. "The proposal before us is this: shall we, representing the human race, agree to an alliance with the alien race we know as the Greenies? The terms of this alliance are that the Greenies shall aid us in technological advancement, both directly and through education, the distribution of which shall be determined jointly between the Greenies and this committee, and handled largely by the human race."

Brice made such a show of drawing breath that Dubba J smiled and Charlie chuckled. But then a thought occurred to him.

"Wait!" said Charlie. When he had everyone's attention, he said, "I hate to bring this up, but we gave the Greenies a chance to modify their offer. Do we owe it to the Grays to give them the same chance?"

"About that," said Kyna. When Charlie looked up at her, she said, "That was one of us, I'm afraid, in the wheat field with Brice. You see, right now the Grays are in touch with your governments, trying to make a bargain that would keep us out."

"They've hated us," said Mynack, "ever since we helped them reach the stars."

"We couldn't just tell you that," said Kyna, "though we felt that we should let you know you had another offer. But coming from Mynack or me it wouldn't have sounded believable. So one of our people made the offer to you on their behalf. And if the six of you had tried to contact the Grays the way we suggested, it would have worked. They would have come and you'd be dealing with them instead of us."

"Honestly, though," said Mynack with a sad shake of his head, "they were one of our early mistakes. They'll still just as selfish and capricious as the day we found them. Whatever arrangement you agreed to with them would not have lasted."

"Do we have to worry about them?" said Charlie.

"No," said Mynack. "They won't touch a planet we're helping."

"All right then," said Brice. "All in favor of forming this alliance under the new terms signify by saying 'aye.'"

"Aye," said Charlie, loud and strong, in a voice that was echoed by everyone else at the table.

"Motion carried!" said Brice, tapping his water-glass-gavel.

PART V

RETURNING VICTORIOUS

57

Brice had given talks and speeches at many places over the years. It started with his stand-up work in small clubs and dives and continued on to venues that could seat a hundred or more. Most comedians didn't look at their routines as talks or speeches, but deep down Brice always thought of them that way. He would stand in the spotlight and deliver a speech, albeit one intended to make people laugh rather than impart information.

And once he had his talk show, the opportunities came from all directions. He spoke at town halls and gave talks to organizations. He even donned a cap and gown to deliver commencement addresses at universities. Not to mention the huge public rallies for one cause or another.

Talking in public to large groups might have been one of the major fears of the modern American, but for Brice it was business as usual.

Today, however, was different.

Today, Brice had to address the United Nations in their general assembly hall.

The hall was a cavernous round room, done up in warm wood

tones with a gold backdrop behind the speakers and the symbol of the United Nations perched above the stage like an all-seeing eye. Hundreds of seats in the room itself, and tiers of windows where even more people would be listening in. The translators worked up there, if Brice recalled correctly.

But the seats in the room itself would be filled by hundreds of delegates from around the world. Proud, accomplished men and women, some of whom would be furious at what he had to say. And that was a problem he couldn't ignore. After all, if the United Nations got together and told the Greenies to take off, what could Brice do about it?

The international press would be here too. Everything he, Dubba J, and Kyna had to say would be simulcast live all over the world, broadcast over both television and radio, and streamed over the Internet.

Brice wouldn't just be addressing the delegates. He would be addressing the whole world. And the way the media had hyped the event, more than two billion people were expected to be listening. Hanging on his every word.

Two. Billion. People.

Air conditioning kept the building chilly, but Brice was sweating anyway where he stood backstage. The four of them waited in a small office room with a meeting table and a half-dozen roller chairs. It also had a mini-fridge filled with bottles of water, but Brice knew his stomach would refuse any.

He checked his tie again, powder blue and straight as far as he could tell. He turned to Laetitia, beautiful as always and resplendent in her white pantsuit.

"Is my tie straight? It doesn't feel straight."

"It's fine," she said, and ran her hands down the lapels of his navy blue suit. "You look impressive. They'll listen to you."

Brice gave her a fond smile. Teesh had been so excited when he told her the plan. Of course, that was about ten hours after he got back, because the two of them had a lot of time to make up, and then he couldn't tell her the resolution without telling her everything he had to go through to get to it.

And he told her everything, just as he had promised.

Her response? "Sounds like the perfect retirement job for you. And there *better* be a role for me."

With her organizational skills? She'd be a gift from heaven.

"I'm going second, right?" said Dubba J, interrupting the private moment. "You're not making me go first."

Brice clapped Dubba J on the shoulder. The kid looked on the verge of throwing up his lunch. Brice had warned him about lasagna before a speech. He'd dressed to impress though. Dubba J could have modeled for Brooks Brothers in that blue-gray suit. Even tied back his dreads for the occasion.

"Don't worry," said Brice. "I'll lead things off. Tell them about the committee, a little about the tests — no details, don't worry — and about the arrangement we came to with the Greenies. Then you come on and explain how the committee will work, and say just enough about implementation to reassure them that humans will be in charge, and that we'll start by focusing on stabilizing the poorer regions of the planet first."

"Then it's my turn," said Kyna, stepping up. She still wore that silver spacesuit with the knee-high boots that left her arms and thighs bare. But she was an alien. She could get away with it. "I tell them how we'll be working with the committee to guide it, and to protect the implementation, to make sure *all* the aid goes exactly where it's supposed to."

"Then I step back up and answer questions," said Brice. "Or at least, I'll do my best."

"What if they say no?" said Dubba J, but that was just his nerves talking. Brice understood the urge. Go over and over the things he already knew to make sure they were cemented in his head and ease his fears.

"Any country who refuses aid doesn't have to take it. But once one country does, just one, others will follow. And still more when the results start showing up online."

"Usually there are a few holdouts in the early days," said Kyna. "But in the end, everyone wants the benefits too much to let suspicion rule the day."

The crowd began to gather. Aides and techs started bustling about backstage, kids who didn't look old enough to Brice to have graduated high school, but had to have been at least college age. All races, and all of them, boys and girls, wearing the same uniform black suits with headsets.

"They dress like that every day?" asked Dubba J.

"I think this is a special occasion," said Brice. "I'm pretty sure at least the techs don't have to wear suits most days. That would be un-American."

As seats filled, Brice's nerves amped up. He got jittery in the knees and he didn't seem to know what to do with his hands. Every way he held them was wrong. He finally settled for holding them behind his back, one hand gripping the other wrist, while he tried to look sagely.

Laetitia blew the moment by sticking her tongue out at him.

Brice started laughing. Then Dubba J — who'd been growing more and more restless as Brice did — started laughing too and the tension just bled out of Brice.

He was smiling when they called him up to the podium, and the right words came easily. He didn't even get heckled, which made the speech better than most of his standup gigs, and more than a few of his public talks.

And for all his pre-show jitters, Dubba J took to the podium like a Frenzy!Video camera, voice smooth and earnest as he played his part.

Kyna handled her turn like she'd done the same thing many times, which she probably had.

When the applause came at the end, not every country joined in. But at least twenty nations did, and that was a start.

Brice was just sweeping Laetitia up in a celebratory hug backstage when a clearing throat interrupted the excited chatter of Dubba J to Kyna.

"Mr. DePaul, may I have a moment of your time?"

Brice reluctantly released his wife and turned to see two men in black. Talky and Walky, from his little meeting before the tests all began.

"Anything you have to say to me," Brice said, "you can say in front of them."

"I'm not altogether certain I agree." Talky gazed meaningfully at Kyna, while Walky loomed behind him. "My words are intended only for citizens of the United States, and although Ms. Kyna has been accorded the position of a foreign dignitary, she is not, in fact, a citizen."

"Your agency doesn't officially exist," said Brice, "and you threatened me the last time we spoke. I'll feel much more comfortable if Kyna stays."

"He threatened you?" said Laetitia, narrowing her eyes.

"Typical," said Dubba J.

"If Brice feels threatened," said Kyna, "then I think it best if I remain. But if it makes you feel better, you may speak in hushed voices across the room."

All the humor and pleasantness drained out of Kyna's blood orange eyes. Brice felt a chill run down his spine.

"But rest assured, gentlemen," she said, "I can defend him as easily from there."

Brice smiled as though he hadn't been creeped out by that moment, and gestured the men in black to join him in the corner. Laetitia and Dubba J flanked Brice in a show of support.

"I didn't want this to be an unpleasant conversation," said Talky, "but since it seems it can't be anything else. I want you to realize that right now you, Mr. DePaul, and you, Mr. Whitehead, could both be charged with treason."

"Treason?" said Brice while Dubba J laughed.

"Not just you two either. Laura Jefferson, Jesse Carter, and Charlie Evans as well. Alita Luna isn't a citizen, but I assure you the charges she could face would be no more pleasant."

"How do you—"

"Each of you was asked to assist the United States government in dealing with the alien situation. Each of you agreed, then reneged on that agreement, and formed a cabal that struck a deal with a foreign power that undermines the United States in its powers and roles both foreign and domestic."

"*It was the government that insisted we do this. You even threatened me.*"

"And once there you failed and refused to comply with your orders."

"If we didn't get rid of your bugs, we would have failed the tests." Brice threw his hands up. "We did the best we could for the whole human race."

"Your first responsibility was to the United States. You were to pass the Greenies' tests if possible. You were never granted power to negotiate on behalf of the United States."

"We didn't," said Dubba J. "We passed the tests. And when we did, they stipulated that they would work with us."

"And if we were negotiating for the United States," said Brice, "why weren't we speaking on behalf of the United States a few minutes ago?"

"Nevertheless," said Talky, "you are United States citizens who entered into an arrangement with a foreign power without authorization. Now if you don't want us to charge you with treason, and I mean all of you, you will need to work with the United States government to ensure that the Greenie technology is distributed in a manner consistent with—"

"No," said Kyna, who was suddenly standing behind Talky and Walky.

To their credit, neither man in black looked surprised. Brice, Dubba J, and Laetitia all jumped at her sudden appearance.

"I'm afraid," said Kyna, "that the only way the United States government — or indeed any government — will benefit from what my people have to offer, will be their full cooperation with the six chosen representatives."

"The Alien Committee," said Brice.

"The Alien Committee," she said. "Work with the Alien

Committee and you will benefit in your turn. Try to hinder or perse-cute them and watch your neighbors outgrow you."

Brice couldn't see either man's eyes behind their sunglasses, but he felt a sudden certainty that they were about to draw weapons.

"The whole world is going to change," said Brice. "Don't try to hold it back."

"I'll have to consult with my supervisors," said Talky, addressing Kyna.

She nodded, with a pleasant smile.

Talky and Walky left then, and once the door closed behind them Brice let out a sigh of relief he felt all the way down to the soles of his feet.

"We'll hear from them again," said Dubba J.

"And we'll be ready," said Laetitia.

58

A-Day-Plus-Sixteen. Six-Sixteen P.M. Eastern Daylight Time

The air conditioner in the limousine was a godsend. The tests had seemed to take so long that Laura was sure she'd be well into fall by the time she saw New York again, but no. Still August. Still too damned hot.

And Laura was not wearing an outfit for sweating. A curve-hugging little black dress that showed just the right amount of leg and cleavage. Off the shoulder, too, which meant that sweaty pits would get obvious all too quickly.

And then there was her makeup, which was already done and ready for the public. Wouldn't do to have any of it run, which would not have been a threat in the dry heat of L.A., not with the industrial grade spackle that must have served as the base for this makeup brand. But here in muggy New York? Fuggedaboudit.

At least she wore her hair down. Simple. No fancy hairdo would have survived this heat wave.

She liked her scent though. It was one Alita had turned her on to, citrus and sandalwood. Not enough to drown out the special savor of New York mire, but still, here in the limousine it made life more bearable.

"Crank that A.C., if you would, Peter," Laura said to the driver, while putting her face directly in front of a vent.

"Should we have picked you up an ice pack?" asked Jesse from the seat opposite her. "I bet if you rolled a cold bottle of beer across your chest on the stage we'd double our donations."

"Not that kind of crowd, thank God," she said without deigning to look at him. Truth was, she didn't mind the teasing. He was easier to deal with, now that they'd had a long talk. They might even be able to grow into a kind of friendship, if he promised to never talk about his conquests.

"Don't kid yourself." Jesse slipped off the jacket of his tuxedo and raised his arms in front of another vent. "I don't care if the GNP of that room exceeds a trillion dollars, most of them are still heterosexual men who'd flip over seeing *you* do that kind of rock video move. Possibly a few lesbians too."

"Well," she said, adjusting so her vent could hit her neck, "you better do something like that too then, for the straight women and the homosexual men. Fund the whole nonprofit in ten minutes."

Finally, their temperatures moderated, they both settled back onto their seats.

"You think this'll work?" said Jesse.

"We cherry-picked for a reason. Every one of the people attending tonight has a history of donating to causes like the one we're starting. I only see one possible sticking point."

"The ones who want to be on the board."

She nodded. It was something they'd all discussed. There was too much work for the six of them, but they had to be the ones to oversee everything. Their biggest donors would be the ones who wanted to be the most involved. The nonprofit only needed their money though, not their guidance.

"We've got to have naming opportunities," said Jesse.

"You've been saying that for days."

"And I'll keep saying it until the rest of you listen. People like to see their names on buildings. Feels permanent."

"We won't have many though," she said. "Maybe a headquarters

or two, but that's about it unless they want to name vehicles or something. Maybe warehouses. A school or two, possibly."

"We need more."

"They'll have to settle for being on the honor roll. The donors
who made it happen. Who helped usher in the *golden age of
humanity*." Laura shrugged. "If that's not good enough, I don't know
what is."

They sat in silence for a few minutes. They'd both done this kind
of fundraising gig before, so there wasn't much to say. Get up on a
stage and say the right kinds of things, which would be easy in this
case. Mingle with the crowd over drinks and appetizers. Smile at
everyone and be just flirty enough to make the men feel good without
giving them false hope or upsetting their wives.

Then came dinner. Her at one table, Jesse at another. Each of
them surrounded by eleven people who'd paid extra for the chance to
share dinner with a movie star. She'd charm them and tell stories,
and listen attentively to any tales they wanted to tell.

That was how the game was played. The donors knew it. Laura
and Jesse knew it. Every once in a while she met someone she could
actually develop a passing friendship with, but for the most part, it
was just another public appearance.

All for the cause.

"You're going to go out with him," said Jesse. "Aren't you?"

"Who?"

Jesse gave her a flat look.

Oh, she realized. Charlie.

"Don't tell me you don't approve," she said.

"I don't. He has no idea what he's getting into."

"Actually," she said with a slight smile tilting the corners of her
mouth, "after what the six of us just went through, I'd say he has a
better idea than most of the guys I've gone out with."

"You know what I mean." Jesse puffed out an exasperated sigh,
head moving back and forth as though looking for support. "People
like you and me, we're high maintenance. We don't live normal lives.
You think he'll be able to handle that?"

Laura snorted, and looked at Jesse like he was an idiot. This was not the first time she'd given him that look, but she was surprised to need it again so soon.

"Exactly what about his life do you expect to be 'normal' now?" Laura fluttered her eyelashes. "Hmm? You think he's just going to go back to freelancing and forget all about—"

"You know what I mean." Jesse shook his head. "And you're still going to sit there and act like you can be the kind of girlfriend he's used to."

"Look." Laura leaned forward to make sure she had Jesse's attention. "I get that you're worried about him. And that's nice. But don't come off like I'm some kind of shark who's going to take two bites out of him and leave him to die. I like Charlie. And he's not like anyone I've gone out with before."

She leaned back in the seat now as she continued.

"And he didn't just ask me on a date. He said he wanted to get to know me better. And I think he really does. So we'll get together and we'll do something and we'll talk. A lot. And if that works for us?" Laura smiled as the limo rolled to a stop. "Then maybe I'll kiss him again and see what happens."

"Again?" said Jesse.

"Game face on, Jess." She turned to the door. "It's show time."

"Wait! What's this 'again?' When did you kiss him before?"

"A lady doesn't kiss and tell," she said as the door opened.

Laura stepped out onto the curb and smiled for the photographers.

59

A-Day-Plus-Thirty-Seven. Eleven-Forty-One A.M. UTC+3

Charlie had expected it to be hotter. For some reason, when he thought of Uganda, he imagined steamy, hundred-plus temperatures. But according to his cell phone, San Jose was fifteen degrees hotter today. Wouldn't be as humid though. Alita'd been right to warn him to dress in white linen.

Honestly, with the breeze coming in off the lake, he felt almost cool.

Alita dressed the same way, though she'd added a hat with a broad brim to keep the bright sun at bay.

Kyna, of course, dressed in the silver spacesuit and knee-high boots that seemed to be her skin. Charlie might have believed it *was* her skin, if Jesse hadn't been so eager to talk about what lay underneath that shiny silver fabric.

Charlie had also expected the smells to overpower him. Lush, jungle scents from plants he could only imagine. Instead the air smelled damp, and slightly of decay and decomposition as some of those plants went the way of all things.

The three of them stood at the edge of an island in the middle of Lake Victoria, the largest lake on the African continent and the largest tropical lake in the world. Behind them was a section of jungle proper, so thick Charlie wasn't sure a machete would have been enough to cut through it. He thought he recognized some ferns and a palm tree or two, but for the most part it was a sea of greens he couldn't fathom.

And the sounds coming from it almost unnerved him. Buzzing and clicking insects, chattering monkeys, and so many different bird-songs they clashed into a cacophony.

Not a place to go hunting for a banana, though they probably grew nearby.

"You're sure we don't want a press conference for this?" asked Alita. "I don't know how flashy it'll be, but even a few scientists with measuring devices to show off the difference in pollution level when you're done would be a boon."

"Not for this one," said Kyna. She smiled at both Charlie and Alita. "The first time we clean something on a planet is a sort of sacred moment for us. It's not a time for skeptics or newsmen with agendas. It's something we only share with a chosen few."

The smile faded for a moment. "I wish the others could be here."

"Me too," said Charlie. "But we all have our roles to play. If we're going to handle this without you teleporting us everywhere, we'll need money, passports, visas..."

"Of course." Kyna held up a handful of blue, chalky cubes, none more than a quarter-inch across. She smiled again. "These are easier to make than you'd think, when your scientists are ready. It won't be that long. But for now..."

Kyna handed a few each to Alita and Charlie.

"On three," said Charlie. "One. Two. *Three!*"

They threw their cubes into the lake.

"Will that really be enough?" said Alita.

"Watch," said Kyna. And she began a low chant, full of words and syllables whose meaning Charlie couldn't guess.

Everywhere the cubes touched, the lake began to glow gold. And the glow spread. Slowly at first, but then faster and faster until it covered the lake as far as Charlie could see.

The glow flashed bright, then vanished.

"There," said Kyna. "The first step on a long, long road."

"What were you saying?" asked Alita. "Was that a prayer?"

"No. The cleansing is pure science. That was just ... poetry. Something I always say at a first cleansing."

"Kyna," said Charlie, "what do you really look like?"

Kyna laughed.

"Still worried that I'm some sort of tentacled horror?"

"No. Well. Maybe. I don't know."

"All right. I'll show you. But just this once. Mustn't give people the wrong idea."

Alita turned away.

"You don't want to see?" said Charlie.

"I don't need to."

Kyna raised her eyebrows at Charlie, giving him the opportunity to back out.

"Sorry," he said. "You don't have to do this if you don't want to. I just can't help my curiosity."

"Curiosity is the best reason to ask," she said.

A golden glow enveloped Kyna, and the body within the glow faded, faded, faded, vanished. Finally there was only the golden glow, which lost its Kyna-shape and seemed more of a three-dimensional oval.

Charlie's eyes grew wide, and his jaw slipped open without his noticing. Seeing her like this was like standing alone in the middle of nowhere and staring into the stars until he felt tiny and insignificant. He stared for a time before he could bring himself to speak.

"Kyna?" he asked in a small voice.

"It's still me," she said, then reformed the Greenie shape Charlie had grown accustomed to seeing. "That's my natural form."

"That's—"

"A bit much for people who aren't ready to see it." To Alita she said, "You can turn around now. Besides..." She stretched her arms. "It's fun having a body."

Charlie blinked, still trying to absorb what he'd just seen. His voice was a fragile thing when he asked, "Just how long have your people been around?"

"A long, long time, Charlie." Kyna smiled, and Charlie felt a little like himself again. A little.

"Well, if we're not doing any publicity," said Alita, "we should get back."

"You're right," said Charlie, strength coming back into his voice. "We have a lot of work to do."

SIGN UP FOR STEFON'S NEWSLETTER

Stefon loves to keep in touch with his readers, and loves to keep you reading. The best way for him to do both is for you to sign up for his newsletter.

Sign up at http://www.stefonmears.com/join

If you sign up for Stefon's newsletter, you get...

- Monthly updates about his publishing and travel schedules
- His latest news, in brief, and answers to reader questions
- A free short story for signing up
- List-only offers and occasional specials
- Plus a free short story every month!

ABOUT THE AUTHOR

Stefon Mears tends to insist on an option C. Stefon has more than thirty books to his credit, and he never stops writing. He earned his M.F.A. in Creative Writing from N.I.L.A., and his B.A. in Religious Studies (double emphasis in Ritual and Mythology) from U.C. Berkeley. He's a lifelong gamer and fantasy fan. Stefon lives in Portland, Oregon, with his wife and three cats.

Look for Stefon online:
www.stefonmears.com
himself@stefonmears.com